"Good thing he's a gifted surgeon. He'll be able to repair all the hearts he breaks."

Yes, that about sums him up, Dana thought. After all, she had personal experience with Trevor MacAllister's charm. But that was in the past. As far as she was concerned, Trevor was just another doctor.

Then she saw him. He, of course, looked incredible. Tall, tanned, perfect masculine features. But Trevor was more than model perfect—he was a tremendously gifted and compassionate surgeon. His colleagues respected him, his patients worshiped him, women desired him.

The man should come with a warning label, she thought. *Lethal, operate at your own risk.*

Because Dana absolutely, positively refused to be attracted to Trevor MacAllister. No way, no how, not ever again. She'd sung that song, danced that dance. And just because she now had to work with him didn't mean she would fall for his wily charms again…or would she?

Dear Reader,

During this holiday season, don't forget to treat *yourself* special, too. And taking the time to enjoy November's Special Edition lineup is the perfect place to start!

Veteran author Lisa Jackson continues her FOREVER FAMILY miniseries with *A Family Kind of Gal*. All THAT SPECIAL WOMAN! Tiffany Santini wants is a life of harmony away from her domineering in-laws. But there's no avoiding her sinfully sexy brother-in-law when he lavishes her—and her kids—with attention. Look for the third installment of this engaging series in January 1999.

And there's more continuing drama on the way! First, revisit the Adams family with *The Cowgirl & The Unexpected Wedding* when Sherryl Woods delivers book four in the popular AND BABY MAKES THREE: THE NEXT GENERATION series. Next, the PRESCRIPTION: MARRIAGE medical series returns with *Prince Charming, M.D.* by Susan Mallery. Just about every nurse at Honeygrove Memorial Hospital has been swooning over one debonair doc—except the R.N. who recalls her old flame's track record for breaking hearts! Then the MEN OF THE DOUBLE-C RANCH had better look out when a sassy redhead gets under a certain ornery cowboy's skin in *The Rancher and the Redhead* by Allison Leigh.

Rounding off this month, Janis Reams Hudson shares a lighthearted tale about a shy accountant who discovers a sexy stranger sleeping on her sofa in *Until You*. And in *A Mother for Jeffrey* by Trisha Alexander, a heroine realizes her lifelong dream of having a family.

I hope you enjoy all of our books this month. Happy Thanksgiving from all of us at Silhouette Books.

Sincerely,

Karen Taylor Richman
Senior Editor

Please address questions and book requests to:
Silhouette Reader Service
U.S.: 3010 Walden Ave., P.O. Box 1325, Buffalo, NY 14269
Canadian: P.O. Box 609, Fort Erie, Ont. L2A 5X3

SUSAN MALLERY

PRINCE CHARMING, M.D.

Silhouette®

SPECIAL VEDITION®

Published by Silhouette Books

America's Publisher of Contemporary Romance

To Christine Flynn and Christine Rimmer, who are friends and two of my favorite writers. Thanks for including me in this project. It's been a lot of fun, and I have really enjoyed working with both of you. Here's to wild success for our "Honeygrove honeys."

 SILHOUETTE BOOKS

ISBN 0-373-24209-3

PRINCE CHARMING, M.D.

Copyright © 1998 by Susan W. Macias

Books by Susan Mallery

SUSAN MALLERY

lives in sunny Southern California where the eccentricities of a writer are considered fairly normal. Her books are both reader favorites and bestsellers, with recent titles appearing on the Waldenbooks bestseller list and the *USA Today* bestseller list. Her 1995 Special Edition *Marriage on Demand* was awarded Best Special Edition by *Romantic Times Magazine*.

The Pledge

Graduation day

We, the undersigned, having barely survived four years of nursing school and preparing to go forth and find a job, do hereby vow to meet at Granetti's at least once a week, not do anything drastic to our hair without consulting each other first and never, ever—no matter how rich, how cute, how funny, how smart—marry a doctor.

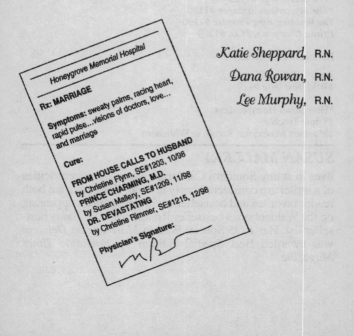

Katie Sheppard, R.N.

Dana Rowan, R.N.

Lee Murphy, R.N.

Honeygrove Memorial Hospital

Rx: MARRIAGE

Symptoms: sweaty palms, racing heart, rapid pulse...visions of doctors, love... and marriage

Cure:
FROM HOUSE CALLS TO HUSBAND
by Christine Flynn, SE#1203, 10/98
PRINCE CHARMING, M.D.
by Susan Mallery, SE#1209, 11/98
DR. DEVASTATING
by Christine Rimmer, SE#1215, 12/98

Physician's Signature:

Chapter One

"Good thing he's a gifted surgeon. He'll be able to repair all the hearts he breaks."

Dana Rowan took a sip of her coffee and resisted the urge to roll her eyes. She'd made a special effort to get to the meeting early enough so she could have her pick of seats. She'd deliberately chosen one in the back...as far from the podium as possible. She wanted to avoid gossip, her nurses—who had, collectively and overnight, seemed to have lost their minds—and most especially the "gifted surgeon" in question. So far she hadn't seen any sign of Dr. Trevor MacAllister, so she'd accomplished a third of her goals. Guess that would have to be enough for now.

The two women sitting in front of her continued to talk about "young" Dr. MacAllister, differentiating him from "old" Dr. MacAllister, who was Trevor's father and the chief of staff at Honeygrove Memorial Hospital.

"Have you seen him?" Sally asked, then continued without waiting for an answer. "He's gorgeous. Serious stud-muffin material." She leaned back in her plastic chair and sighed loudly.

"I know," Melba said. "Don't forget I grew up here. I was a few years younger than him, but I remember Trevor back when he was in high school, and let me tell you, he was just as good-looking then." She strained her neck as she peered toward the open door. "I'll bet time has only improved him."

Dana wished there were somewhere she could move to. She didn't think she would be able to stand listening to this kind of talk through the entire staff meeting. Unfortunately, judging by the buzz flying around the room, she would have to leave the hospital or possibly even Honeygrove itself to escape the excitement generated by Trevor MacAllister's return.

"He's just a man," she muttered. "He puts his pants on one leg at a time, just like other mortals. No doubt he has other human frailties, like an occasional bad temper and morning breath."

But the nurses weren't listening, and even if they had been, they wouldn't have cared. She wasn't saying what they wanted to hear. In the world of hospital gossip and lore, Trevor was a godlike creature. A hometown boy returned to the fold after making his name out in the world.

She took another sip of coffee and tried to disconnect from everyone around her. Regardless of what she personally thought of the man, he was now a surgeon at the hospital. Her job was to schedule surgical nurses and keep the OR operating—pardon the pun—efficiently. That meant working with "young" Dr. MacAllister. Fine, she would put her personal opinions aside and be as professional as the job required. She would survive the minimal contact and do her best to ignore the inevitable stories that would circulate. After all, they meant nothing to her. Like Melba, she'd grown up in Honeygrove and had first-hand experience with Trevor's considerable charm. She'd fallen hard and she'd been burned big-time. If she allowed herself to examine her heart, she might even still see a few of the scars. But that was in the past. As far as she was concerned, Trevor was just another surgeon. As such, he held no interest for her.

Sally tucked a loose strand of dark hair behind her ear and leaned close to her friend. "He's divorced," she whispered, although not softly enough to keep her words from drifting back to Dana. "It's been two years and he hasn't gotten serious about anyone since. Think he's trying to get over a broken heart?"

"Are you crazy?" Melba asked. She made a dismissive gesture with her hand. "A man that good-looking? You don't actually think his wife left *him,* do you? I'm sure he's been real busy these past two years. From what I've heard, he's already been out with a couple of nurses here and he hasn't officially started work yet. I'm not saying you couldn't have fun with him, but don't make it more than it is or you'll end up with a broken heart."

Amen, Dana thought, and hoped Sally would listen to her friend. The brunette was pretty enough to tempt Trevor, but he'd never been much on commitment.

Sally grinned at Melba. "You're warning me off so you'll have a clear shot at him yourself."

Melba smiled in return, her teeth flashing white against her honey-colored skin. "I wouldn't mind having a little fun with the good doctor, but I'm not going to make it more than that. He might have grown up, but I don't think he's changed all that much."

She bent to pick up the plastic coffee cup she'd tucked under her chair. As she straightened, she caught sight of

Dana sitting behind them. Her smile turned sheepish. "We don't usually get this worked up over a new doctor."

"I know," Dana told her. "Under the circumstances, I understand the appeal. After all, this *is* Trevor MacAllister we're talking about."

Melba caught her note of sarcasm, but Sally missed it completely. She spun in her seat so she faced her boss.

"Exactly," the twenty-five-year-old surgical nurse said. "So you're going to help, right? I'd like lots of rotations that put me right at Dr. MacAllister's side." She swayed to inaudible music. "I can see it right now. We'll look at each other across the patient's body. Our eyes will meet—the music will start."

"You'll drop an instrument and blood will spurt everywhere," Melba put in.

For the first time that morning, Dana chuckled. "Not an attractive thought, but probably accurate. I'll be handling business as usual, Sally. Nothing has changed."

The young woman pouted. "Of course it has. After all—"

There was a commotion by the door. Sally spun back to face front, then drew in an audible gasp. "It's him! Oh, look, Melba, he's stunning. I want him desperately."

Then you'll probably get him, at least for the night, Dana thought. While everyone in the room stopped talking and focused on the new arrival, Dana took a last sip of coffee, crushed her napkin and placed it in the empty plastic cup. She set both under her chair, after which she straightened in her seat. Only then did she glance toward the door.

He stood under fluorescent light that turned most people's skin an unappealing shade of muddy yellow. He, of course, looked incredible. Tall, tanned, with the perfect masculine features of a movie heartthrob. She was too far away to distinguish the color of his eyes, but she knew them to be an impossible shade of hazel green.

Several doctors moved to greet him. The older man at his side, his father and the chief of staff, introduced him with obvious pride. Trevor was more than model perfect—he was also an incredibly gifted and compassionate surgeon. His colleagues respected him, his patients worshiped him, women desired him. A true paragon, she thought grimly.

Dana was faintly annoyed by all the fawning. Wasn't there supposed to be a meeting in progress? So a new doctor was on staff. It happened all the time. Why did they all persist in acting as if they were being visited by a religious icon?

The meeting room was about thirty feet square and she was nearly as far from the door as possible. A couple dozen other people milled around talking now that the initial hush had receded. Dana had felt confident that she would be neither noticed nor acknowledged. So when Trevor looked in her direction, she didn't bother to turn away.

"He's looking at me!" Sally exclaimed.

"Don't be ridiculous," Melba told her.

Dana barely heard them. Despite the physical distance between them, despite the number of years since she'd last seen him, despite the stern lectures she'd given herself to avoid making a fool of herself over this man ever again, once he caught her attention—she couldn't turn away.

Those hazel green eyes trapped her. Trevor seemed to single her out in the crowd. All his attention, all his considerable energy, flowed toward her, around her. She felt it as tangibly as a touch…or a kiss. Heat flared in her thighs and her chest, working up and down, making her want to fan herself…or run for cover.

She was, she realized with dismay, not breathing, so she

rself to inhale and exhale slowly and deeply. ...ses in the room faded to faint buzzing, while the corners blurred into nothing. A wanting as powerful as a force-three hurricane built inside her.

Trevor's father said something and the object of everyone's attention shifted toward the chief of staff. For Dana, it was like breaking free of a tremendously powerful tractor beam. Her breathing once again became involuntary. The heat waned, as did the desire. The room returned to focus and she could hear what everyone whispered.

If she'd been standing, she would have collapsed into the nearest seat. As it was, all she could do was lean weakly against the chair back and wait for her strength to return.

What had just happened? She shook her head. Scratch that—she didn't want to know the answer. She absolutely, positively, *refused* to be attracted to Trevor. No way, no how, not again. She'd sung that song and danced that dance. If nothing else, she had the ability to learn from her mistakes. He might have the gifted hands of Michelangelo, but he had the morals of an alley cat.

Dana shook off the residual effects of her momentary weakness and forced herself to look at the hospital's chief of staff. Walter approached the podium and nodded to a few friends. The room quieted. From the corner of her eye she watched as Trevor made his way to an empty chair in the front row. He never once glanced her way, so she could only assume what she'd experienced before had simply been the result of low blood sugar or the placement of the moon or something. Obviously Trevor hadn't been looking at her.

She wasn't sure how long the meeting lasted. In some ways it felt as if she'd been sitting in her chair for days; in other ways, it seemed only a few seconds. But as soon as Walter excused everyone, Dana sprang to her feet and hurried toward the door. She told herself the real reason she was fleeing was that she had piles of work waiting on her desk, that it had nothing to do with avoiding Trevor. Besides, she need not worry. Already a crowd was collecting around him. A crowd of mostly women, she noted with some disdain. Even if he only greeted them individually, he would be stuck there for an hour.

She continued to walk forward purposefully. The corridor—and freedom—were in sight, when someone touched her arm.

She didn't have to turn around to identify the person. She knew the same way bats know how to fly in the dark or cats know how to land on their feet. She knew because, despite the years and the past, or maybe because of them, a part of her still recognized him.

She stopped and, without turning to face him, said, "Hello, Trevor."

"Dana!"

The pleasure in his voice made the heat return. It washed through her, a liquid warmth that dissolved will and purpose along with bones.

Because there was no way around it, she shifted until she was facing him, then glanced up. It was like tumbling out of a tree. For a moment she had a wonderful sensation of free-falling for eternity. Then she hit earth with a *thump* and had all the wind knocked out of her.

She couldn't move; she couldn't breathe. She could only look at him and wait for him to blow her away. He did. He smiled. A perfect mouth curved over perfect teeth, exposing a perfect dimple. The man should come with a warning label. Maybe something from the surgeon general or the military—lethal, operate at your own risk.

"I was hoping I would run into you," he said, and placed his hand on her arm, just above the elbow.

The polite gesture allowed him to guide her out of the room and into the corridor. She thought about protesting, but she hadn't gotten her breathing going again, so words were impossible. She could only stare mutely and try to figure out why on earth he sounded so pleased to see her.

People passed them. She had a sense of movement and bodies. By the time she had herself nearly under control, they were in the elevator, heading down. She forced herself to remember what had happened all those years ago. How he'd humiliated her in front of the entire school. The anger had long faded, but the sense of shame lingered. Now she focused on that, willing the emotions from the past to push aside the heat and desire she refused to acknowledge. No matter what, she would not want this man again. Ever.

"What are you doing?" she asked when she realized they were alone in the elevator and Trevor was staring at her with a smile tugging at his lips.

"Taking you for coffee."

She made a show of glancing at her watch. "I'm very busy."

He shrugged. "So am I, but this is important. Don't worry, it won't take long. I just want to get a few things straightened out."

She didn't like the sound of that, but before she could complain, the doors opened and two nurses stepped inside. They took one look at Trevor and simpered. There was no other word for their flirty expressions and open body language.

"Good morning, Dr. MacAllister," they said in unison.

Dana thought about sticking her fingers down her throat and making a retching sound, but doubted anyone else would appreciate the humor in the gesture. The attention was nauseating. How did the man stand it?

Silly question, she thought, glancing at his handsome

features. He accepted the adoration with the equanimity of one born to greatness. Women had been fawning over him since he was in the cradle and no doubt they would continue until he was on his deathbed.

"Doesn't it get boring?" she asked as they exited the elevator, collected mugs of steaming coffee and made their way to a quiet table in the corner. She took the seat facing the rest of the room because she wanted to watch the reaction of the women already there. Most had already seen him and were staring hungrily.

Trevor settled next to her, oblivious to the attention. "Doesn't what get boring?"

"The women. Or have you grown so used to being worshiped that it's just matter-of-fact?"

Instead of responding glibly, he took a drink of his coffee, then set it on the small table between them. "I see my reputation has preceded me."

There was a trace of regret in his tone. Dana dismissed it as wishful thinking on her part. He was too pretty to have values or anything close to a conscience.

"What did you expect?" she asked. "Honeygrove isn't exactly a small town, but people do know one another. They remember what you were like growing up. Combine that with the hotbed of intrigue one normally finds in a hospital, throw in a fascinating and eligible surgeon—" she motioned to the room behind him "—it's high drama."

"You're right."

He leaned forward and rested his elbows on the table. The traditional doctor's white coat flattered his tan and made already broad shoulders seem wide enough to support a building. She told herself that her attraction was a meaningless physical response to having been without a date for months. In the past couple of years she'd thrown herself into her career. She had a great promotion and raise to show for her efforts, but her social life bordered on monastic.

A moment of silence fell between them. Dana used the time to compose herself, trying to still the faint tremors in her arms and legs and slow her heartbeat. She was a grown-up. She could easily handle this situation. Her gaze settled on his face, on well-defined eyebrows and a straight nose. She bit back a sigh—okay, so he was a fine-looking specimen. But that extraordinary body hid the heart and soul of a rogue. She would do well to remember that.

Dana leaned back in her chair and crossed her legs. "Well, Trevor, you called this meeting. What did you want to talk about?"

"You've been avoiding me for nearly a week. I want to know why."

His statement made her stiffen slightly. "I'm not avoiding you. I've been busy." She didn't make a habit of lying and had a bad feeling she didn't do it well. Hopefully Trevor wouldn't catch on.

"I've left several voice-mail messages about setting up an appointment so you and I could talk. My office is ready to start scheduling patients, but we have things to work out first."

Dana nodded. He was right. It was her job to keep the surgical unit working smoothly. There were dozens of details—personnel and their schedules, supplies, equipment, repairs, purchases. A new surgeon coming on staff required coordination between her team and his.

"I wasn't avoiding you," she said again, hoping repetition added conviction to her voice. "However, I'll be happy to set up a meeting for later today or tomorrow. If that's convenient?"

His hazel green eyes never looked away. The force of his attention was as tangible now as it had been earlier. She found herself wanting to promise him anything he requested. When she started to involuntarily lean toward him, she straightened quickly and forced a quick, tight smile.

"Thank you," he said.

Even his voice was tempting, she thought with disgust. Low and sexy, the well-modulated tones were designed to make women whimper. It wasn't Trevor, she told herself firmly. Maybe her flu shot had worn off early and she was coming down with something. That was it. A mild case of food poisoning or the plague. Anything but him.

"If that's all…" she said, pushing to her feet.

"It's not." He put his hand on her forearm to hold her in place.

Dear God, he was touching her. Heat flared again, racing from the point of contact to the rest of her body. Fire collected in her breasts and between her legs. She would never survive this. Never. After all this time, nothing had changed.

She sank back weakly, wondering why her body had to betray her. Hadn't the lesson been painful enough? Weren't the emotional scars a reminder of all he'd done? She shook her head. Apparently her hormones didn't care about broken hearts or shattered dreams.

Slowly, she pulled her arm free and placed her hands in her lap. "What else, Trevor? I can't afford to extend this break much longer. I have a pile of work waiting for me on my desk."

"This won't take long." He stared at her. "I suspect you'll deny it, but I can tell you're still angry with me. It's been years, Dana. You need to let the past go. We're going to have to work together, and it's time to put our history in perspective."

He spoke calmly, but it was all she could do not to shriek at him. How dared he bring that up? "Perspective? Easy for you to say. You're not the one everyone talked about for weeks afterward. You went on with your life, while I was left to deal with a ruined reputation."

Not to mention a broken heart, she added to herself. She was still shaking, but this time from reaction to his words rather than from attraction. Her face felt hot. No doubt she was blushing. She kept her head high, refusing to let him think he was going to get the best of her.

"I'm not that innocent young woman anymore," she continued. "I don't care what you do with your personal life, but while you're dealing with me, you will remember we are business associates and nothing else."

He'd handled the whole situation badly. Trevor cursed silently. He'd been a fool to think Dana would have let go of the past. It might have been a long time ago, but obviously the memories were still fresh in her mind. The worst part was, her anger was justified. Unfortunately, he couldn't do anything about it.

"If I could change the past, I would," he told her.

"How nice for both of us. Tell me. What would you change? Would you still pretend you cared about me to get me to sleep with you, only this time you wouldn't tell the entire school? Or would you just avoid the whole messy entanglement?"

Fire flashed from her blue eyes. She kept her chin high, her gaze steady. She'd always been tough...that was one of the many things he admired about her. Dana had a survivor's strength. Life hadn't always treated her well, but she'd come through. If he told her he admired her though, she would throw his compliment right back in his face.

"I would change two things," he said. "This time I would make you listen to the truth. You wouldn't hear it then, but I'm hoping you'll hear it now."

"As you said, it's been a lot of years. Why should any of that matter?"

Because you're still hurting, he thought. Instead he said, "Just listen. Please."

She continued to glare at him, but she didn't move from her seat. He took that lack of action as assent.

He sucked in a breath. After all this time, he was finally going to tell her what really happened that weekend. The hell of it was, she wouldn't believe a word.

"I really cared about you, Dana," he began. Cared. What a silly word that didn't come close to describing his feelings. She'd been his whole world—only she'd never known. She'd seen what everyone else had seen. The handsome facade, the easy laughter. Not the young man he'd been or the tender heart he'd done his damnedest to hide.

"That weekend meant the world to me."

She snorted in disbelief, but he ignored her and went on.

"I didn't tell the whole school that we'd been lovers."

"Then why did everyone know?" she asked. "It was all anyone talked about for a week. That Dana had done it with Trevor." She pressed her hands to her cheeks. "I was humiliated."

"I know." He leaned toward her. "I'm sorry. I never wanted for you to be hurt."

"Yeah, right."

"Dana, I give you my word. I only told one person. Joel Haddock. He spread the rumors, not me."

Her gaze narrowed. "That's low, even for you. Joel was your best friend."

Trevor nodded. "Definitely. *Was.* Our friendship ended that Monday when I found out what he'd done." He studied her face. "You don't believe me." It wasn't a question.

"Of course not. Joel was good to me. After everyone knew what we'd done, the boys wanted to talk to me only because they thought I was easy. They tormented me, cornering me in the halls, trying to touch me.'' She shuddered at the memory. "Joel was there. He listened and he kept me safe.''

Trevor felt old anger surfacing. He knew what Dana had gone through and he'd been helpless to protect her. "Joel was there because he always had a thing for you. He started the rumor to break us up." He laughed harshly. "It sure worked. You never spoke to me again. Until today."

"You said you would change two things," she told him. "The first was to get me to listen to the truth, such as it is. What's the second?"

She didn't believe him. He could see it in her eyes and read it in her body language. He told himself it didn't matter. He and Dana had to work together, not be friends. But he'd hoped for more. Maybe some forgiveness, or at least a little understanding.

"I wouldn't have told Joel," he said. "That was my other mistake. If he hadn't known what happened, or how I'd fallen for you, he wouldn't have tried so hard to break us up." He rose to his feet. "I know that semester was difficult for you. I'm sorry for my part in what happened. But I won't apologize for that time we spent together. I've never forgotten it or you." He flashed her a smile. "Not that I expect you to believe me."

"Good, because I don't."

She stood, also. She wore a dark-peach coatdress. Chin-length, dark-blond hair had been brushed back from her face. She'd changed from high school. Her features were less rounded, her expression more wary. But her athletic body still moved with a grace that made him think about sultry afternoons and tangled sheets.

"I don't know that we've cleared the air," Dana said. "But at least everything is out in the open. I'm good at my job, Trevor. Just as you're good at yours. We're now forced to work together. I don't have a problem with that if you don't. As I said before, I don't care what you do with your personal life—just don't do it on my time. I can't tell you not to see my nurses, but I will ask that you keep your flirtations to a minimum. If I see them affecting the running of this hospital, I won't hesitate to report you."

The insult was undeserved, but not unexpected. He told himself Dana was reacting to the truth as she saw it. But it was hard to just let it go.

"No problem," he said, then headed for the door before he exploded. Several women called out greetings. He nodded pleasantly as he walked to the elevator. Once he was inside and the doors closed, leaving him alone, he gave in to his rage.

He swore long and loud, then hit the wall with a closed fist. Dana thought he was little more than a gigolo, which was what most people believed. That Trevor MacAllister had a woman in every port—or in the case of the hospital, a nurse on every floor and in every department. That he went out with a different one each night, bedded them all in legendary fashion and forgot about them the next day. Out of sight, out of mind.

He didn't want to make any part of his reputation a reality, but she—like the rest of the world—wouldn't be interested in something as boring as the truth. The only part of the legend he wanted to be real was the bit about forgetting. If only he could put it all out of his mind—let the past go. He could save himself a lot of sleepless nights...and a lot of pain.

Chapter Two

Dana pulled open the dishwasher and began unloading the machine. Despite the beautiful April morning, she felt distracted and edgy. Knowing what caused the feelings didn't help. Had she been a jogger she would have gone out for a ten-mile run. Maybe she would regrout her shower tiles—anything to take her mind off the source of her trouble. Trevor MacAllister.

She grabbed a handful of silverware and crossed to the drawer next to the refrigerator. It wasn't fair. After all these years he'd waltzed back into her life as if nothing had ever happened. "For him it hasn't," she reminded herself aloud. While he'd been the only guy she'd ever had a crush on in high school, and her first lover, she'd only been one in a line of conquests for him. She hated that she couldn't stop thinking about him.

The past week had been long and difficult. She'd managed to get through their start-up meeting with a minimum of reaction. At least that's what she told herself. He couldn't possibly have known that the entire time he sat so casually in her office, her heart had been pounding and her knees growing weak. She'd felt a flush on her cheeks, but had hoped her makeup was enough to cover it.

So that should be the end of it. Trevor was on staff. Any questions she had could be answered by his office. There was no reason she should have to see him, talk to him or even hear his name. But it wasn't that simple. For one thing, nearly every female in the hospital was still buzzing about him. For another, she couldn't seem to escape him. Every time she rounded a corner or exited an elevator they ran into each other. One time he'd been pulling on his white coat over tailored shirt and tie. The height and strength of him had sucked the breath right from her chest. Another time he'd been coming out of surgery, tired, sweaty, with stained scrubs hanging loosely on his body. She shouldn't have noticed. She *never* noticed doctors. But she wasn't that lucky with Trevor. Something about him drew her. Like a moth to a flame, she thought humorlessly. And like that little moth, if she wasn't careful she would end up a charred piece of nothing blowing away on the breeze.

"This is crazy," she told herself as she picked up the pot in the top rack of the dishwasher. She carried it to the cupboard, then shoved it in place. "I refuse to spend my weekend thinking about this man. What I need is a distraction."

She walked through her three-bedroom town house. There were plenty of weekend chores. Cleaning, laundry, some bills to pay. All necessary, but none taxing enough to occupy her thoughts for very long. She considered calling her best friends, but Katie would be busy with Mike, and Lee had mentioned something about going away for the weekend. Which left her on her own.

She eyed the wallpaper in the dining area, but decided stripping the walls was a bit much, even for someone in her condition. Besides, she liked the subtle pattern. Would redecorating really get Trevor out of her head?

She moved back into the kitchen and poured herself some coffee. She could have handled seeing him again, and even talking to him, if only he hadn't brought up the past. The more she thought about what he'd told her, the more she grew confused. No way did she believe that Joel Haddock had been the one to tell her entire high school what she'd done with Trevor. Yet she couldn't accept the fact that Trevor was lying. He was many things she admired and many things she despised, but he'd always been completely honest. It didn't make sense. Maybe—

A rumble caught her attention. She carried her mug to the front bedroom that doubled as her at-home office and stared out the window. A moving van had pulled up in front of the town house next door. She'd heard that the place had been rented. This was exactly what she needed. She would go over, introduce herself to her new neighbors and offer to help. A couple of hours spent carting boxes around and unpacking would be a great distraction.

She left her mug on the counter in the kitchen, pocketed her keys and stepped outside. Three men were already lowering the tailgate of the trailer. She looked around for a passenger car. A sleek, silver Mercedes pulled into the nearest visitor parking slot. Dana stared at the vehicle. A knot formed in her stomach as she realized it looked familiar. A man stepped out of the car and the knot tightened.

"Please, God, no," she murmured as Walter MacAllister raised an arm in a gesture of greeting, then headed toward her.

The chief of staff was tall and fit, with chiseled features that made him look younger than his sixty years. The long stride was familiar because his son had inherited that powerful walk, along with the elder MacAllister's good looks. She told herself not to panic, that Walter's being there didn't *mean* anything, but she knew she was lying. Walter and his wife had a beautiful house outside of Honeygrove. They had no reason to rent a town house...at least not for themselves. Which left another possibility too hideous to consider.

"Dana."

Walter reached her side and took her hands in his. He was caring and friendly with all his staff, frequently hosting dinner parties at his house. His was an open-door policy that kept morale high and turnover low. Dana knew it was just his management style at work, yet she'd always felt he'd taken a special interest in her career. He was the one who had recommended her for her current position.

"While it's always a pleasure to see you, Walter, these aren't your normal stomping grounds."

He released her hands and glanced around the complex. "It's as lovely here as you said."

She followed his gaze, taking in the delicate pink flowers on the black hawthorn trees, the trimmed ornamental bush, the quiet trickle of the water in the brook flowing through the grounds. "It is nice," she agreed cautiously.

Another rumble filled the morning. She didn't want to turn around and find the source of the sound. The knot in her stomach had doubled, as had her sense of foreboding. It would be too cruel of fate to do what she thought it was considering.

A black convertible pulled into the space next to the garage. Dana focused on the car because she had a bad feeling she already knew the driver.

The sports car was low and powerful, with scoops on the hood and wide racing tires. No doubt it could drive circles around her sensible Honda. She'd never been in a convertible—with over forty inches of rain a year in Honeygrove, they weren't exactly practical. Still, it looked like fun. A metal decal by the passenger door showed an upright snake, while letters on the rear bumper spelled out Cobra.

Dana raised her eyebrows. She would have figured someone with the nickname "Prince Charming, M.D." would drive an expensive foreign luxury car. Not an American-built muscle car.

She kept her attention on the vehicle as long as possible, but when Trevor came to a stop next to her, she had no choice but to look at him.

He flashed her a grin. She doubted it was his best one—he probably saved those for the actual seduction. This was his everyday smile, the one he gave away without thought. She tried to tell herself it wasn't special, that there was no reason for her visceral reaction to his presence. For all the good it did. Her heart rate increased as her body responded to Trevor's powerful magnetism. Damn the man.

"Dana," he said, as if actually pleased to see her. "What do you think?" He motioned to the large moving van. "We're going to be neighbors."

She'd already suspected as much, but it was one thing to think it and another to hear him say the words. "Really?"

Walter nodded. "You always said such nice things about your complex that when Trevor asked me about a place to rent while he had his house built, I instantly thought of here. Fortunately, one of the units was available."

"Talk about luck," Dana muttered, shoving her hands into her back jeans pockets. This couldn't be happening. Trevor couldn't move in next door. It wasn't just that she would have to see him from time to time; she would have to *hear* him. Their units shared two common walls. One was the living room, which wouldn't be a problem, but the other was the bedroom. She resisted the urge to groan. She didn't want to spend her evenings listening to him play Don Juan to whichever woman he might have up there.

"We're ready, sir," one of the movers called.

"Sure." Trevor walked to the man and spoke with him briefly, then headed for the front door. He was gone for a few seconds, then the garage opened and he reappeared. "I know where I want all the furniture," he told the men. "The boxes are marked by room."

The movers began unloading the van. Trevor helped, giving directions when necessary and carrying in boxes. His red polo shirt hugged powerful muscles in his shoulders, back and chest. Worn jeans—obviously designed to drive women insane—had faded to white at the hips seams, the knees and the crotch.

Walter looked at Dana. "Is this going to be a problem for you?"

She had to forcibly withdraw her attention from his son. She probably looked like a hungry wolf eyeing a rabbit as a potential meal.

His hazel eyes were shrewd and saw far too much. Did he expect her to tell him the truth? She smiled broadly. "Not at all. In fact, I came outside to offer my help."

The older man raised his eyebrows. "That was before you knew the identity of your new neighbor. I can tell what you're thinking, Dana, but you don't have to worry about Trevor. He won't be making noise and keeping you up late. Rumors of his exploits are exaggerated."

"Thank you," she said, wondering if there was a parent alive who didn't think the best of his offspring.

The three men continued to carry furniture into the town house. Dana trailed after them and found Trevor in the master bedroom. He told them where to set the large dresser.

She wasn't sure what she'd expected as far as decor, but the simple wooden pieces in the bedroom looked faintly conservative. Maybe he saved flashy for the sheets. Black satin or possibly silk.

"I'm here to help," Dana said. "What would you like me to do?"

Trevor glanced at her. "I appreciate that, although I'm a little surprised."

"That I would be neighborly?"

He nodded. "I don't think I'm who you would have chosen to live next door."

He had that right. Still, he was her boss's son and she could make the best of a bad, albeit temporary, situation. "Not a problem. I hope you're not worried about me. Cramping your style and all."

"You'd be surprised how little that concerns me. There isn't as much style as you think."

"Good looks *and* modesty. Gee, Trevor, it's amazing some woman hasn't snapped you up before now." She'd intended the comment to come out sarcastically, but oddly, as she spoke the words she found that she meant them. She knew from personal experience that he could be as charming as the devil himself. If he ever combined that with sincerity, he would be irresistible.

He ignored her statement and led the way down the hall. "I have a lot of books, so if you really do want to help, you can start there." He motioned to the neatly stacked boxes in the center of the room. Two of the walls contained floor-to-ceiling built-in bookcases.

"Dr. MacAllister, could you let us know where you want the sofa?" one of the movers called.

"Be right there." Trevor walked to the door. "Thanks, Dana. I appreciate your help."

When he was gone, she moved to the pile of boxes and opened the first one. Inside were medical texts. No surprise there. She took an armful and placed them on the bookshelves. So much for escaping from what was on her mind, she thought with a grin. She'd gone from the frying pan into the fire. Now she wasn't just thinking about Trevor—she was actually in his house. Oh joy. And they were going to be neighbors. Could it get worse?

She mentally withdrew the question, not wanting to tempt fate any more than she had. The only good thing about the situation was that she would see him with an assortment of women. That should take care of her wayward hormones. Even they would eventually figure out he wasn't worth lusting after. Not when he was more interested in quantity than quality.

Time passed quickly. She worked efficiently, flattening the boxes as she emptied them. There were tons of books. Not just the medical texts, but a collection of mysteries and bestsellers, three boxes of biographies and some books on travel. Surprisingly, all looked well read. She fingered the spine of a battered techno-thriller about a Russian submarine escaping to the West. He couldn't have read all these himself. When would he have had the time? He worked long hours in his office and in surgery, and he was out every night. But she didn't think Trevor had bought the books used.

"You're looking serious about something," he said, walking into the room and carrying two canned soft drinks. He handed her one. "I thought you might be thirsty."

"Thanks." She took the drink and popped the top. "I was just admiring your collection."

He eyed the full shelves. "I like to read. It's how I relax after surgery."

"I'm surprised you have the time."

"When something's important to me, I make the time."

She sensed a double meaning there, one that made her uncomfortable. "Are the movers finished?" she asked.

"Yeah, they left about twenty minutes ago. So did my dad. You want the nickel tour?"

"Sure." Easier to trail after him than to keep looking at him, she thought as her body once again betrayed her.

He led her through the three-bedroom town house that was a mirror image of hers. In the three years she'd lived in the complex, this unit had always been a rental. The walls were cream, the carpet a neutral beige. Cream vertical blinds allowed in light.

They started in the living room. Like the furniture she'd seen in his bedroom, the pieces were conservative and tasteful. A dark-blue leather sofa with a matching recliner stretched across the back wall. A television and other complex-looking electronic equipment filled an entertainment unit opposite. The end and coffee tables were oak, over-sized but simple. A few paintings leaned against the wall—a couple of oil seascapes, and three watercolor scenes of a bay—along with a collection of photographs that looked to be blowups from several different trips. Knowing what she did about him, she would have pictured something flashier.

The room she used as an office he'd filled with exercise equipment. She didn't dare picture him in shorts, and a cropped T-shirt, covered with sweat—her pulse was already rapid. In the master suite, several boxes stood open. She saw piles of linens—not silk or satin, but plain colors in cotton. Even the comforter was a sensible shade of blue and not the least bit exotic.

"What do you think?" he asked as he led her back to

the living room. He motioned for her to take a seat on the sofa.

"It's very nice," she said, not sure how to reconcile what she'd seen with his life-style. She settled in the far corner, sinking onto the soft leather cushion. "You're living here temporarily?"

"Until my house is built. I bought a piece of land."

He sat down just left of center, which put him far enough away that they didn't touch but not so far that she could forget about him. Of course, that might require his moving to an eastern bloc nation.

"Have you started construction?" she asked, pleased her voice sounded normal. That was something.

"I'm still working with the architect. I have some definite ideas, but I don't know if they're practical. We're still figuring out things."

So he could be her neighbor for a while. Great. She took a sip of her soda. Silence filled the room. She glanced at the coffee table, then at the fireplace in the corner.

"You'll like that—"

"You don't have to—"

They spoke at the same time. Dana shifted in her seat. "Go ahead."

"You don't have to stay if you have plans," he told her. "I appreciate your help, but I don't want to take advantage of you."

If only he did, she thought before she clamped down on her wayward thoughts and willed them into submission. She looked at her watch. It was barely noon.

"Expecting someone for lunch?" she asked, then covered her mouth in horror. She hadn't really said that, had she?

He finished his soda and set the can on the coffee table. A lock of dark hair fell across his forehead. "Not at all. I meant what I said. I don't want to keep you, but if you'd like to stay, I'd enjoy your company.''

Dana wondered how he could say that. She wasn't being especially nice, which made her feel slightly ashamed. She wasn't sure how to respond to him.

"Come on," he said, rising to his feet. "You can talk to me while I unpack my desk."

She followed him up the stairs. The last bedroom was a combined office and guest room. There was a gray-and-white striped sofa that folded out into a sleeper. His desk was relatively small and L-shaped, with a computer set up on one side. He reached for one of the boxes in the center of the floor.

"The moving company packed for me," he told her as he opened the top. "It makes unpacking a treasure hunt. I'm never sure what's inside."

She pointed to the writing on the side of the box. It said Office. "I guess that's not much help."

He chuckled and reached inside. Instantly his smile faded. He pulled out a framed photograph.

"What is it?" she asked, moving toward him.

He turned the frame toward her. It held an eight-by-ten photo of a beautiful dark-haired woman. She had wide green eyes and a perfect smile. For a second Dana thought she must be a fashion model and tried to figure out if she'd seen her on any magazine covers. Then the truth sank in.

"This must be the former Mrs. MacAllister," she said, wondering if she sounded as shocked as she felt. It was one thing to know intellectually that someone like Trevor would marry a stunningly gorgeous woman; it was something else to see proof. Even more shocking was the realization that, if the rumors were true, he'd been the one to dissolve their marriage.

"Vanessa," he said, turning the photo faceup and gazing at it. "I'm not sure why I've hung on to this."

"Maybe to remember what you lost," she said.

"Possibly." He set the frame photo-side down on his desk. "Like many who've gone through a divorce, I have regrets."

"Maybe you should have thought of that before you left her."

"I did," he said quietly. "She didn't give me a lot of choice."

Dana perched on the edge of the sofa. "I know this is none of my business and I have no right to ask. I probably shouldn't even mention it."

"But?"

She drew in a breath. "Vanessa is obviously a beautiful woman. Why on earth would you leave her? Was it so very important to run around with other women?"

He stiffened. His arms dropped to his sides and he stared at her as if he'd never seen her before. "That's what you think." It wasn't a question.

"I don't know what *to* think. I guess some people are different. Not wrong, just different."

"You mean about wanting a stable, faithful marriage?"

"Exactly."

"You see me as one of the different ones?"

"Aren't you?"

Hazel green eyes darkened. A muscle in his jaw twitched and she realized he was angry.

A twinge of guilt rippled through her. "I'm sorry, Trevor. I told you I had no right to ask that question. It's none of my business."

He reached into the box and pulled out several file folders. "Too late now, Dana. You've expressed your opinion.

I'd hoped for better, but, hey, why would you give me the benefit of the doubt?''

''I didn't mean it like that.'' She stared at the can in her hand. She wasn't sure what to do or say. Leaving would be too much like running away. Why had she spoken without thinking?

''You want to know why I left my wife?'' he asked, his voice little more than a growl.

She didn't want to know anymore. She had a bad feeling she wouldn't like what he had to say. But she'd been the one to start this line of questioning, so she had no one to blame but herself. ''Why?'' she asked in a small voice.

He smiled, but it was without humor or beauty, more a twisting of his perfect mouth, as if he were in pain.

''I found her with another man.''

Dana caught her breath. That was impossible.

''I see by the look on your face you're surprised,'' he continued. ''I couldn't believe it, either. That's why I forgave her. The first time. When it happened again, I packed my bags and I left.''

''Why on earth would she cheat on you?'' she blurted out without thinking.

''If that's a compliment, thank you.'' He tossed the empty box aside and sat on a corner of the desk. ''I don't have an answer for that. I was a surgical resident, so I was gone a lot. When I was home, I was exhausted. That's not by way of an excuse.'' He shrugged. ''I tried to understand, to explain it all away. The first time, I managed. But I couldn't do it again.''

''I'm sorry.''

''Me, too.'' His eyes were flat and devoid of emotion. ''The worst part of it was I didn't miss her all that much. Hell of a thing to say. After I left Vanessa, I had the uncomfortable realization I might never have loved her at all.

But I missed being married. It was hard getting used to being alone. I guess I kept her picture to remind me of what should have been rather than what was.''

Dana couldn't believe what she was hearing. Not only that Trevor's wife had cheated on him, but that he mourned the loss of his marriage. She wouldn't have thought he would. Wasn't the freedom to pursue as many women as possible his ultimate goal?

"Why'd you come back to Honeygrove?" she asked. "You've made a name for yourself. You could have gone anywhere."

This time when he smiled, it was genuine. She found her lips curling up in response.

"I missed home. I wanted to be near my folks. They say L.A.'s the place, but it's too much of a big city for me."

She might have been more surprised if he'd broken into song and dance, but not by much. He missed his family? He wanted to live in a smaller town? Maybe aliens really did exist and they'd taken over his body. Or maybe Trevor MacAllister wasn't who or what she'd imagined him to be.

He glanced at his watch. "I've kept you long enough. I really appreciate the help, Dana, but I don't have the right to claim your entire Saturday."

She found herself oddly reluctant to leave. She wanted time to explore this new and possibly improved man. But she rose to her feet and allowed him to guide her toward the entrance.

His fingers were warm and strong where they rested on the small of her back. As they passed the kitchen, he took the soda can from her and placed it on the counter, then he held open the front door.

"Thanks for everything," he said.

"No problem. I was happy to help." She gazed up at

him. He was so incredibly perfect to look at. It was wrong for one man to be so very beautiful.

He leaned one shoulder against the door frame. "If I get lost at the grocery store, will you come lead me back home?"

He was flirting with her. That she could accept. It was her eagerness to respond that made her cranky. "I don't think there will be a shortage of volunteers for that job," she told him, trying to ignore the excitement spreading through her.

An odd light glimmered in his eyes. Something that made her think *he* was thinking about kissing her. She told herself she should be insulted if he imagined she was that easy to manipulate. And yet…the thought of his kiss made her lips tingle and her body hum. She remembered his kisses, the strength of him, his power, his taste, the sensation of drowning in something sweet and wonderful.

"Bye, Dana," he said, then straightened and reached for the door.

He was going to close it behind her, without kissing her. She was both disappointed and confused.

"Bye," she told him as she stepped off his porch and headed for her own place.

"Dana?"

She paused and turned toward him. "What?"

"Don't believe everything you hear. The truth isn't as exciting as people want it to be, but that doesn't make it any less the truth."

He shut the door before she could ask him what he meant.

She stalked toward her place, annoyed that she regretted leaving him. What was wrong with her? She couldn't possibly want anything to do with him. But she hadn't wanted to go and… As she paused in front of her door, she pressed her fingertips to her temples. She felt as if she'd just been on a roller-coaster ride that had left her hanging upside down for too long.

Hours later, she was just as confused and out of sorts. It was nearly nine on a Saturday night and she could hear Trevor moving around next door. As far as she could tell, he didn't have company. Did that mean he was actually staying in? Had she been wrong about him? If so, did that mean she was wrong about what had happened fourteen years ago?

She wasn't sure she wanted to know that. If Trevor hadn't betrayed her, she'd had no reason to hate him then and no reason to mistrust him now. But she sensed with a certainty she couldn't explain that it was necessary to go on mistrusting Trevor. Especially if she wanted to keep her life sane and her heart in one piece.

Trevor leaned against the balcony and inhaled deeply. If the power lines were about fifty miles due west, he would be able to smell the Pacific Ocean. He was a hell of a lot more used to living in Los Angeles, but he did spend his daily jogs along the beach. Still, living like this was a small price to pay for coming home.

Home. He smiled at the thought. He'd waited so long to get back. College or three years, a six-week furlough through medical school, internships and residencies—and here he was, back where he'd started. Good thing all these fine homes would be worth extra money.

He moved away from the railing and sank onto the white plastic chair that lined the corner. The night was cool but clear. He told himself he should go in and get something for dinner. It was nearly nine and he hadn't eaten yet, but instead of moving, he relaxed and let his head rest against

Chapter Three

Trevor leaned against the balcony and inhaled deeply. If the town house were about fifty miles due west, he would be able to smell the Pacific Ocean. He hadn't liked all that much about living in Los Angeles, but he did miss his daily jog along the beach. Still, giving that up was a small price to pay for coming home.

Home. He smiled at the thought. He'd worked so hard to get away—college in three years, a fast-track through medical school, internship and residency—and here he was, back where he'd started. Considering all, there was no place he would rather be.

He moved away from the railing and sank onto the white plastic chair tucked in the corner. The night was cool but clear. He told himself he should go in and grab something for dinner. It was nearly nine and he hadn't eaten yet. But instead of stirring, he relaxed and let his head rest against the chair back. Here it was, a Saturday night, and he was all alone. Who would believe it?

One corner of his mouth twisted up. His reputation was an amazing thing. He'd always been impressed with the stories that circulated about him. How did they get started and why did people believe them? If he went out as often as the rumors claimed, he would be existing on less than three hours' sleep a night. If he was intimate with as many women as those rumors maintained, he would have the libido of Don Juan and the endurance of a triathlete, not to mention the IQ of a gnat. In this day and age, casual sex was more than stupid—it was deadly.

The irony usually amused him. The contrast between what the world believed and reality was as great as that between water and fire. The truth was, he spent most nights alone...even Saturday nights. He preferred it that way. But sometimes he thought about what it would be like to have a special woman in his life. As he'd told Dana earlier that day, he might not regret leaving Vanessa, but he did miss being married.

Dana. The quirk at the corner of his mouth turned into a genuine smile. He was sorry he'd missed the look on her face when she'd realized they would be neighbors. She'd probably wanted to spit nails, but instead she'd been gracious. Some of that, he knew, was because of his father's presence. She wasn't about to curse him out in front of the chief of staff. Ironically, Walter was the person she should blame for Trevor's current living conditions. That sly old dog. Matchmaking again.

Trevor thought back to his parents' multiple attempts to fix him up with women. "Nice ladies," his father called them. Women with humor and brains; some pretty, some not; all the type to be put off by his reputation. He'd dated a couple and they'd been among his most successful relationships. Both his parents had warned him about Vanessa, not wanting to interfere yet wanting him to know she was more interested in marrying someone as attractive as herself than in a genuine relationship. She'd wanted to be part of a handsome couple. Unfortunately, her pretty face hid the morals of an alley cat. His parents had been right about her. He wished he'd seen it sooner. Once he'd decided to move back to Honeygrove, his father had started a subtle campaign to remind him of a girl he'd dated in high school. What his father didn't know was that Trevor didn't need any help remembering Dana. If anything, there were days he would like to be able to forget her.

A car pulled up nearby. He couldn't see the vehicle, but he heard it stop and the doors open. A man and a woman stepped out, their voices carrying on the faint breeze. Another door opened, then a young girl laughed. From her conversation and the sound of her voice, she was around five or six. The family talked together as they headed for their town house.

Trevor swallowed the envy that welled inside him. He'd hoped for children, but Vanessa had convinced him to wait. At the time he'd been devastated, but now he was glad. He wouldn't want her to be his child's mother. Not after he'd learned the truth about her. But his ultimate goal hadn't changed. He wanted what that couple had, what so many others had found. A loving mate, happy children, a contented home life.

The elusive dream. He closed his eyes and asked, as he had a thousand times, what combination of features and characteristics, what movements, what words, conspired to make people—women—assume the worst about him. He was not interested in sex for sex's sake, nor did he crave a different woman every night. If the world knew the few number of ladies he'd actually made love with... He grimaced. No one would believe him.

For the most part he ignored the rumors, until they hurt someone he cared about or kept him from someone he really wanted to know. Someone like Dana.

He told himself the past was long over and getting lost in it again was a waste of time. He reached for the bottle of beer sitting on the plastic table next to him and took a drink. He tried to think of other things, of the surgeries he had scheduled for next week, of the two patients he'd admitted to the hospital that Saturday morning. He even toyed with the idea of renting a video. But it wasn't enough. Silent and unwelcome, the past intruded, slipping by his defenses and swirling through his mind like thick fog.

He didn't even have to close his eyes to remember. The image was so clear, so striking, it was almost like looking at a life-sized photograph. He could see Dana in black jeans and a fuzzy peach sweater the exact color of her tempting mouth, clutching her books to her chest. She'd been all of fifteen, a sophomore in high school. Big eyes and a smile that lit up the room.

He'd told himself she was too young. After all, he was a senior, only a few months shy of graduation. But something about her had appealed to him. Maybe it was the way she blushed every time he caught her looking at him. Or the faint stutter when she'd managed to return his casual "hi" after the championship basketball game.

He told himself not to go there—the past would offer nothing but heartache. The past was finished and couldn't be changed. He was ten kinds of fool for wanting to relive it. Still, he relaxed in his chair and closed his eyes.

He could smell the rain of the afternoon. Ironically, it had been April, as it was now...only a lifetime ago. He recalled standing by his locker as one girl after the other

said hello to him. Even then he'd had an undeserved reputation for having a way with "chicks." They, his friends
joked, playing on the word, "flocked to him." At seventeen, he hadn't understood the phenomenon any more than
he did now, but back then it had seemed more of a blessing
than a curse. He could get as many dates as he wanted,
with any girl he wanted. After taking out a few of the
prettiest ones, he found he needed more than someone to
look at. He wanted to care about the girl he was with; he
wanted to be intrigued. Which was why he'd finally gathered the courage to talk to Dana.

Trevor smiled at how nervous he'd been. He'd felt terror
that she would notice his shaking and sweating or that his
voice would betray him by cracking. She'd been standing
with her two close friends, Katie and Lee, friends who were
still important to her. The three girls had looked at him,
but he'd seen only Dana.

"Hi," he'd managed, pleased his voice didn't crack.

She'd blushed, but had managed to hold his gaze. "Hi,
Trevor."

Idiotically, he was thrilled she knew his name. In his
head he understood that he was a popular senior and many
underclass students knew who he was. But this was Dana.
That *she* had taken the time to figure out who he was made
him feel he could conquer the world.

"How's it going?" he asked.

"Fine." Her voice was low and soft.

He pointed to her math text. "You taking Murphy's
class?"

She nodded.

Mr. Murphy was known for his Friday tests and not grad-
ing on a curve. "How are you doing in algebra?"

"Pretty good. He's hard, but I like math, so I don't
mind."

He tried to think of something funny to say, or something that would put her at ease. But his usual wordplay had deserted him. He could only think about how much he wanted to make her smile, and maybe hold her hand.

"I was, ah—" he cleared his throat "—going to the library tonight to study. About seven-thirty. You want to come?"

Technically, it wasn't a date. In the peculiar world that was Honeygrove High School, the library was considered neutral territory. A safe place for a potentially interested boy and girl to test the waters. Many a relationship had blossomed or fizzled between the tall rows of dusty books.

From the corner of his eye he saw Lee and Katie exchange amazed glances. Seniors didn't date sophomores. Trevor knew he would take some heat from his buddies, but he didn't care. There was something about Dana. Something that made him—

"I'd have to be home by nine-thirty," she said, and squeezed her eyes shut. "Dumb, huh? But it's a school night and my mom insists."

When she didn't open her eyes, he realized she was waiting for him to mock her. Instead, he wanted to grab her in his arms and give her a bear hug. Or shout his pleasure to the world. In a roundabout way she'd just said yes.

"No problem." Now that he'd been accepted, his ability to be cool returned in spades. "I'll pick you up at seven-thirty."

Her eyes popped open, along with her mouth. She blinked. "You will?"

"Sure. See ya."

He walked casually down the hall, greeting friends, acting as though nothing extraordinary had happened. Of course, no one knew that his heart pounded like a jackhammer as he worried about finding a secluded table at the library and at the same moment tried to figure out how he would have time to wash his car before he picked her up.

When he reached his classroom, he glanced back. Dana stood with her friends. The three girls were talking frantically and gesturing. Dana's smile was so wide she looked as if she'd just been crowned a beauty queen. His lips curved up in response. Tonight couldn't come fast enough.

It was 9:16. Trevor let his wrist rest casually over his steering wheel so she wouldn't know he'd been checking the time. Dana's mother had been pretty impressed with him. Parents usually liked him well enough, so he doubted Mrs. Rowan would mind if her daughter was a few minutes late. But he was determined to get Dana inside on time. He'd learned that by sticking to the rules from the beginning, he and his date found it easier to negotiate changes later. Besides, he didn't want to make Dana uncomfortable. A voice in his gut told him this wasn't going to be a casual relationship. He was in it for the long term and he could afford to take it slow.

Which didn't mean he wouldn't kiss her. If she cooperated.

She was staring at the algebra book on her lap. Her left index finger traced the edge of the spine up and down. He could feel her nervousness, her uncertainty, and he guessed she'd never been out with a boy before. Which probably meant she hadn't been kissed. The thought of being her first pleased him.

He leaned forward slightly and rested his right hand on her shoulder. "I had a good time."

She looked up, eyes wide like a cornered animal. She nodded. "Me, too."

"You're pretty smart."

Dismay filled her face. "Oh. Sorry."

"No. Don't apologize. I like smart girls. I can talk to them. They say stuff back." He grinned now, remembering their heated discussion about the right way to solve a word problem. "You're not afraid to tell me what you think."

"My mom says I'm too outspoken."

She was warm and the peach sweater was as soft as it looked. He moved his hand closer to her neck, then stroked the delicate skin under her ear. Her breath caught and he felt a shiver race through her.

"Outspoken is good," he said lightly, relieved it was dark in the car. She wouldn't be able to see his predictable reaction to her nearness. It was embarrassing. He'd gotten hard the second he'd seen her and things hadn't changed in the past two hours.

"You think so? I'm not sure. My mom says—"

He leaned over the console between them and angled his head. She stopped talking and froze in place, her mouth slightly parted, her eyes still wide. His lips touched hers.

Lightning ripped through him. Heat and need and feelings he'd never experienced before. He was trembling and felt as if he were about to explode. Fighting the desire to haul her hard against him, he kept the kiss light and still, trying to give her time to get used to what they were doing. After about a minute, he drew back somewhat.

Her eyes were closed, her mouth still parted. She smiled and touched a hand to her lips. "Wow." Her eyes opened and she covered her face with her hands. "Oh, no. I didn't really say that, did I?"

He chuckled. "Yeah, you did, and I'm glad. I thought it was a 'wow,' too."

She peeked at him between her fingers. "You did?"

"Promise."

He cupped the back of her neck and drew her closer. This time she melted against him. Her slender arms settled around his neck and he felt the tentative touch of her fingers in his hair. Her mouth yielded to his. He thought about deepening the kiss, but he was conscious of the time and of not wanting to go too far, too fast. She was special and he wanted to enjoy every moment they had.

"Dana, I have to take you in," he murmured against her mouth.

"Oh." She nodded. "I guess you're right."

"Can I see you tomorrow?"

"Yes!" she said eagerly. "Of course. I'd like that."

He loved that she wasn't grown up enough to be sophisticated. In time she would learn to pretend a lack of interest, to be coy and hold back. But her enthusiasm only made him like her more.

"Tomorrow is Friday. How about getting something to eat, then going to a movie. What's your curfew?"

She chewed her bottom lip. "I don't know. I've never been—" Even in the shadowed light of the Mustang's front seat he saw her blush. "That is, you're sort of my first, well...date." The last word came out as a whisper.

"I'm glad." He climbed out of the car and walked around to her door, then escorted her to her small apartment. "You can let me know tomorrow at school. I'll talk to you at lunch."

"Okay."

When he took her hand, she stared at him in wonder, then smiled. His chest tightened with pleasure. She was very special, he told himself as he waited while she unlocked the door and stepped inside. He'd finally found a girl he could really like and he promised himself he would do everything in his power to make this work.

"Trevor," she breathed, her voice thick with passion. "I think I like this."

He'd fallen for her, he thought with wonder. It had only been a few weeks and already he didn't know how he'd managed to survive without her. Around Dana, he felt able to take on the world. The rumors about his playing around didn't matter. He was hers and she knew that. She believed in him. He hadn't realized how much he'd needed that belief, until she'd given it so completely. Her honesty, her intelligence, her humor, her adoration, all conspired to make him love her. Which he could handle. It was their sensual playfulness that was getting him into trouble. Her shirt had long since been discarded and he was fighting the temptation to remove her bra.

"This *is* a mistake," he muttered, searching for control. He could hear his hormones laughing at his feeble attempts.

"I'm glad your parents are away for the weekend," Dana said, and dropped a kiss on his mouth. "This is fun."

She rubbed against him again and he groaned. "You can't keep doing that. Dana, I'm serious. You can feel what's happening to me. It means I want you. I know you like the kissing and touching, but you're not ready for anything else."

He placed his hands on her waist and lifted her off him, then rolled into a sitting position and tried to think pure thoughts.

Dana came up behind him and wrapped her arms around him. "I'm sorry. I don't mean to tease you. I like what we do together. But you're right. We should stop."

The lamp on the nightstand provided the only illumination in his room. He stared at the bookshelves in front of him, at the familiar trophies for football and track, at a few car models and some books. But he didn't see any of them.

He turned and cupped her face. "Dana, I wish..."

She smiled. "I know. I love you, Trevor."

His breath caught in his throat. Had she really said those

magic words? He'd never been happier in his life. "I love you, too. I love you so much I—"

She kissed him, cutting off his words. He pulled her close and they tumbled back onto the bed. They were kissing and touching, and suddenly they were both naked and he was stroking her belly, moving closer to that place he'd never been before.

He nuzzled her breasts, tasting them, tasting *her,* hoping she didn't notice how much he was shaking. He'd experimented with girls before, but he'd never made love.

As he prepared to enter her, he asked, "Should I stop?"

She shook her head. "I love you."

He drew in a shuddering breath and slowly entered her. The pressure was unbearable, as was the pleasure. He tried to hold back, to think of something else, but it was like trying to control the tide. One more thrust of his hips and he lost it.

When the spasms had faded, he looked at her. Dana touched his face. "I thought it would take longer."

Typical Dana, who didn't know enough to pretend to salvage his male ego. He kissed her fiercely. "Don't ever change," he told her. "I love you exactly as you are."

She wrinkled her nose. "What does that have to do with anything?" She shifted against him.

Amazingly enough, he felt himself become aroused again. He started to move. "Let's try that once more," he said. "This time it will be longer."

She pulled him close and kissed him. "I think I'd like that," she murmured against his mouth.

On Monday Trevor got to school late. He'd had a dentist appointment and for once he hadn't minded having his teeth cleaned. In fact, he figured he could have flown to school instead of driven. He'd never been so happy in his life.

Friday night had been magical. His only regret was that Dana had spent the rest of the weekend with her mother—some family obligation she hadn't been able to get out of. But he would see her tonight.

He walked into school just in time for fourth period. He slid into his seat next to his best friend, Joel, who gave him a knowing wink. The two boys had hung out the previous afternoon and Trevor had confessed what had happened with Dana.

As his history teacher lectured on the precursors to Pearl Harbor, Trevor noticed he was getting more attention than usual.

Karl, a fellow football player and full-time jerk, leaned over and whispered, "I heard about you and Dana. Way to go."

Trevor frowned. The comments continued when he left class. By lunch he realized the entire school knew. He was furious for both Dana and himself and concerned for her. While making love was seen as a rite of passage for males, females could easily be labeled sluts. He didn't want anyone saying anything bad to Dana.

He searched for her through lunch, but never saw her or her friends. Finally, he cut his last class and drove to her apartment.

She was pale, her cheeks tearstained, her shoulders slumped as she answered the door. Her pain was so tangible he felt it cutting through him, too.

"Dana, what—"

She held up her hand to stop him from talking. "Don't," she said harshly, her voice cracking with sobs. "Just don't. You got what you wanted. I almost understand that. What

I don't understand is how you could have told everyone."
Fresh tears filled her eyes and trickled down her cheeks.

"I didn't," he said. "I swear." He didn't tell anyone.
Except Joel. Joel, who had always watched Dana, had always made cracks about her. Trevor hadn't thought about
it one way or the other until that moment. Had his friend
wanted Dana for himself?

"Do you know what they're saying about me?" she
asked. "Do you know what they called me today?"

He was bleeding to death. He could feel the gaping hole
in his chest. "Dana, listen to me. I love you. I would never
do anything to hurt you."

"Liar."

She said the single word with a finality that told him
she'd already made up her mind.

"I never want to see you again," she continued. "Don't
come over here or talk to me. Don't even look at me. I'll
hate you forever. I swear I will."

He'd tried everything. He'd written notes, spoken with
her friends, called her daily. But he had nothing he could
offer her as proof. Joel had denied everything, then taken
Dana's side, as if he, too, believed Trevor had been the one
to spread the rumors. Trevor's only relief had come the
following fall, when he'd finally left for college.

Trevor reached for the beer on the table at his side and
gave his head a quick shake, hoping to dislodge the memories. He knew better than to spend much time in the past.
It had a way of grabbing on to him and never letting go.
Dana had thought their brief relationship meant nothing to
him, yet she was the reason he'd completed his undergrad-
uate degree in three years instead of four. At first he'd
buried himself in his studies to forget. Eventually he got
caught up in the process, until the work consumed him and
became its own reward. And now she was back in his life.

He knew he hadn't returned to Honeygrove because of her, yet he couldn't be sorry she was around. He didn't expect to pick things up where they'd left off, but he would like a chance to make things right. For reasons he didn't want to explore, he would prefer that Dana not think of him as the bad guy. When that was resolved, he would make some effort in his personal life. It was time to find someone and settle down. He wanted a loving relationship and a couple of kids. Goals most men found easy to accomplish, although he'd had a hell of a time making that happen.

All he wanted was someone to see him for who and what he was on the inside. Someone to care about him, to believe in him and the truth instead of the rumors.

He finished the beer and stood. If that didn't happen, there was always work. He could bury himself in it just as he'd buried himself in his studies. It was one lesson he'd learned very well.

"We went dancing," Sally said. "You know, that new club downtown? The one with the really cute D.J.?" She sighed rapturously and wrapped her arms around herself. "He held me close and I thought I was going to die."

"You're going to wish you had if you let yourself fall for him," Melba intoned ominously. "I'm telling you, don't go getting serious about Trevor MacAllister."

Angie, a blond nurse pretty enough to make other women dislike her on sight, came up and joined the conversation. "Listen to Melba," she said, and gave a slow, self-satisfied smile. "You might have had him Saturday night, Sally, but I had him all Sunday night, and I do mean all." She gave a little wink, then walked over to the elevator and pushed the Down button.

Dana wished there were a means for her to gracefully

escape from the conversation, but she was trapped between Sally and Melba, with no way to tell them she wasn't interested in the object of their conversation. Worse, she was stuck waiting for him. He needed to talk about several changes in the current surgery schedule.

"Like I said, we went dancing," Sally repeated, speaking loudly so that Angie could hear. She tucked a strand of dark curly hair behind her ear. "Some of us don't believe in putting out on the first date. You know, some of us believe we're worth more and have some class."

Angie glanced over her shoulder and grinned. "Some of us got asked and some of us didn't." She rolled her eyes. "I'm so tired. I swear, I didn't get but a couple hours' sleep. I would blame him completely, but he kept telling me he was inspired."

Dana gritted her teeth. She told herself she was annoyed at being kept waiting, then shook off the thought. No point in lying to herself. She knew better. She was cranky because she'd actually started to believe Trevor's "I'm so alone" act. To think that she'd gone over and actually *helped* him unpack. He must have been laughing when she left. All that talk about his ex-wife and how he'd found her with another man.

She clutched her clipboard and wished she could toss it across the room. To make matters worse, she'd truly felt sorry for Trevor. Like an idiot, she'd assumed he'd spent Saturday night in. After all, she'd heard his television playing until nearly nine at night.

She turned to Sally. "I know that Trevor moved over the weekend," she said. "He must have been busy unpacking. What time did he pick you up?"

Sally looked surprised that Dana had joined the conversation, but she answered quickly enough. "Late. The club doesn't really get going until almost eleven."

There went that theory. By ten Dana had been reading in bed. She wouldn't have heard Trevor leaving the town house. Not that it was any of her business.

She knew that her irritation was fueled by the fact that she'd been so taken in by him, and had been feeling guilty for being slightly less than pleasant during their conversation. She'd seriously considered inviting him over for dinner on Sunday. Good thing she hadn't.

Never again, she told herself. She would do her best to avoid the man like the wart scum he was. The next time she saw him, she would—

The elevator doors opened and Trevor stepped out. All conversation ceased as the four women turned their attention to him.

"There you are," he said.

Dana blinked. He'd walked right past Angie and Sally with little more than a nod, but he was giving her one of his better smiles. That didn't make sense. How could he ignore those other women? He'd *dated* them. According to Angie, he and the pretty nurse had done the wild thing through most of the night.

"Dr. MacAllister," she said, ignoring the frenzy stirred up by her suddenly out-of-control hormones. Bad enough that he was a skirt chaser. Worse that her own body betrayed her by melting on command every time she saw him and he bestowed a smile on her. Why couldn't she grow up? A crush at fifteen was excusable. A crush at her age made her look really stupid.

"I'm sorry about having to make changes," he said, motioning for her to lead the way to her office.

She glanced back and saw the three nurses eyeing them. He still didn't acknowledge any of them. How strange.

"The schedule is more flexible than usual this week," she said. She entered her office and moved to sit behind her desk. Trevor took the chair across from her. He pulled a sheet of paper out of the front right pocket of his white coat.

She watched him as he read the sheet. "You look tired," she said. "Rough night?"

The words popped out without warning. When he glanced at her, she was determined to bluff her way through and tried to smile casually. She wasn't sure how it actually looked.

"I was up late unpacking," he said.

"You didn't have a date?" She heard the incredulity in her voice and wished she could call back the question.

"No. I stayed in. What about you? Anything fun over the weekend?"

Her social life was incredibly dismal, but he didn't need to know that. "I prefer to keep conversation strictly business."

"I see." Perfect eyebrows arched. "You *were* the one asking about my personal life."

"I know. I apologize. For a moment I forgot myself."

He leaned forward and rested his hands on her desk. "Forget away."

Her brain screamed at her to watch out. Trevor was lethal when he flirted. She'd already suffered once at his hands and didn't see any reason to do it a second time.

"This is none of my business," she said slowly. "But I want to remind you that hospitals are notorious for gossip. While there's no policy against staff members dating, it can create tension in the workplace. You might want to remind your dates that they should be discreet."

"My dates?" He studied her for a moment. "I see. How many did I have this past weekend?"

"Two that I heard about."

Hazel green eyes stared at a place over her left shoulder.

His facial expression didn't change, but suddenly she couldn't read what he was thinking. It was as though an invisible screen had fallen to shield him.

He handed her the piece of paper. "These are my changes in the surgery schedule. If there's a problem, I would appreciate you contacting my office."

He was gone before she could say anything else. Dana was left staring after him, wondering why on earth she felt as if she'd disappointed him.

Chapter Four

"Who ordered this?" Lee Murphy asked as their waiter delivered a basket of steaming cheese garlic bread.

Dana shook her head. "Don't look at me. I wouldn' have ordered it, but I don't mind helping everyone eat it.'

Katie Sheppard smiled. "You know they just bring i unless we tell them we don't want any. It's a tradition."

"Calories," Lee said, eyeing the basket, then grabbing a slice. "Unnecessary calories."

"But if we didn't actually order the food, the calorie don't really count," Dana said.

Her two friends laughed. When the waiter reappeared they gave him their order, then settled in for a chatty lunch Dana sipped her diet soda and listened while Katie talked about her wedding plans. The affair would be simple, with only family and close friends.

"I'm not going to have a maid of honor," Katie said her brown eyes crinkling as she smiled. "I want the two of you to be my attendants, though. Just like we promised in high school.''

Dana looked at Lee. "I can't believe I'm about to get all teary."

Lee grimaced. "Terrible, isn't it? We should be annoyed because she broke the pact. Next thing you know we'll be planning a wedding shower."

Dana shrugged. "I was thinking about a brunch."

"Me, too," Lee admitted, then laughed. "We're hopeless."

Katie addressed them both. "So you're really all right with this? I know we promised, but..." She smiled. "I can't help it. I love him."

"We understand," Lee told her. "What's a little promise among friends?"

Katie picked up a piece of garlic bread. "I feel badly about that. Really I do. Does it help to remind you two that I really meant it at the time?"

Lee touched Katie's arm. "You don't have to explain. Dana and I aren't mad at you. Why would we be? You've found a wonderful man who loves you, and you're going to spend the rest of your life with him. We'd be pretty crummy friends to want to stand in the way."

"She's right," Dana added. "Be happy, Katie. That's what this time is all about."

"Thank you." Katie reached down and pulled a magazine out of her oversized purse. "I was hoping you'd say that. So I brought a copy of a bridal magazine. There are a few dresses I think you'll like."

Lee and Dana groaned in unison. "Nothing with ruffles," Lee said. "I mean that, Katie. No cute bows, no little capes on the shoulders and definitely no trains."

Katie held up her hands in mock surrender. "That was

never my plan. I was thinking more along the lines of simple and elegant.''

She opened the magazine and angled it toward Lee. Dana glanced at the picture, but found her attention drifting from the conversation of dress styles and colors. Not that she wasn't interested in her friend's wedding. She was still adjusting to the fact that Katie was marrying a doctor.

Years ago, after graduating from nursing school, the three lifelong friends had signed a pact swearing none of them would ever marry a doctor. They all had their reasons. Katie's doctor father had always been available to everyone but his family. Lee's father, also a doctor, had gotten Lee's mother pregnant, then left her with an illegitimate baby. Dana's father had also left. She had watched her mother wasting her life, waiting for a man to come rescue her after her divorce. Her fantasy had always been to marry a doctor, and she'd refused to go out with several honest, decent men simply because they didn't fit her preconceived notion of what she wanted.

Until a few months ago, the three friends had kept their promise. Then Katie had gotten involved with her close friend Mike Brennan. Dana couldn't blame her. Mike was one of the good guys and wildly in love with Katie. Marriage was the next obvious step in their relationship. Turning her back on a very special life of love would be as foolish as Dana's mother's insistence on holding out for a white knight, who never showed up.

But... Dana bit back a sigh. She hated to admit it, even to herself, but at times she was envious of her friend. She didn't want to get involved with a doctor, but she did want to find someone she could care about. Someone who would care back. Like most women, she wanted a family—including children and a husband. Focusing on her career hadn't left her much opportunity to socialize. Maybe now that she'd received her promotion she could start taking care of her personal life.

"So what do you think?" Katie asked, turning the magazine so Dana could see the photograph of the bridesmaids' dress.

The dark-green gown had a boat neck and long sleeves. The simple bodice set off the floor-length, tulip skirt.

"This part comes off," Katie said, pointing to the skirt. "See the knee-length panel underneath? It's really a shorter skirt, so you can wear the dress again, to a party or something." She chewed on her lower lip. "Do you like it?"

Dana glanced at Lee and nodded. Her friend smiled. "We love it. No frills, no ruffles and no bows, which pleases me. But this is your wedding, Katie. Are you happy with it?"

"Yes. I looked when I went shopping for my dress, and I really like this one best. We need to arrange a time to go order them."

Before they could continue, their waiter returned with their food. All three had ordered grilled-chicken salads. Dana thought about all the lunches they'd shared since graduating from nursing school. By now they should have their own table at the restaurant. Or at least a plaque on the wall, commemorating their patronage. The thought made her chuckle.

An hour later, she and Lee started across the street toward the hospital, while Katie got into her car to make a quick trip home to check on her father. He was doing better, but was still not as strong as before his heart attack.

"You were quiet at lunch," Lee said. "Is everything all right?"

"Fine," Dana told her. "I was just thinking about things. Katie marrying Mike. I'm really happy for her, but it's strange."

"To think about her marrying a doctor?" Lee asked. "But if it makes her happy, that's what counts." She glanced at Dana. "It's none of my business, but how are you doing, now that Trevor's back in town?"

"Tough question," Dana admitted. "I'd feel better if we weren't neighbors." She'd already filled both women in on that particular detail. "As far as dealing with him at the hospital...I guess I'm doing as well as can be expected. Nothing has changed. The nurses are lining up to date him. He's already been out with two that I know about. At least I don't have to worry about having a crush on him."

Lee stiffened slightly. "A crush wouldn't be so bad."

"It would for me. I gave Trevor my heart once and he trampled all over it."

"I know. I'm sorry. That was really difficult for you."

They walked into the hospital. Dana paused by the reception desk. "Trevor and I have talked about the past," she said, her voice low so that they wouldn't be overheard. "He brought it up when he first came here."

Lee raised her eyebrows. "I'm surprised. Did he apologize?"

"Not exactly. He said he wanted to explain. He swore he wasn't the one to spread the rumors about him and me. He said the only person he told was Joel Haddock."

"Who?"

"You know, the dark-haired skinny guy I was friends with that summer. He'd been close to Trevor. Trevor claims Joel wanted to go out with me himself, and that when he found out about Trevor and me, he spread the story to break us up."

"Do you believe him?" Lee asked.

"I don't know. Trevor has a lot of flaws, but he's always been honest. He has no reason to lie this many years after the fact."

"Does the past still matter?"

Dana shook her head. "There's a hard question. I guess it shouldn't, right?"

"Only you can answer that. Trevor was important to you once. You were hurt badly by what you thought were his actions. Would knowing none of it was his fault change anything?"

Dana wanted to say that it wouldn't. She wasn't that fifteen-year-old girl anymore. Trevor was no longer the center of her world. She'd grown up and moved on. Yet, in ways she couldn't explain, it did matter.

"I'm confused," she admitted.

"It's a start," Lee said, and glanced at her watch. "I'm really sorry, but I'm running late. I have to get to the clinic."

Dana gave her a quick hug. "No problem. Thanks for listening. I'll talk to you soon."

Lee waved, then headed down the hallway. Dana walked to the elevators and pressed the button for the third floor. When the doors opened, she stepped inside. Two young nurses were talking. She glanced at them and wondered if they'd set their sights on Trevor yet. If not, it was just a matter of time. In the slang of the day, Trevor was a chick magnet. He'd already dated Angie and Sally. Who else had fallen victim to his considerable charms?

At least she was safe. She'd received her inoculation back in high school and that kind of immunization lasted for life.

"So much for being immunized," Dana muttered two days later as she walked past the television. The sound was down and she didn't even glance at the show on the set. "This is disgusting. I'm completely humiliated for myself. If anyone had a clue." She sighed.

The good news was no one had a clue. The bad news was she was worse than pathetic. This was just like driving by a boy's house back in high school, only worse, because now she was a grown-up and she knew better. Instead of cruising in a car, she was pacing in her living room, hovering by the common wall, trying to pretend to herself that she wasn't actually listening to see if Trevor was home. The only thing more humiliating would be holding a glass to the wall and listening.

She heard a faint sound and froze. It came again. The unmistakable rumble of a laugh track on a TV sitcom. He *was* home. Granted it was a Wednesday night and many people didn't go out during the week. But he wasn't just anyone, and hospital scuttlebutt had it that he'd been out continually since his return. But if the sound coming from his town house really was his television, as she thought, she would swear he'd been home the previous two nights...not that she'd actually eavesdropped at the wall.

She flopped onto her sofa and told herself she should be ashamed. She was acting like a kid with a crush on a rock star. Worse, she was lying to herself about it.

"I need a hobby," she said aloud. "Something to occupy my free time."

She glanced at the book she'd been reading, but for once her favorite mystery author couldn't hold her attention. Too many thoughts raced around in her head. The OR had scheduling problems and she needed to sort them out. She was on three different committees and they all required reports she hadn't started. Her sock drawer was in pretty bad shape....

The laugh track sounded again. Dana stared at the wall. What was going on? Was he really home, or did he leave the TV on when he went out? Something didn't add up. Angie and Sally seemed to be his two favorites, but a couple of other women claimed to have been out with him. When did he find the time? And why wasn't he more exhausted during the day?

Don't think about this, she told herself. She needed a distraction.

As if in answer to her prayers, a knock sounded on the front door. She bounded off the sofa and walked to the foyer. "Who is it?" she called, even as she started to unlock the dead bolt.

"Trevor."

She froze in the act of releasing the lock. A tremor rippled through her. She glanced down at her faded sweatshirt and much-washed jeans. It was nearly seven in the evening, so she doubted a scrap of makeup remained on her face. She gave herself a mental shake. It was just Trevor. Her appearance was unimportant.

"Hi," she said as she pulled the door open. Her smile was polite, although it was tough to keep it in place, what with her jaw wanting to drop.

He wore the masculine version of her outfit. A dark-blue sweatshirt over faded jeans. The difference was, she looked relaxed and slightly scruffy. He looked like a highly paid model on his way to a photo shoot. Stubble darkened his cheeks. Weariness shadowed his eyes, until the green faded completely.

"I'm having a crisis," he said, and held out a wad of paper.

Dana took it from him and realized it was sticky. "What is this?"

"Contact paper. I'm trying to line my shelves. Obviously I'm doing something wrong. Is this a female thing, like knowing what colors go together? Am I missing the shelf-papering gene?"

She thrust the ball of sticky paper back at him. "I suspect

what you're missing is the will to line your own cupboards. You're just looking for free labor."

"Ouch," he said, and pressed a hand to his stomach. "That's a low blow." A slow smile turned up the corners of his mouth and made her toes curl. "If I offer you beer and pizza, the labor wouldn't be free."

She told herself to say no. He was dating. Let Angie or Sally or whoever trot on over and line his shelves. They would be thrilled to spend the time with him. Of course, then she would be forced to listen to their voices and the sound of laughter drifting through the common wall.

"Please," he said. "I'll change the oil in your car."

"I just had it done." She told herself she was being neighborly, nothing more. "Okay, I'll help. But I want mushrooms on the pizza, and a deep-dish crust."

"Deal."

Telling herself she would probably regret this, Dana grabbed her key and stepped outside. After locking her door, she followed him to his place.

She hesitated before stepping inside. What would she find? A typical bachelor pad? She wasn't sure she wanted proof of his wild social life. The stories were already more than she could handle. Then she reminded herself that the furniture she'd already seen had been completely normal. No reason to think that he would have strange pieces of art or pictures. She walked into the foyer.

The town house was much as she remembered, with oversized but conservative furniture. The prints and photographs had been hung on the walls. Mostly outdoor scenes and seascapes. Nothing provocative. She could see into the living room. Magazines lay scattered on the coffee table. Most of them looked like medical journals. A spy-thriller bestseller sat open on the floor next to the couch. No signs of any female presence here. Come to think of it, none of the nurses had mentioned being at his place. That was a relief. She hoped he kept that policy intact.

"I think I'm doing something wrong," Trevor said, leading the way into the kitchen. "Maybe because I don't understand the purpose of shelf paper. I had a cleaning service come in and scrub all the cupboards. Why do I have to line them, too?" He pointed to a half-dozen rolls of contact paper. "I wouldn't bother, except my mom sent it over and I know she's going to check when she comes to visit me."

"Will she yell at you if you don't use it?"

"No." He shifted uncomfortably, looking more like a little boy than a successful doctor. "But, you know. It's my mom."

It was nice some woman had power over him. She bit back a smile and moved to stand in front of the pantry. Boxes of food sat on the floor, but nothing in the cupboard. The top shelf had been lined already. Sort of. The paper was certainly attached, but it was crooked, with several large bubbles in the center. The edges were jagged.

Dana grabbed a loose corner and pulled the paper free. "Somehow I don't want to know how you put this in. Didn't you measure first?"

He raised dark eyebrows. "Of course I measured first. What do you think? That I'm a complete idiot?"

His outrage was so realistic she knew he was bluffing. She wadded up the used paper and tossed it at him. "You didn't, did you?"

He tossed both sticky balls into a trash bag sitting in the corner. "No. I guessed how big the shelf was."

"And you were wrong."

"'Wrong' is a strong term."

"But accurate," she teased. "Hand me the tape measure."

She showed him how to measure the shelves and, if they

were all the same size, to cut one piece, then use it as a template. Trevor was a born cutter, but he was lousy at anchoring the paper by one side, getting it straight, then gently peeling off the back so that the sheet laid down perfectly.

"Just leave it," Dana said when he'd twisted his third attempt. "We don't have enough paper for this. You measure the other cupboards and cut the right sizes. I'll come behind you and do the peel-and-stick part."

They worked well together, Dana thought as they moved around in the kitchen. The relatively close confines required occasional contact, but she tried to ignore her body's reaction every time he was near. Hormones were powerful things, she told herself as her heart rate increased in direct proportion to his closeness. If only... She smiled to herself. Yeah, right. If only Trevor were for real. All the things he already was—funny, smart, gifted and, okay, good-looking—plus a few others, like faithful and loving. Then he would be a completely irresistible package. As it was now, he was very nice to look at, but she knew better than to touch.

He stopped work long enough to order the pizza and grab them a couple of beers from the fridge. "So you're staying in for the evening," she said. "That must be a nice change of pace."

He handed her one of the open bottles and frowned. "You made a similar comment the last time we spoke at the hospital. You know, when you lectured me on the pitfalls of dating among the ranks. Has it ever occurred to you that I might *not* be seeing anyone right now?"

"That's not what I hear."

"I see." He took a swallow of beer. "I don't suppose there's a chance the rumors might be just that—rumors?"

Oddly enough, she wanted them to be untrue, although

she didn't dare analyze the reason why. Too much risk in that one. "Are they?" she asked.

Instead of coming back with a quick, humorous response, he held her gaze. "Would you believe me if I said yes?"

He was asking more than a simple question. A shiver rippled through her. Not one of desire…not this time. It was something more dangerous. A wanting she couldn't define. Trevor had once been the brightest star in her universe. When that star had gone out, it had taken her a long time to make her own light. She didn't want to have to go through that again. Oh, but she was woman enough to admit he tempted her.

Someone knocked on the door. "That must be the pizza," she said, grateful for the interruption.

Trevor paid the delivery guy and returned to the kitchen. Dana had found both the place mats he owned and set the table. The overhead light fixture made her gold blond hair shine. Her face was scrubbed clean of makeup, her clothes casual. She looked the way he remembered her from back in high school. If only life could be that simple again.

He wanted to pursue their previous conversation. He, too, had heard the rumors that he was dating several nurses at the hospital. The truth was, he hadn't been out with anyone in nearly two years. Not since he'd walked out on his ex-wife after finding her in bed with another man for the second time. It didn't matter that he kept telling himself he had to get on with his life. His plans for having a loving family that included a wife and children would have a much better chance of coming true if he started going out. But he couldn't face the process. There were too many explanations. Too many women unwilling to believe.

Like Dana. He hated that he gave a damn about her opinion, but for reasons he didn't understand, what she thought mattered.

"I looked over the schedule for next week," Dana said, pulling a slice of pizza out of the box. "You have a lot going on."

"Just a couple of extra cases."

"They were marked as special. Are you working with a national charity foundation?"

He nodded. "I got involved with one when I had my fellowship in Los Angeles. They work with the hospital to reduce fees—I donate my time for the surgery." He shrugged. "I think it's important. My father did the same thing when he was still in practice."

Walter had taught him to always give back. Trevor knew he'd been blessed with a gift. For some, surgery was a mystery they could never conquer; for others it was merely plumbing; but when he began a procedure, he felt completely in tune with his patient's body. It was as if the organs and cells whispered to him, telling him the best place to cut, to mend, to heal. He took another swallow of beer. Pretty fanciful stuff for a simple guy like him. Obviously he'd been spending too much time alone.

She handed him the plate with the pizza slice, then took one for herself. "I'm impressed."

"Don't be. There are at least a half-dozen other surgeons in the area donating their time."

She tucked a strand of short hair behind her ear. "Do you know how many surgeons there are in Honeygrove? Believe me, you're in the minority." Her gaze focused on his face.

"Let me guess," he said, trying not to sound cynical or weary. "You never would have expected me to do something like this."

"You're right. I wouldn't have expected you to volunteer your services, but now that I'm thinking about the situation, it makes perfect sense."

Her words pleased him because her good opinion mattered.

Dana took a bite of pizza and chewed. When she'd swallowed she said, "Whatever differences I may have with you over your personal life, I respect and admire your abilities in the OR. I've watched you work, Trevor. What they say is true—you're amazingly gifted."

"So I'm more than a pretty face?"

She smiled. "Apparently so."

They were treading on dangerous ground. He wanted to pursue this line of conversation because he wanted to explain everything. He wanted to tell her that he wasn't what people thought—that he didn't date every single female in a fifty-mile radius, that he wasn't shallow and insensitive, that he wanted a normal life. But he'd tried telling women that before. Oh, they pretended to believe, but they didn't really. Experience had taught him people couldn't be told— they had to take the time to discover who he was for themselves. Usually it didn't matter, but with Dana...

Telling himself she'd just been some girl in high school didn't help. He'd fallen for her, and without meaning to, he'd hurt her badly. They'd been each other's first time. Maybe that was a bond that could never be broken.

She finished her slice of pizza. "You've always been more than a pretty face. You're intelligent, funny, easy to talk to."

"A paragon."

"I don't think paragons have harems."

He raised his eyebrows. "Neither do I."

"That's not what the nurses are saying."

"And it's not possible they were making things up? What if I told you I hadn't been on a date since I came back to Honeygrove?"

She laughed. "Trevor, come on. You don't have to play

this game with me. I remember you from high school. You were the most popular guy on campus.''

"I had an exaggerated reputation.''

Her smile faded and her eyes clouded with memories. He knew what she was thinking.

"Dana, about that weekend.''

She shook her head. "No, don't let's talk about that. It's not important anymore. Time has a way of fixing things. I'll admit I was a little unhappy when I found out you were coming back, but now I'm fine. We're working well together, don't you think?''

"Yeah,'' he muttered. "It's great.''

She finished her beer, then rose to her feet. "It's getting late,'' she said. "I have to be at work early tomorrow, so I'm going to head home.''

He followed her to the door. "Thanks for helping me.'' He wanted to say more, to maybe invite her back, but he figured she would make up an excuse to refuse. She wouldn't believe it was anything but a come-on. Of course he was lonely—but he wasn't just looking for company; he was specifically interested in spending time with Dana.

She paused by the front door and looked at him. The overhead light illuminated her face. Her skin was clear, with a faint blush of color at her cheeks. Her full mouth tempted him. He wanted to know if the kissing would be as magical now as it had been all those years ago. He wanted to take her in his arms and remember what it had been like to hold her close.

Just one friendly kiss, he thought, wondering how she would react. Then he thought about the other friendly things he wanted to do with her and knew he wasn't ready to stop at a kiss.

"Thanks again,'' he said.

"No problem. See you at work." She gave him a quick wave and started out the door.

He watched her walk around to her front door. What was she thinking right now? Did she imagine that he had a hot date lined up? Probably. He would love to tell her what was really going on—or actually what wasn't—then watch the look on her face. Assuming she believed him.

Chapter Five

Dana hummed cheerfully as she dealt with last-minute schedule changes. A couple of emergencies had tied up surgical equipment, rooms and personnel into the morning, but she'd already shuffled everything around. With a little luck, no scheduled surgery would get bumped. She knew that preparing for surgery was traumatic for patients and she hated the thought of telling people they had to wait another day. She also had to worry about having enough staff, not to mention making sure recovery wasn't overloaded. Sometimes her job was like juggling, trying to keep a dozen or more balls in the air. The pressure could be intense, but she enjoyed the challenges and the fact that every day was a little different.

After making the last call to confirm a surgical nurse's availability, Dana leaned back in her chair and sighed contentedly. She'd made it all happen. Moments like these, when she knew she'd done her best and it had come out right, she felt validated in her career choice. So what if she'd focused nearly all her energy on her job? Wasn't it worth it?

She turned her chair and reached for the coffeepot she kept on her credenza. After pouring a cup, she pulled out a file and started checking paperwork. But thoughts intruded. Thoughts of Trevor.

She'd fallen asleep thinking about him. It was, she knew, a dangerous precedent. Bad enough that her body responded every time she was near him, but she didn't want to have to worry about an overactive imagination, too. Still, she had to admit she'd enjoyed lying in bed, remembering the sound of his voice as he'd talked with her. He'd made her laugh while they'd worked on the shelves. There was something about him, something almost sincere. If she hadn't known better, she would have sworn he was lonely and really happy with her company. A ridiculous thought considering his active social life. Or was that really true?

What had he said about the rumors? That they might not be accurate? He'd also hinted that he hadn't been on a date since he'd come back to Honeygrove. She frowned. That one didn't make sense. After all, both Sally and Angie had said they'd dated him and neither woman had a reason to lie. Did Trevor? Hadn't she always thought of him as honest? So what was the real story?

Someone knocked at her door. "Come in," she called.

Sally stepped into her office and smiled. "'Morning, boss. I just wanted to thank you for scheduling me with Trevor."

Dana leaned back in her chair. "I scheduled you for a surgery because you're qualified and available. I don't make adjustments based on your desire for a personal life."

"I know. I'm teasing."

Sally plopped into the chair opposite Dana's. The young

woman hadn't tied her hair back yet and dark curls spilled over her shoulders. Blue scrubs brought out the color in her cheeks and added a honey glow to her tanned skin. She was, Dana had to admit, very pretty. And very young.

"But he is amazing," the nurse added.

"Trevor?" Dana asked, pretending ignorance, while trying to squelch the flash of annoyance that flared in her chest.

"Uh-huh." Sally sighed dramatically. "So sweet and charming. You know most surgeons are remote and demanding, but not Trevor. Oh, he can be a terror in the OR if someone makes a mistake, but privately, he's a very special man."

"I see."

"Last night we—"

"You saw him last night?" Dana asked, cutting her off. "But he was home."

Sally straightened in her chair. "How would you— Oh, that's right. He moved into your town-house complex. Does he live close?"

Dana was already regretting her outburst. It had nothing to do with Sally and everything to do with her own foolishness. Once again she'd been sucked in by the charm. What had she been thinking? Trevor had wanted her to help him with his kitchen because he didn't want to do the work himself. She'd been foolish enough to go along. Not to mention foolish enough to fall asleep thinking about him. Was she crazy? Did she actually think he was interested in her? Okay, he might be intrigued, but so what? Apparently anything female under fifty and still breathing interested him.

"His town house is a short walk from mine," Dana said, avoiding the technical truth that he lived next door. "I, ah, happened to see his car when I took out the trash last night.''

No way was she going to admit she'd been in the man's house eating pizza until nine. That she'd actually thought they might be friends this time around.

"I see." Sally rose to her feet and stretched. "We were supposed to go dancing, but decided a quiet evening would be better, so we stayed in. He had a lot to do at home, so he didn't get over to my place until about ten.''

Dana resisted the urge to throw something. Damn. So while she'd been lying in bed, thinking warm fuzzy thoughts about Trevor, he'd been across town, warming Sally's bed.

"I'm glad things are working out between you," she said, mustering as much sincerity as she could. Hopefully, the younger woman didn't notice the tension in her voice.

"Thanks. I think we have something very special going on." She gave Dana a quick smile, then left.

Dana stared after her, feeling both old and stupid. "Never again," she said aloud. She would not be tricked by him anymore.

But as she tried to focus on her work, a voice in the back of her head whispered that Trevor hadn't done anything wrong. He'd asked for her help and she'd agreed. He'd bought her pizza and had been a pleasant companion. He hadn't broken any promises or mistreated her in any way. They had no understanding—their evening together hadn't been a date. So why was she so upset? Why did the thought of Trevor staying the night with Sally bother her?

"Don't go there," she told herself. "Some things are better left unexplored."

"It makes me nervous when my staff members start talking to themselves."

She glanced up and saw Walter MacAllister standing in

the doorway. "I wasn't talking to myself," she said quickly, then grinned. "I was, ah, practicing a speech."

"Of course you were." Walter stepped in and took the seat Sally had recently vacated. He wore a shirt and tie under his white jacket. "The advantage of talking to oneself is that one is always assured an intelligent response. At least, in your case that's true. With some other people I'm not so sure."

"Thanks for the compliment, but I'm not always sure about myself, either."

He set a folder on her desk. Despite his white hair and trimmed white beard, he appeared much younger than his sixty years, which made Dana think about how great Trevor would look at his dad's age.

"There was quite a mess in the OR this morning. First, those car accident victims, then the emergency bypass. You did an excellent job of coordinating the scheduled surgeries. I received calls from a couple of surgeons who were pleased you'd managed to keep their patients from having to come back later in the week."

"Thanks. I know it's stressful for patients, so I try to avoid that."

Walter nodded. "You're good at this, Dana. As I knew you would be, I suppose it's only fair I take all the credit."

"Of course, Walter," she said, and laughed. "I wouldn't expect any less."

"I suspect one day I'm going to regret that you're not more frightened of me."

He'd been teasing, but she responded seriously. "Walter, I have the greatest respect for you. You don't terrorize your staff because you know it's not the right way to get them to do their best. You lead by example and you've set a high benchmark for us to achieve. I work hard because I believe in doing my best and because I want to measure up to your standards.''

''You've excelled, Dana. Look how far you've come since you graduated from nursing school. I knew you'd do well and you have. Now, if we're done mutually affirming each other, I'd like to mention a couple of things.''

''Sure.'' She pulled out a notepad. Walter held regular meetings, but he also tended to drop in on his staff and discuss some issues one-on-one. She ran a quick mental check on what was going on in her department, trying to pinpoint any problems. To the best of her knowledge, everything was running smoothly.

''Next Saturday Maggie and I are having a small dinner party. We'd like you to come.''

''Thanks, I'd love to.''

Walter and his wife frequently entertained hospital personnel. Not just the doctors, but everyone from nurses to kitchen staff, surgeons to janitorial assistants. The food was always excellent, the conversation eclectic, and the relaxed atmosphere allowed people who worked together but would otherwise never speak have a chance to get to know one another.

''About seven. Do you want to bring a date?'' He pulled a sheet of paper out of his right front jacket pocket and paused.

Dana pretended to consider the matter, a face-saving measure designed to make Walter think she might actually have a man she could invite. ''I think I'll come by myself.''

''Great. We're looking forward to it. Maggie and I always enjoy your company.'' He scribbled a note and tucked the paper away. ''The second matter involves business. I have good news. At least I hope you'll consider it good news.'' He leaned forward in his chair and smiled. ''The hospital is sending you to the FMR Management seminar. The course starts in two weeks.''

Dana stared at him. All the doctors and senior staff were required to attend the week-long management program in the northern California wine country. It was prestigious and expensive, with the hospital picking up the tab. The material was designed to expand problem solving by moving from linear to three-dimensional thinking.

It was rare for someone in her position to be sent to the seminar. Obviously Walter had nominated her and the committee had agreed.

Elation filled her. ''I'm thrilled. Thank you.''

''I think you'll enjoy your time there. They have some very innovative programs.'' He grinned. ''Just don't go in expecting a lot of classroom-type activities. You'll be surprised by what they ask you to do. Be open and plan to have fun and I'm sure you'll have a great time.''

''And learn something,'' she added.

''You can't help that part.'' Walter stood. ''I have a meeting with some angry family members who want to threaten us with litigation. So thank you for this pleasant interlude, Dana. Maggie and I will see you next Saturday.''

''Bye.''

She waited until he was gone, then allowed herself one loud ''Yes!'' of victory. She was going to the management seminar. What a coup! She couldn't wait to tell Katie and Lee. Just think, a whole week away at a luxury hotel in a beautiful part of California. As a bonus, she would have an entire week in which she wouldn't have to think about Trevor MacAllister even once.

Walter and Maggie MacAllister's house had a view of Honeygrove in one direction and the mountains in the distance in the other. Dana paused to glance around before ringing the doorbell. The first time she'd been invited here she'd been quaking in her newly purchased pumps. The luxurious 5,000-square-foot custom home was a far cry from the small apartment where she'd grown up. If Katie and Lee hadn't been with her, she would have turned tail and run. Fortunately, they had given one another courage and the night had been a success.

That felt like a long time ago, she thought, remembering how in awe she and her friends had been of the chief of staff. Now, while she still felt a twinge of nervousness, she knew she would find the host and hostess gracious, the food incredible and the company friendly. Even the most difficult staff members relaxed at the MacAllisters' house. The welcoming atmosphere didn't come from expensive furnishing or designer wallcovers but was a by-product of the family who lived there. Walter and Maggie were charming people who enjoyed the company of others and it showed.

She turned so she could gaze at the city stretched out before her. The night was surprisingly warm and clear. Streetlights twinkled, as if reflecting the stars up above. She drew in a deep breath and smiled. Things were going very well for her and she was content. Nothing could mar her pleasure at the evening ahead.

A rumble cut through the quiet. Dana stiffened slightly as she recognized that particular car engine. It was quite distinct and one she heard daily. Trevor left for his office long before she left for work. She was usually still in her bathroom getting ready when she heard him back out of his garage. Inevitably, she was forced to picture him freshly showered and shaved, still smelling of soap, in a crisp shirt and tie. If she wasn't careful, she could waste several minutes lost in the reverie of what Trevor would look like as he dressed...or while still in the shower.

She shook her head to clear it and told herself to hurry

inside. For some reason, it had never occurred to her that Trevor would be here tonight, although it made sense that he'd been invited. To the best of her knowledge, this was the MacAllisters' first dinner party since their son had returned to town.

She didn't want him to catch her standing on the steps. Better to already be at the party, talking with someone so she could pretend not to notice that he'd arrived. If she was careful, she might be able to avoid saying much of anything to him. Sometimes the crowds were large enough to allow people to get lost.

But she couldn't get the message from her brain to her feet. It was like being at the sight of an accident when one orders oneself to look away but finds the task impossible.

Telling herself she was a fool, she waited for him and whomever he'd brought with him. At least she would have tangible proof that, despite what he claimed, he really *was* dating. Maybe that would help her clear him from her mind.

But the tall, handsome man walking lightly up the walkway steps was alone. He paused when he saw her and smiled. "Dana? I didn't know you were going to be here. We could have driven together."

His comment required a response on her part, but she couldn't seem to think of one. She told herself it wasn't her fault. For one thing, he was giving her his best smile, the one that could reduce steel to a puddle, never mind the effect it had on her bones and muscles. For another, he was in a suit. Dark slacks and jacket, cream shirt, red striped tie. He was stunning.

He continued to stare at her, waiting for her to say something. What came to mind was a brief prayer of thanks that she'd worn her ivory silk dress, picked up at nearly two-thirds off during a going-out-of-business sale at a boutique in a neighboring town. The fabric emphasized curves, making that which was modest appear lush, while the softly flowing cut of the skirt added the illusion of grace to her walk.

"I didn't know you were going to be here, either," she managed at last. While it wasn't witty repartee, it was at least something closely resembling conversation.

Trevor joined her by the front door. "It's my first time," he said, and winked. "I'm a little nervous, so I'm going to depend on you to show me the ropes."

"This used to be your home. You grew up here. How can you be nervous about anything?"

He took her arm and led her to the door. She told herself to ignore the heat that flared under his fingertips, and the darting sparks that seemed to fall from the heavens, only to land in tingling explosions on her skin.

"I don't have a problem coming to visit my folks," he said as he knocked on the door. "But this is my first hospital party with the chief of staff and his wife."

"I'm not sure I believe you," she muttered, hoping that she didn't break into a sweat from all the heat his nearness generated. There was definitely something wrong with her hormones and it had to be more than just a lack of social life. She'd had long stretches without dating, but she'd never reacted like this. Maybe it was some yet undiscovered virus. She refused to believe it was directly related to Trevor himself.

The door opened and Maggie MacAllister welcomed them. Trevor's mother was tall and slender, with dark hair like her son's. Her face and body defied her age and she dressed in conservatively elegant styles that flattered her figure. The first couple of times Dana had been up at the house, she'd been terrified of putting a foot wrong. But Maggie was so friendly she'd quickly put Dana at her ease.

"Hello," Maggie said, motioning for them to come inside. "We're so glad you could make it." She leaned close to Dana and gave her a hug. "You look beautiful, my dear. Such a lovely dress, and you flatter it perfectly."

Dana inhaled the scent of Maggie's subtle perfume and felt her own tension ease.

Maggie turned to Trevor and hugged him, as well. "So, I understand you're the new surgeon at our hospital. What do you think of Honeygrove, Dr. MacAllister?"

Trevor chuckled. "You can't pretend you don't know me, Mom."

"I'm just trying to treat you like everyone else." She stepped back. "Come in. We're out in the family room. There's an open bar and snacks. We're doing Italian tonight and it's wonderful, so save plenty of room." She leaned toward Dana. "I found this wonderful little restaurant and they're catering for me. I know I should cook, but I'm still awful at it. This is so much easier."

"I'm sure you're a great cook," Dana said politely, trying to remember if she'd ever eaten anything Maggie had prepared. But these dinners were always catered.

"No, she's not," Trevor said. "But we love her anyway." He put his arm around his mother. "What's for dessert?"

"I see you haven't changed. I'm not going to tell you, because I don't want you picking at your dinner just so you'll have room for seconds of dessert. And I will be watching to make sure you eat all your vegetables."

"Mo-om."

Dana burst out laughing. At that moment Trevor sounded more like a ten-year-old than a grown man. "He doesn't eat his vegetables?"

"I have to bully him into it. Lord knows what he eats when he's on his own. One would think a doctor would care about nutrition."

"I care," Trevor protested.

"Yes, but not enough to do something about it."

They entered the large family room. There were about fifteen other guests. Dana knew everyone and was soon caught up in conversation. Time passed quickly and she was surprised when Maggie announced dinner. It was only when Trevor was pulling out her chair that she realized he hadn't left her side. Somehow they'd stayed near each other as they'd moved from group to group. She wasn't sure what that meant, then told herself it didn't mean anything. It was coincidence, nothing more. After all, they weren't the only people without dates. Several staff members had come with spouses, but an equal number were alone.

"I'm starved," Trevor said, taking the seat next to her, then pouring her a glass of red wine. "I've heard the food from this place is excellent."

"Even the vegetables?" she teased.

He grimaced. "Now you sound like my mother. Let me guess. You're going to watch to make sure I eat at least one serving of them."

"Not at all. You're a grown-up. If you want to flirt with malnutrition, that's your business."

"Great. Now I'll feel guilty if I don't eat some."

"Whose fault is that?"

Hazel green eyes dilated slightly. His lips curved up in a slow smile. "Yours."

A ripple of pure desire started low in her belly and moved up. Her breath caught. All this attention was more than her nervous system could handle, yet she couldn't think of anywhere she would rather be.

Danger! a voice in her head screamed. She knew what it meant. Trevor was trouble for her. He always had been. This time, however, she had the advantage of age and experience. She wasn't going to blindly fall for him again.

This time she would keep her wits about her and stay out of trouble.

Maggie took her seat at the foot of the table. Three servers, hired for the occasion, brought out large bowls and dishes of steaming food. "As usual I ordered way too much," she said. "Please, eat as much as you can. I hate leftovers."

Conversation was lively between bites of food. Trevor reached for the bread and passed the basket to Dana.

"I understand congratulations are in order," he said. "My dad told me you were promoted to your current position just a few weeks ago."

She took a roll and handed the basket to her left. "I guess it's been about a month and a half."

"You're very good. Not only organized, but calm in a crisis. Based on what I observed, I'd figured you'd been doing the job for at least a year. I'm not surprised, though. You always were brainy as well as beautiful."

He made the comment lightly, then glanced up when someone asked him to pour more wine. The person on his right made a comment about a recent medical-malpractice case in the newspaper and Trevor offered his opinion. Dana tried to follow along with the discussion, but she found it difficult to focus. Too many thoughts whirled through her head.

First of all, had Trevor really been talking to his father about her? Had this been in the context of a more general conversation or had she been the subject? There wasn't a way to find out, which was frustrating to say the least. Second, she was thrilled that he thought she was good at her job. While she told herself his opinion didn't matter, she knew she was lying. She *did* care about what he thought, even though she hated that fact. But the most intriguing and confusing and exciting comment of all had been his last one: "Brainy as well as beautiful."

Had he really said that? Had he really meant it? Did Trevor think she was attractive?

Stop it! she commanded herself. She was slipping into dangerous territory. It was one thing to find Trevor incredibly appealing and have her hormones do the dance of joy and exultation every time he was around. It was quite another thing to actually start to hope or believe or anything like that. She knew this man. She knew he didn't believe in monogamy or long-term relationships. She doubted he had any desire to get married or have a family and those were things she really wanted. Not that he'd indicated he was the least bit interested in her.

"You're not eating," he said, leaning toward her. "Don't you like it?"

"Yes. Everything is delicious. I..." She glanced at her nearly full plate and wished she hadn't taken so much in the first place. "I guess I have a lot on my mind."

"Anything I can help with?"

His sincere expression made her want to dump all her problems on his impressively broad shoulders. If anyone was strong enough to lean on, he was. Unfortunately, she couldn't tell him about her biggest problem because he *was* the problem.

"Just some work stuff," she said. Which was almost true. "I'll be fine, but thanks for asking."

He rested his hand on her forearm. Her silk sleeve did little to protect her from his heat. She quickly placed her fork on her plate before the trembling got so bad she dropped it.

"I meant what I said, Dana. I would like to help, or just listen. We're neighbors and we work together. I thought it would be great if we could be friends. That is, if you're willing to let go of the past.''

She hadn't thought about the past in days. Apparently she had let it go. Friends. Could she stand that? Did she want to hear the intimate details of Trevor's personal life?

Before she could formulate an answer, Walter stood up and raised his wineglass. ''I'd like to thank all of you for coming tonight. I always enjoy our dinner parties, but this one is special because Maggie and I are pleased to have our son back with us.'' He motioned to Trevor.

Trevor nodded and smiled, but Dana sensed he was uncomfortable with the attention.

''Welcome home,'' his father said. ''I'm pretty easy on new staff members, so consider yourself lucky. But when you get back from your trip, the break-in period is over.''

They all laughed and raised their glasses. A couple of other people offered toasts, mostly thanking the Mac-Allisters for their hospitality.

Dana leaned close to Trevor. ''Where are you going?'' she asked, her voice low.

''A management seminar. It's in northern California and starts in about a week. Apparently all senior staff go. Are you familiar with it?''

Dana swallowed, then set down her glass. So much for getting away from him, she thought.

''Yes,'' she said. ''The hospital has been using that program for a few years now. As a matter of fact, I'll be attending that seminar, as well.''

He smiled. The good one. Her blood heated while hormones and pheromones and Lord knows what other chemicals poured through her body, creating a chain reaction of excitement and wanting.

''Great. We can drive down together.'' He winked. ''In my car, of course. If the weather's decent, we can put down the top. And if you promise not to go over a hundred, I'll even let you drive partway.''

She thought about his powerful sports car, of the low, leather seats and how close they would be sitting. It would take several hours to reach the hotel in the middle of the northern California wine country. All that time, trapped…just her, Trevor, his tempting body and her wayward desire.

Chapter Six

Dana scribbled a couple of notes in the margin of the
schedule she'd printed out, then shook her head. Everything
will be fine, she told herself. She was only going to be
gone a week, and a trip to a seminar in northern California
wasn't exactly a space flight to another galaxy. If something unexpected happened, she could be reached by phone,
or someone else would handle it.

But she couldn't quell the butterflies line-dancing in her
stomach, and she would rather think they were from concern about her job than anticipation that she was going to
be alone with Trevor for the long drive...not to mention
the fact that they were attending the seminar together.

"Not together," she said softly. "At the same time.
There *is* a difference."

"Uh-oh, the boss is talking to herself. It's the first sign
she's getting ready to crack." Melba leaned against the

door frame and grinned. "Obviously you need this time away, Dana."

"I'm not about to crack. I'm concerned about details."

Melba raised her eyebrows. "Uh-huh. Sure. Don't you worry about a thing. I've heard they're working miracles with drug therapy these days."

"Thanks for the vote of confidence."

Melba stepped into the room. "Seriously, Dana, go and have a good time. You've been working hard. This will be a lot of fun. If nothing else, you'll have some great scenery."

Dana knew she wasn't talking about the wine country surrounding the hotel, but she pretended ignorance. "You're right. I've always wanted to visit the area. I'm hoping we'll have an afternoon or two off so that I can go to one of the local wineries."

Sally walked into her office. "I heard that. I can't believe you're serious. You'll be spending an entire week with Trevor and you're talking about wine tasting?" She rolled her eyes. "This is such a waste. If they sent me, instead, I could really appreciate the opportunity."

"From the way you've been talking, Trevor will need the break from you." Melba nodded at her friend. "Rumor has it you're wearing out the poor man."

Sally flipped her dark curls back over her shoulder. "I'm doing my bit, but Angie's the one who's insatiable. To hear her talk—"

Dana held up her hand to stop the flow of conversation. "As interesting as all this is, ladies, I've got to be going. I'm meeting Dr. MacAllister downstairs in—" She glanced at her watch and groaned. "I'm already ten minutes late."

She picked up her suitcase and started for the door. The two nurses fell into step with her.

"So how much would it cost to convince you to trade places?" Sally asked.

Dana laughed and thought about naming a ridiculously low price. A dollar, maybe two. But she didn't. Not only because she felt her ambivalence toward Trevor wasn't something she should joke about with her staff, but also because a part of her wasn't unhappy with the situation. She hated to admit it—in fact, she would have lied under threat of torture—yet the truth was, she was actually looking forward to spending the time with him. Sort of.

By himself he was fun. They got along well, talking easily about the hospital, what was going on in the world, their favorite kinds of music. The trouble occurred when other people were involved. Except everything had been fine at the dinner party they'd both attended recently. So it wasn't that. If only he didn't feel obligated to date every single nurse at the hospital.

Maybe what you really object to is the fact that he's dating every single nurse at the hospital except you.

The little voice inside her head spoke softly, but the words were still powerful. Dana came to a stop in front of the elevator and stared at the Down button without pushing it. Was that it? Was she secretly jealous of the attention he gave other women? Did she want some of it for herself?

She clamped her teeth together. That couldn't be true. She wouldn't let it. She was absolutely not interested in Trevor. She'd learned her lesson already. Hadn't she?

"See," Melba said, pressing the Down button. "She's not going to name a price. She wants to go off with him, too. Not that I blame her."

Shaken by a revelation she didn't want to be true, Dana had trouble focusing on what the other woman was saying. "What I really want," she managed at last, "is to go to this seminar. I'm neutral on the subject of who else will be there.''

"I wish I could be neutral," Sally said with a sigh. "The only good thing is that even though I won't see him for a week, Angie won't, either."

The two women accompanied her downstairs. The elevator opened on the main floor, by the lobby. There were the usual crowds—patients waiting to check in, visitors, staff members going to lunch. Probably at least two-dozen people milling around. Dana didn't notice any of them. The world reduced itself to one man standing by an aging brown sofa.

It wasn't his height or his good looks that drew her. It might have been the worn jeans hugging long legs and narrow hips, or the long-sleeved white polo shirt that emphasized broad shoulders. Maybe it was the welcoming smile that curved his perfect mouth up at the corners, or the way he took a quick step toward her to grab her luggage. Or maybe it was the scent of him, half masculine temptation, half some intangible breath of soap and shaving lotion and clean skin.

Her knees buckled slightly and she had to consciously force herself to remain standing. She could feel the fluttering of her heart and the sudden rush of desire. So much for remaining neutral, she thought grimly.

"Sorry to keep you waiting," she said, hoping he couldn't tell what she was thinking. Fortunately, she didn't have to worry about the other two women. They were too busy drinking in the sight of Trevor to notice her weakness.

"I barely got here myself," he said, leading the way out the front of the hospital. "It's a beautiful day. Would you mind if we put the top down on my car?"

The Mustang Cobra was parked in front. Its black paint gleamed in the warm sunshine. He was right about the day.

The sky was clear and blue. According to the weather report the previous night, the whole west coast was in for a huge series of storms later in the week.

She eyed the sleek car. "It would be a shame not to take advantage of the afternoon while we can," she admitted, knowing she would enjoy having the wind blow through her hair. She'd been cooped up at her job for too long, she thought with a flash of anticipation.

Trevor put her suitcase next to his in the trunk. The two small bags filled the tiny space. He smiled. "Okay, so I didn't buy it to carry things around."

Sally slipped past Dana and moved close to him. "I adore this car," she said, and gave him a winning smile.

Dana braced for the lovers' departure. She told herself it didn't matter what he did in his private life, and she didn't care if they wanted to make a spectacle of themselves.

But instead of pulling Sally close or making a personal comment, Trevor merely said, "Thanks," then walked to the passenger door and held it open.

Dana frowned. That didn't make sense. Why would he practically ignore one of the women he'd been seeing? Unless they'd already said their goodbyes in private and he didn't want to do that again in public.

She shook off the faint feeling of resentment toward Sally. None of this was the nurse's fault. If she, Dana, had a problem with Trevor, she should either bring it up with him or get over it.

"Don't I get to drive partway?" she asked teasingly as she started to slide onto the leather seat.

"Absolutely," Trevor said. "Want to go first?"

Dana stared at him. At his hazel green eyes and the laughter lurking there. "Are you serious?"

"Of course. Can you handle a manual transmission?"

"I learned to drive one."

"Then go for it, kid." His grin turned mischievous. "But I warn you, this car has a lot of power, so be careful if you don't want to get a ticket."

Dana got out and walked around to the driver's side. As she slid onto the seat, he handed her the keys. She glanced back at the two nurses and saw identical expressions of envy on their pretty faces. She knew it didn't come from wishing they could drive the car. They wanted to be going away with Trevor.

"See you in a week," she called as she pulled her seat belt across her lap and chest, then snapped it into place. The car started instantly. The rumble sent a thrill through her.

"Bye. Have fun."

Trevor waved absently at the two women watching them. "You ready?" he asked Dana.

She nodded. In her jeans and light-blue sweater, she looked more like the high schooler he remembered than the professional woman he saw every day. He liked the contrast. He also liked the excitement on her face.

She eased the car into gear and let out the clutch. They moved forward slowly.

There wasn't much traffic on the way to the interstate. Dana kept them just under the speed limit as she got used to the powerful car. He liked the way her hands held the steering wheel with a sureness that showed she was in control. The wind whipped her short gold blond hair away from her face. Dark glasses hid her eyes, but her mobile mouth kept him apprised of her moods. Currently, she was having a blast.

They stopped at a light before turning onto the freeway. "Will you get nervous if I go fast?" she asked.

"Not at all. She can handle it." He patted the dashboard. The light turned green. Dana released the clutch and punched the gas in one smooth movement. The car leaped forward. They flew down the on-ramp and merged with traffic. It was a full minute before his seat belt unlocked sufficiently to allow him to lean forward enough to see the speedometer. Then he laughed.

"Should I mention there's a speed limit?"

Dana glanced down and gasped. "Wow. She has a lot of power. Okay, I'll slow down."

She did. A little. Then laughed. The sweet sound made him respond in kind. Although he tried to leave his work behind when he left the hospital, some of the tension always stayed with him. Now he felt it ebbing as the wind whistled by and the sun warmed him.

A car full of teenagers pulled up next to him. A couple of boys looked at Dana and yelled encouragement.

"I'm not going to race them," she muttered.

But Trevor saw the speedometer inch up. Then she shook her head and they slowed down. The teenagers roared past them.

"They weren't just interested in the car," he said.

"What on earth do you mean?"

"You're a beautiful woman. The car only highlights the fact."

She glanced at him. "Oh, please, Trevor. Don't use your good material on me. It's wasted."

"Hey, this isn't material. I mean it."

She shook her head as if she didn't believe him. He refused to let that fact spoil his good mood. They would be at the seminar for a week. He planned to use the opportunity to get to know Dana again. Although they'd spent some time together, it had been disjointed at best. He knew the rumors circulating around the hospital kept her at a distance. But if they could spend several days together, away from all the talk, she might start to see him for the man he was. He wanted that more than he should.

She changed lanes to go around a slow-moving vehicle. "You always had the coolest car," she said. "I remember the Mustang you had in high school. It was perfect."

"I didn't think you noticed."

She shrugged. "I noticed everything about you, Trevor. Everyone did. You were the most popular boy in the school. Or don't those past conquests matter anymore?"

"There weren't as many conquests as you think, and yes, some of them matter very much." You matter, but he didn't say that. She wouldn't believe him. Not yet, anyway. But soon. Maybe.

"High school was a long time ago," she said. "We've all changed."

"How are you different?" he asked.

"I've grown up." She brushed her hair off her face, then laughed when it blew back. "I suppose the biggest difference is not being poor anymore."

He remembered her small apartment and her mother's run-down car. He'd always thought Dana dressed really well, but he'd heard the other girls talking about her clothes and the fact that many of them had been hand-me-downs from friends or purchased at a thrift store.

"You worked hard," he said. "You've accomplished a lot."

She nodded. "My mom used to tell me not to bother. That the best way out was to wait for a man to rescue me. She waited for that for years after my dad walked out on her."

"Where is she now?"

"In Florida. She finally got her rescue. But even back in high school I knew I wanted something different. I wanted to be responsible for my own future. That's why I went to college and then on to nursing school.''

"My dad told me you had a scholarship for college, then a grant for nursing school.''

She gave him a quick look before turning her attention back to the road. "You were talking about me?''

"Yes.''

"Oh.''

He could feel her questions. She wanted to know why he was interested in her and what other things his father had volunteered. But she didn't ask any more questions and he didn't offer the information. Better for her to wonder.

"Is your life what you thought it would be?'' he asked.

"Sometimes. Right now I don't have a lot of balance, which can be a problem. For the past couple of years all I've thought about is work. Therefore my social life is pretty sad. Now that I have the job I want, though, I suppose I can think about making some changes.''

"Marriage and a family?'' he asked.

"Something like that.''

He wondered if she had anyone special in mind.

"What about you?'' she asked. "Are you where you wanted to be?''

"Career-wise, yes. I always dreamed of being a surgeon. But personally—'' He shrugged. "Obviously I'd hoped for better.''

"Do you have any contact with your ex-wife?''

"No. I prefer it that way. There's nothing left to say. Vanessa wasn't interested in a career or even finishing college. She wanted to play. I was a little too sincere and hardworking for her. Last I heard she had married the eldest son of a wealthy plastic surgeon. She should be happy with him.''

''If nothing else, she'll get to look young for a really long time.''

''There's nothing wrong with a few wrinkles,'' Trevor said. ''I think living life makes women beautiful.''

Dana opened her mouth, then closed it. ''Wow. You sound like you mean that.''

''I do.''

''Such deep thoughts for a man who drives a convertible. You're right. You're a lot more than a pretty face.''

Her teasing made him laugh. Dana was easy to be with. That had always been the way with them and he was pleased it hadn't changed.

''I have an assortment of personal questions,'' she said. ''Don't feel you have to answer any of them.''

''Fire away.''

''Do you miss Vanessa?''

''No.'' He probed his heart. ''I don't feel anything for her, either. It's been over for a while.''

''Did you lose the baby early in Vanessa's pregnancy?''

He frowned. ''We never had a child together.''

''But I thought...'' Her voice trailed off.

Trevor's confusion faded and he had to hold down a flare of anger. ''Amazingly enough, I thought I was in love with her, Dana. I proposed to Vanessa because I planned to spend the rest of my life with her, not because I thought she was pregnant.''

Dana's mouth twisted. ''Really?''

''Don't sound so skeptical.''

''I'm not. And you sound angry.''

''It's a hell of an assumption. That the only reason I would marry a woman is that I got her pregnant? Do you really think that about me?'' He took a deep breath, his good mood suddenly lost. ''Never mind. I don't want to know your answer to that.''

They didn't talk for a few minutes. He tried to concentrate on the road, but he wasn't driving, so the light traffic didn't keep his interest. Why did he even bother? She wasn't going to change her mind about him.

After a while, she reached out and placed her hand on his forearm. "I'm sorry," she said. "That was a terrible thing to assume. I don't blame you for being angry with me. Can we please start over?"

"Sure. Whatever."

"Trevor, I mean it. I *am* really sorry."

"I know. It's okay. I'm used to it."

"To people assuming the worst about you?"

"Yeah. It happens all the time." He thought about the rumors currently circulating through the hospital. He hadn't heard all the details, but from what he'd put together, he was supposedly dating at least two nurses regularly, maybe three. And having casual sex with God knows how many others.

"How do you handle it?" she asked.

"I ignore it and hope it will go away. I've given up trying to explain. It doesn't help."

"So you're saying I shouldn't believe the stories?"

"Not if you want the truth. Yes, there are women interested in me, but it's a whole lot more about my reputation than who I am. I'm selective about who I get involved with and I date much less than the grapevine would have you believe."

She glanced at him, then focused on driving once more. "Why are you telling me this?"

"Why do you think?"

Her mouth opened, then closed. "Oh." She was silent for a minute, then repeated, "Oh."

Trevor smiled. At last he was making progress.

* * *

They arrived at the resort in the late afternoon. Dana stared at the imposing glass-and-wood structure and was grateful she hadn't come alone. Nothing like a five-star rating to make her remember her humble roots.

Trevor handed his car keys to the valet and gave the young man both their names. Yes, they were attending the management seminar; yes, they were there for the week. He waited until she'd climbed out of the sports car, then placed a hand on the small of her back and led her inside.

The ceiling soared three stories. Plants gave the lobby an outdoor feeling inside, while the furniture groups created an air of intimacy. The floors were marble, the walls and columns wood, the trim brass. It was the kind of place that prided itself on attention to detail. Instinctively, Dana took a step closer to Trevor. She knew he wouldn't let her put a foot wrong.

He pointed to a small sign near the registration desk. It told seminar attendees to go to the main ballroom. She swallowed hard. Had Walter made a mistake sending her here? Maybe she should have refused or thought up an excuse to put the experience off.

They walked into the ballroom. Huge crystal chandeliers hung from the ceiling. About sixty people were milling around. Dana resisted the urge to run back to the car. She knew that everyone could tell she was out of her element.

Trevor leaned close. "I hate stuff like this," he whispered. "It makes me uncomfortable."

"Really?"

He nodded.

His confession made her feel better. "Me, too," she admitted.

"So promise you'll tell me if I get spinach in my teeth, and I'll do the same."

She chuckled. Something leaped between them. It wasn't

exactly an electric current, but it was close. She thought about all they'd discussed in the car. His irritation when she'd assumed he'd gotten married because Vanessa was pregnant, and his assurance that the rumors about his dating habits were just stories and not the truth at all. Mostly she thought about his hint that he was interested in her. She clutched the information to her chest and prayed that it was true.

A petite and very pregnant Asian woman walked to the podium set up at the front of the room. "Good afternoon," she said, distracting Dana from her thoughts and the feel of Trevor's hand at the base of her spine. "Welcome to our week-long seminar."

"She's going to pop any second," Trevor said, eyeing her stomach. "My back hurts just looking at her."

"Imagine how hers feels."

"I don't want to."

"My name is Shelly Jones and I'll be leading the seminar this week." She touched her stomach and smiled. "Don't be fooled. I know I look huge, but I have at least three weeks to go."

"Is that all?" Dana murmured, wondering if the woman had a family history of early delivery.

Shelly's dark hair hung past her shoulders. She wore a navy dress and low heels. "We have an eclectic group with us this time. Everyone from middle managers at a large telecommunications firm to a surgeon."

Dana nudged him. "That would be you."

"Gee, thanks."

He whispered the words close to her ear and his warm breath fanned her face. She felt a flicker of response deep in her belly.

"We have many goals for the seminar," Shelly continued. "Lots of different exercises. We hope you enjoy your time with us. First, we're going to start with an ice-breaker exercise. Several staff members are going to walk around with baskets. Inside are pieces of paper. Take one and read it, but don't let anyone else see what's written.''

A young man in a hotel uniform passed by them. Dana and Trevor each took a slip of paper. Dana opened hers and read ''Somewhere Over the Rainbow.'' She frowned. What did it mean?

''The first order of business is to get to know one another.'' Shelly smiled. ''In case you haven't guessed, these are song titles. I want you to start humming your song, then walk around humming until you meet up with others who have your song. We should end up with five groups of twelve. Ready?''

There was a moment of stunned silence in the room. Shelly laughed. ''This is just the beginning. By the end of the week, this will seem tame. I promise.''

''Like that's good news,'' Trevor muttered. ''I can't sing and I don't hum much better.''

Dana didn't know whether to grin or run screaming for the car. She decided to play along. She began humming her song. Trevor looked at her.

''That doesn't sound like 'Getting to Know You.'''

She shook her head.

''See you around, then,'' he said, and turned away.

He cleared his throat several times, then emitted a sound that wasn't anything like music. Dana started to laugh.

Three hours later she was still laughing. The exercise had been great fun and she'd made friends with several people. Following the session, they'd been fed dinner and assigned rooms.

Trevor took her key and held it up next to his. ''Rooms 306 and 308. Looks like they're adjoining.'' He winked.

"I'm hoping to catch up on my sleep, so try not to keep me up too late with your wild parties."

"I don't have wild parties," she insisted. "You're the one with the reputation."

"'Still waters run deep.'"

"I'm—" She paused, not willing to say she wasn't deep. "I promise not to party."

"I don't mind, as long as you invite me."

They halted in front of her door. He handed her the key, then leaned against the door frame. "Did you enjoy tonight?"

She nodded. "It was great. I think I'm going to learn a lot."

"Me, too."

He was staring at her. Dana told herself it didn't mean anything, but her suddenly pounding heart didn't believe her. Had it gotten really hot all of a sudden? And what had happened to her ability to breathe? Her chest was tight and her lungs ached. Maybe it was...

She knew exactly what it was. What it always was. Trevor.

She stared back at him, willing him to move closer, to kiss her. That's what she wanted. His mouth on hers, his arms around her. Only then would the aching inside go away.

She leaned toward him. He touched her cheek. "'Night," he said, and walked to his door.

Dana stared after him, confused and obviously ready for more than Trevor was willing to offer.

Chapter Seven

Despite the threat of rain later in the week, the next morning dawned clear and warm. Trevor stared out at the manicured gardens of the hotel and told himself he had no one but himself to blame for his lack of sleep. He'd known better than to start thinking about Dana as he'd gone to bed. He should have read one of the many medical journals he'd brought with him. The information would have provided a distraction, and occasionally the articles were dry enough to use as a sleep aid.

Instead, he'd stretched out in the dark and thought about their drive together, about all she'd talked about and how she'd looked behind the wheel of his car. He'd pictured her soft hair blowing in the wind and the way her mouth had turned up when she'd smiled. He'd recalled their conversation, how she'd talked about keeping her grades up in college so she wouldn't lose her scholarship. She'd worked hard to achieve all that she had and he admired that. He admired her.

But he wasn't sure what else he felt where she was concerned. He respected her and her abilities. He knew he liked her. He thought she was bright and funny. Obviously he wanted her. A few minutes in her presence provided physical proof of that fact. So many times he'd wanted to kiss her. Not just yesterday, but other times. Last night had been the worst, though. Watching her at the opening session, hearing snippets of her conversation with the other participants and her laughter. He'd felt drawn to her. And like that foolish moth, he was at risk of getting fried.

A tap at his door distracted him. He crossed the carpeted floor and unfastened the lock. Dana smiled up at him from the hallway.

"I wasn't sure if you'd already left for breakfast, so I thought I'd check. Would you like to go down together?"

The seminar brochure had stressed the need for casual clothing so everyone could be relaxed during the exercises. Dana wore black jeans and a red sweater. Gold hoops dangled from her ears. He could smell the scent of soap and shampoo; she rarely wore perfume.

The wanting came hard and fast. He tried to convince himself some of it was about not having been with a woman in so long, but he knew it was specifically about Dana.

"Breakfast sounds great," he said, and picked up his room key. "How'd you sleep?"

"Fine. It's quiet out here."

"I noticed," he said, remembering the stillness as he'd lain awake in the king-sized bed. He'd imagined he could hear her stirring on the other side of the wall.

"I went through the materials they gave us last night," she said as they waited for the elevator. "There wasn't much on the program."

"I saw that, too. I don't think they want us to have time to prepare."

She looked at him and wrinkled her nose. "I keep telling myself this is for my own good. Walter wouldn't have sent me unless he thought I could handle it."

"You'll be fine," Trevor told her, placing his hand on the small of her back and motioning for her to precede him into the elevator.

"Easy for you to say. You're the one with the natural charm."

"As opposed to unnatural charm?"

She chuckled. "As opposed to those of us who muddle our way through social situations."

Her confession of feeling inadequate surprised him. He'd always viewed Dana as completely together. "You don't muddle—you do great. Everyone admires you."

He'd kept his hand on her back because it was a socially acceptable way to touch her. She hardly needed his assistance or guidance. It was a ploy to stay close to her, touching her, absorbing her warmth and the pleasure her presence brought him. So he felt her start of surprise at his compliment.

"Trevor," she began, as if going to ask him to explain himself. Then the doors opened and they joined the other seminar participants walking toward the large ballroom at the end of the hallway. There wasn't another chance for private conversation.

The ballroom had been divided into several smaller rooms; the largest was being used for breakfast, with eight round tables set for eight.

"I don't see any nameplates," Dana said, moving close to one of the tables and glancing at the place setting. "I guess it's not assigned seating."

"Works for me, but what are those?" Trevor asked. He

pointed at the small white boxes sitting next to each plate. The boxes weren't much bigger than a medium-sized apple.

Shelly, their very pregnant leader, walked to the front of the room and took a microphone from its stand.

"Good morning," she said. "Please sit anywhere. There's a surprise waiting for you at the table, but we'd appreciate it if you waited to open it until after breakfast. However, we'd like you to write your name on the tags provided so we can all continue getting to know one another."

"How about over there," Trevor said, deciding to assume he and Dana would sit together.

"Great."

When he held out a chair for her, she slid into it and smiled at him. His body reacted with the same embarrassing speed as when he'd been all of seventeen. He settled on the seat next to her and moved close enough to the table that no one would be able to tell.

The food was as good as it had been the previous evening. Everyone was friendly and soon a spirited discussion was underway at their table about the contents of the mysterious white boxes.

"Chocolate," Dana said firmly.

"For breakfast?" Trevor asked.

"Chocolate is a food group that works at any meal."

Two of the people sitting with them were women. They smiled at each other. The guys looked confused. Trevor had long since realized females had a relationship with chocolate that mere men could never understand.

"Too small for a book. Maybe it's some kind of crystal or meditating rock," a guy named Bill said. He was an executive in the banking industry and a resident of San Francisco. "After all, this *is* California."

They kept guessing until breakfast was over and Shelly

picked up her microphone again. "All right," she said. "Go ahead and open your boxes."

Trevor reached for his. It was lighter than he'd expected and something moved around inside. Not as though it were alive, but he could feel weight shifting.

Dana opened hers first and started to laugh. "What on earth is this for?" She held up an egg.

Trevor opened his box. "I have the same thing," he said, staring at the contents.

"We all do." Bill looked disgusted. "An egg?"

Shelly nodded as if she'd heard him. "That's right, everyone has an egg. For the next week, this is your best friend, your child, your constant companion—whatever you want it to be. The point is, you're responsible for the egg. You'll bring it to classes, take it out with you for dinner. The rules of engagement are the eggs are not to be left alone…ever."

Trevor stared at the egg in its box. "At least it's small. I'd hate to have to be responsible for something heavy like a watermelon."

"They're kidding, aren't they?" Dana asked. "An egg?"

The waiters dropped off a basket in the center of the table.

"Your supplies are being delivered to you right now," Shelly went on. "There are hats, blankets, even some markers if you want to give your egg a little personality. You've got about fifteen minutes until the first workshop starts, so use that time to bond with your egg."

"I've got three kids at home," Bill said. "I've done plenty of bonding." But he dutifully dug through the basket and pulled out a tiny pink cap. "What the hell. With three boys, a girl would be nice." He put the cap on the egg and placed his egg back in its box.

Trevor took the basket from him and picked a blue cap for his egg. He also took a blanket and marker and handed the rest to Dana.

"What are you doing?" she asked as he started drawing on his egg.

"Making a face. This is T.J.—that's short for Trevor Junior."

She rolled her eyes. "I should have guessed." She passed on the basket without taking anything.

"You're not dressing your egg?"

She shook her head and stood. "It's just an egg, Trevor. I understand the point of the exercise, but I think it's silly to dress it up." She took her box and headed for the door.

Trevor shrugged, then put the pen down and studied his handiwork. Two dark eyes stared back at him. He'd added a dot for a nose and a wide, smiling mouth.

"'Morning, T.J.," he said, and tugged on the tiny cap. Nestled in the blanket and tucked in the box, the egg looked like a space alien newborn. Then he followed Dana.

A crowd had gathered by the door. People were talking and comparing "children." Dana turned toward him. "Let me see what you did," she said.

He showed off his egg, oddly proud of the little guy. "He kinda looks like me, don't you think?"

Dana eyed him. "You're taking this so seriously you're scaring me. If I didn't know better, I'd swear you were actually interested in having kids of your own."

"As a matter of fact—"

But he didn't get to finish his sentence. Dana had started turning back toward the door. Someone jostled her. She took an instinctive step to the side. One arm reached out for balance, her hand dropped and her egg fell to the floor with a loud *splat*.

Shelly walked over and stared at the mess. "The cleaning staff here hate this particular exercise." She patted Dana's arm. "Don't worry, there are plenty more in the kitchen. Go tell them you need a new egg."

Color stained Dana's cheeks. "I'm not sure what happened. I got bumped and then it just sort of went flying."

Trevor leaned close. "I was going to suggest we get together later to let our eggs play, but I don't know that I want my egg around yours. I mean, I have a certain responsibility for my egg's safety."

Dana glared at him. "I can't decide if I should laugh or threaten you."

Kiss me, instead, he thought. But he didn't say it. All he managed was a gruff, "I'll save you a seat," as he headed for the classroom and she turned toward the kitchen.

Rain pounded against the tall glass windows. Dana sat in the lobby of the hotel and watched the storm. According to the weather reports, it wouldn't let up until the seminar was nearly over. Oddly enough, she didn't mind. The resort was beautiful, and the various classes and activities kept them so busy there wasn't much free time. She enjoyed the people she'd met, and most of all, she was having fun with Trevor.

She looked up and saw him crossing the lobby, walking toward her. Although it was only their third day, they'd already developed a routine. They took their morning breaks out here, and in the afternoon they relaxed in the garden sunroom in the back of the hotel.

Trevor walked with an easy grace. She'd grown used to seeing him casually dressed in jeans and a long-sleeved shirt or sweater, but she still wasn't used to his magnetic charm or his good looks. She was beginning to think she could go her whole life and not get used to being around him. As he got close, as if on cue her body began coming alive, with odd feelings coming from different sections. It was like an orchestra warming up.

Something fizzled low in her belly. Heat flashed in the center of her chest. Tingling whipped through her fingers, then jumped to her thighs and vibrated there.

Trevor flopped down on the sofa next to her and grinned. "What did you think of this morning's exercise?"

They'd broken up into small groups and had been given a business problem to solve. After an hour, they'd stopped to meditate for twenty minutes, led by Shelly, who despite her advanced pregnancy was still much more limber than Dana could ever hope to be. Following the meditation, they'd returned to their groups and worked on another business problem.

"I'm not sure," Dana said. "My group didn't solve the first problem, but we fixed the second. Was it because we'd learned from our mistakes, learned to work together, or was it really about using the meditation time to focus? It could be a combination of the three, I suppose. What about you?"

He placed his egg on the coffee table in front of them. Their two boxes were side by side. Dana didn't even want to think about the whole-egg exercise. She was having extraordinarily bad luck with her attempts to keep her egg whole.

"My group solved both problems," Trevor said. "But we were much faster and worked better the second time. I can see the advantage of using meditation to facilitate focus. One of the medical journals I've been reading has some information on patients meditating before surgery, then listening to those tapes during the procedure and while in recovery. Some people are suggesting the meditation helps the body heal faster." He leaned back, sitting so close his arm brushed against hers. "Who's to say they're wrong? There's so much we don't know about how the body gets sick and then heals itself.''

"I agree. I remember caring for people who shouldn't have survived, let alone recovered, and they did. Then there were others who appeared to be healthy and strong, yet they didn't make it. Sometimes there's no predicting the outcome.''

She was pleased with herself. After all, she'd strung four sentences together without blushing or stuttering. A miracle, considering the waves of hormones cranking up her desire and making her want to throw herself at him. She settled for a small sigh of contentment as his hand casually brushed against her thigh when he shifted on the sofa.

"I watched the news this morning," he said. "The storm is going to be a bad one. They're talking about the potential for flooding. We might not be able to get out for a while.''

Dana glanced around at the high ceilings in the beautiful lobby, then out at the storm. "It wouldn't upset me too much to be trapped here. The people at the seminar are a lot of fun.''

"What? You don't miss the hospital?" Trevor pretended outrage.

"I miss my friends. While I adore my job, I don't mind taking a break. And what do you miss?" She braced herself to hear that he was longing for his lady friends. Had he been calling Angie or Sally or any number of other women in the evenings? Their activities usually ended about nine. She and Trevor had stayed up with a few other people in either the lobby or the bar, getting to know one another and talking about the day's exercises. But she didn't know what he did once he went back to his room. She found it hard to believe he would be content to be on his own.

"I was just getting settled in my new place," Trevor said. "My work is still exciting, so I would have been happy to stay put. But I'm having a great time here. The company is very pleasant."

She told herself he didn't necessarily mean her, but that didn't stop a warm glow from washing over her.

"Hey, you two." Bill waved and walked over to them. "A group of us are talking about ordering in pizza for lunch. We thought we'd better do it before the rain gets worse. You want in?"

"Sure." Trevor reached for his wallet and handed Bill a twenty.

"I left my purse upstairs," Dana said.

"Don't worry about it," Trevor told her. "I've got you covered."

Bill gave her a wink. "The sunroom in back at twelve-thirty. See you there."

"Thanks," she said after Bill had left. "I'll pay you back."

"It's just pizza." Trevor reached forward and picked up the small box containing her egg.

"But…" She bit her lip. There was no point in arguing. She would just look like an ungracious slob. "Thank you."

She knew why his action made her uncomfortable. Because they knew each other, they'd been spending a lot of time together. Everyone attending the seminar assumed they were a couple. It was an interesting phenomenon. At first, a few of the women had tried flirting with Trevor, but he'd simply ignored them and they'd stopped. Then she'd noticed she and Trevor were being invited to things together. A part of her wanted to set the record straight, while the rest of her was happy to play along. It was a harmless fantasy, right? Like mooning after a rock star or an actor. Trevor was too perfect to be a real flesh-and-blood man.

"When did you get a new egg?" he asked. "Last night?"

She flushed. "I don't know what you're talking about."

"This is a different egg from the one you had yesterday." He pointed to a few brown flecks on the shell. "These are new."

"They were on the other side of the egg," she lied, wondering why it was so hard for her to keep her egg in one piece.

He looked at her and shook his head. "I don't think so. I would have remembered. So what happened?"

She snatched the egg from him and gripped the box in her hand. "Nothing happened." He raised his eyebrows. She exhaled in frustration. "All right. I'll tell you, although I don't understand what the big deal is. I was getting dressed this morning. Like you, I had the television on to catch the weather report. They started talking about the storm just as I was reaching for my watch. I turned away from the dresser and accidentally knocked the box onto the floor."

He winced. "Jeez, Dana, this makes what, three eggs or four?"

"It was an accident."

"Three?"

"Four," she grumbled. She hated the egg exercise. Maybe because she'd gotten off to a bad start. "Don't you be critical of me. I was a maternity nurse for years and I did just fine with newborns. I'm a very caring and careful person. I just can't relate to an egg, okay?"

He held up his hands in a gesture of surrender. "You don't have to yell at me. I'm not saying anything."

"I'm not yelling," she said between gritted teeth. "I'm simply explaining I don't worry about an egg the way I would a child or an adult. An egg isn't alive."

He looked startled, as if she'd suddenly slapped him or stripped off her clothes.

"Don't say that," he commanded in mock horror. "He'll hear you."

She looked around. "He who?"

"T.J." Trevor picked up his small box and cradled it close to his chest. "Hush, little guy. She didn't mean it. Of course you're real. That's it. Smile for Papa. Good boy. You are so darn clever."

Dana felt her mouth drop open. "You're taking this egg thing way too seriously."

She glanced at the box. Every day there had been modifications. On the second morning she'd noticed Trevor had drawn trucks and boats on the inside of the container. For stimulation, he'd told her seriously. Children needed that to develop properly. Today there was a shiny miniature paper airplane and a football, both made out of foil gum wrappers.

"I'm practicing," he said.

"For?"

"Fatherhood. I've always wanted kids and I think I'd be a good dad." He glanced knowingly at her box. "Although we can't say the same thing about you, can we?"

She realized he'd given her the perfect out. "You're right," she said, pretending to be serious.

His eyebrows drew together. "Dana, no. I was teasing you. You'll be a terrific parent."

"Maybe." She drew in a breath, ready to pounce. "But you are right about what you said. I would be a lousy dad."

"You set me up," he said accusingly.

She chuckled.

He set his egg on the coffee table, then lunged for her. She shrieked as he began to tickle her, his long fingers dancing along the side of her rib cage.

"Trevor, stop! Stop!" She gasped for air, laughing and twisting, trying to get away from him. "I'm not ticklish."

''Oh, I can tell.'' He leaned closer and reached for her other side.

''I mean it. This isn't dignified. Oh!''

She inhaled sharply and kicked out. Anything to get away. He didn't give up. Between his size advantage and his superior strength, she didn't have a chance. She thrust out her free hand in an attempt to tickle him back. Unfortunately, he really *wasn't* ticklish.

''Trevor!''

She made one desperate attempt to turn away. Her left arm bumped against the back of the sofa. As soon as her hand connected with the soft material, she knew she was in trouble.

Sure enough, the force of the movement sent her egg flying through the air. It sailed in a perfect arc, narrowly missing the coffee table before falling onto the stone floor and landing with a messy *splat*.

Dana winced. ''This is not my fault.''

''Oh, Dana, what are we going to do with you?''

She looked up and saw Shelly staring at her. Dana pointed to the shattered shell and broken yolk. ''This isn't my fault. Trevor was tickling me and I couldn't get away, and you tell her Trevor.''

He picked up his box. ''I don't know, Shelly. T.J. and I were just chatting with Dana here when she tossed her egg into the air. What can I say?''

Dana ignored the twinkle in his eye and shoved his arm. ''Oh, thank you very much for that support.'' She stood. ''This isn't my fault. You know it and I know it.''

''Where are you going?'' Trevor called as she stalked away.

''To the kitchen, of course. I need another egg.''

''You might want to save yourself the extra trips and just ask for a dozen.''

* * *

Bill passed Dana a margarita. "My favorite was the dog exercise," he said.

Dana chuckled. A couple of days ago they'd been required to stand in front of the group and, in a stern voice, tell Shelly, "Don't you ever, ever, ever let me catch you brushing that dog's teeth again."

Everyone had been weak with laughter watching classmates struggle to keep a firm tone in their voice, but actually getting up to do that had been difficult. The purpose had been to remind everyone that while embarrassment was uncomfortable, it didn't maim or kill and people did survive the experience.

"Not the water-balloon fight?" she asked.

Bill thought for a moment. "That was fun, although I'll have to explain to my wife why I have condoms in my luggage."

Dana nodded. After a particularly tense session, everyone had gone out into the garden and had a water-balloon fight in the rain. They hadn't made a dent in the four jumbo boxes of condoms Shelly had provided. The instructor had taken a lot of ribbing that she was thinking about protection about nine months too late. In retaliation, she'd sent the extras to everyone's rooms.

Trevor took a drink of his beer. "What was your favorite, Dana?"

"I'm not sure, because I really enjoyed everything we did. I can't believe we've been here six days already and we go back day after tomorrow. It's gone by quickly."

Bill glanced out the window. They were in the lobby bar, at a table that usually looked out over the manicured gardens. But for the past three days all anyone had been able to see was rain. "Assuming we can get out of here," he said. "This is the tail end of the storm and it should be gone in the morning, but the flooding has gotten worse.

Did you know the instructors have to spend the night here?''

"Just as well," Dana said. "I know Shelly swears she's got another couple of weeks until the baby is due, and first babies are traditionally late, but to me she looks ready to give birth at any second. I would hate to think of her getting trapped somewhere."

"Yeah. Lucky for her, if she goes into labor early she's got a doctor and a nurse right here."

Trevor shook his head. "Don't look at me. I'm not about to deliver a baby."

Dana glanced at him and smiled. "But you're so good with Trevor Junior."

Trevor shuddered. "I'm keeping good thoughts that Shelly goes to term."

Bill stood up. "Okay. The party is in my room in an hour. We've ordered Chinese food. Are you going to be there?"

Dana opened her mouth to reply, but Trevor beat her to it. "Dana and I have plans for tonight, but thanks for asking."

"No problem. See you two in the morning." He sauntered off to join the next table.

Dana glanced at Trevor. "We have plans?"

He gave her an apologetic smile. "I hope you don't mind me saying that. We've gone to a different party every night and I'm tired of that. I thought it would be nice to order in dinner and spend some time alone together. But if you'd rather join the others, I understand."

She had been in the process of taking a sip of her drink and she had to remind herself to swallow. The icy liquid soothed her suddenly tight throat, but it didn't do a thing for her pounding heart.

Trevor wanted to have dinner with her? Alone? Panic

and anticipation battled it out in her stomach. Over the past six days, she'd gotten to know Trevor. She liked the man he'd become. She enjoyed his company. But...none of that had changed his reputation or her concerns about getting involved with Dr. Love. Still, she couldn't deny he made her come alive. Would it be so very wrong to spend a couple of hours alone with him? Maybe he would finally kiss her and she could know if it was as wonderful as she remembered. Maybe it was a risk, but could she live with herself if she didn't take a chance?

"I'd like to have dinner with you," she said.

He flashed her his best smile. "Great. Why don't you plan to come to my room around seven."

Chapter Eight

Trevor tugged on the collar of his long-sleeved white shirt, told himself it really wasn't too tight, that he was just suffering from a bad case of nerves, and opened the door. Dana stood in the hallway, her blue eyes wide, her expression half excited, half wary.

He knew exactly how she was feeling. He'd tried to convince himself he'd simply invited a co-worker over for dinner, but he couldn't swallow the lie. For one thing, this wasn't his town house back in Honeygrove; this was a hotel room where the largest and most prominent piece of furniture was a bed. For another, he thought of Dana as much more than a colleague. Finally, while his body's reaction to her was simple and predictable, it more than complicated the situation. He could only try to keep her distracted so she didn't happen to glance down.

He took in the white long-sleeved blouse she wore

tucked into jeans and grinned. "So you got my memo about the dress code," he said.

She laughed. "We're twins tonight. That's pretty embarrassing."

"Fortunately, no one has to know." He stepped back to let her into the room. "The wine is here," he said, motioning to the bottle resting in an ice bucket on the tiny table in front of the sofa by the window. "However, dinner is going to be a while. Apparently a lot of people had the same idea of ordering room service and we'll have to wait."

"I don't mind." She walked to the couch and perched on the edge of the far cushion. "I'm not that hungry."

He was, but not for food. Get over it, MacAllister, he told himself. He had to find a way to distract himself. If he didn't, he was going to say or do something they would both regret.

He sat down next to her. The sofa wasn't that long, and even though he stayed on "his" side, they were still close. "I see you found a sitter," he said as he started opening the wine. "I called downstairs, but there wasn't one available. I don't think it'll be a problem, though. T.J. had a pretty busy day and he's a sound sleeper."

He glanced at the small box sitting on top of his dresser. Dana followed his gaze, then laughed. "You're crazy," she told him. "No, I didn't get a sitter. I left my inert egg alone in my room. There, I've admitted what a terrible egg mother I am. Do you want to call social services?"

"I don't think that will be necessary." He handed her a glass of wine. "I guess we have different ideas on parenting," he said, his voice mockingly sad. "I'm a little surprised, but I'll get over it."

"Gee, thanks." She took a sip. "This is nice."

He wasn't sure if she meant the wine or their being alone together. "Yes, it is."

She took another sip and leaned back in her seat. "I can't believe how quickly the week has gone. It's been a great experience."

"I agree." He angled toward her. The lamp behind her cast a warm glow over her blond hair. As usual, she'd brushed it away from her face. The short cut barely came below her ears, but still looked feminine on her. He stretched his right arm along the back of the sofa. His fingertips were inches from her shoulder.

"Are you anxious to get back to work?" she asked.

"Not anxious, but ready. I have heavy surgery caseloads the first couple of days, then it should slow down a little. Oh, I've heard from my architect. He's drawn up the preliminary plans for my house. If you have some time, I'd really like you to look at them. I'd appreciate a woman's perspective on things."

She flushed. He wondered if it was from pleasure or just the wine.

"I'd be delighted," she said. "Although based on our 'egg'sperience here, you could be more adept at that kind of thing."

"I'm willing to risk your opinion."

She tilted her head and stared at him as if confused about something.

"What are you thinking?" he asked.

"I'm wondering why you're asking me. There are many other women who would be happy to go over the plans with you. Or do anything else you'd like."

He set down his glass and leaned toward her. "Maybe, Dana, but yours is the opinion that matters to me."

She blinked slowly. "Trevor, I..." Her voice trailed off.

Some of his good mood faded. "If I were a masochist, I'd ask you to tell me what the rumors are this time."

"I don't understand."

He shrugged. "There are always rumors. You should remember that from high school. People, mostly women, are always talking about me. I'm not sure why. It's frustrating, to say the least." After working up the courage, he asked, "Have you thought about what I said about Joel? That he was the one who told everyone we'd made love that weekend?"

She cupped the wineglass in her hands and looked at him. "I've thought about it. I don't know what to believe. You've never lied to me. To the best of my knowledge, you've never lied to anyone."

"But?"

"But...why would Joel do that?" She shook her head. "I know what you told me, that Joel was interested in me and wanted us to break up. But he and I never went out."

"Did he ever ask you out?"

She was quiet for a moment. "I don't remember. Those first few days passed in a blur and nothing about them is clear. I know he was always around and I think I told him I appreciated his being a friend to me. At the time I felt pretty alone."

Trevor grunted. He wanted to hunt Joel down and beat the life out of him. Damn him for interfering in what was possibly the most wonderful relationship of Trevor's life. If only he'd been able to explain to Dana at the time. If only she'd been willing to listen. They could have been happy together. Or maybe not. Maybe they'd both been too young.

"I'm sorry about that," he said. "I wish I could change things."

"I believe you," she said. "That means a lot to me."

He took her wineglass from her and set it on the table. One of his hands remained clasped around hers and he didn't let her go. "I realize this isn't going to get me a lot of sympathy, but I'm going to tell you anyway. I'm more than just my reputation. There's actually a living, breathing person underneath all the hype." He deliberately made his tone light. "There are even a couple of people who'd be willing to tell you I'm kind of a swell guy."

Her hand was small and warm, and her fingers easily laced with his. He held on gently, not squeezing, but determined not to let go. Was it his imagination, or was Dana leaning toward him? Her eyes were faintly dilated. Wine or desire? Did he finally have her attention?

"I haven't heard *those* rumors," she said. "But I'm willing to bet they might be true. There are times when you're the worst kind of guy, dating everything in sight. Then there are times when you really surprise me. I mean that in a good way."

He was torn between annoyance at her first comment and pleasure at her second. "Despite what everyone says, I don't date."

"Uh-huh." She didn't sound convinced.

He tried a different tack. "Are you seeing anyone seriously?"

"No. Not really. Some of it is career and some of it is that I haven't been asked."

Hope flared, along with desire. "You don't have to justify yourself to me," he told her. "You're bright, beautiful and very desirable. Obviously if you're not seeing anyone, it's by choice."

This time the blush was unmistakable. "Well, thank you. Plus there's the matter of the agreement I have with Katie and Lee. Of course, now it's just Lee, but we're determined to stick with it."

"What are you talking about?"

"Oh. When the three of us graduated from nursing school, we promised one another we wouldn't marry doctors. We saw that they didn't make good husbands or fathers, so we signed this pact." She exhaled. "Then Katie went ahead and got engaged to a doctor. Mike Brennan. You probably remember him from high school. What can we do? They're in love." She paused, obviously waiting for him to comment.

"I guess it was out of your hands."

"Exactly. The problem I have is where I work. Who do I meet? Doctors. They're everywhere. I just can't escape them."

He was more intrigued than annoyed by the thought of her bargain. Maybe it was a mistake to take it as a personal challenge, but that was how it felt. "So if a doctor, such as me, was interested in you, he wouldn't have a chance?"

"That's right."

He tugged on her hand, pulling her closer. She slid toward him on the sofa. Her eyes widened. With his free hand, he tucked her hair behind her ear, then let his fingers linger on her soft cheek.

"There's nothing I could do to change your mind?"

"Nothing at all." Was her voice really breathless, or was it just wishful thinking on his part?

"You're not susceptible to temptation?"

"No," she answered. "In fact—"

But he didn't hear the rest of her sentence. He placed his mouth on hers and cut off her words. As his lips pressed against her sweetness, he couldn't find it in himself to give a damn about what she was about to say.

It was one of those moments when time stood still. He'd kissed women before, although not in a long while. He'd even kissed Dana before…in another lifetime, it seemed.

So he should have been prepared for the intense heat and desire that filled him. He should have known how much he would want to haul her close and deepen the kiss, plunging inside her, tasting her, feeling her, giving and taking in a sensual exploration designed to carry them to the edge of madness, perhaps even beyond.

He held back partly because being this close to her was nearly as much as he could bear. She smelled sweetly of herself and some feminine fragrance. One of her hands rested on his shoulder, a warm weight. Her fingers squeezed his muscles in what he hoped was an involuntary reaction to their nearness and the sensation of his mouth on hers.

He moved slowly, pulling back slightly without breaking the kiss. He explored her lips. He tested different points of contact, savored the quivering response he felt, then lightly touched his tongue to the fullest part of the curve.

She gasped. A sharp but quiet sound. Her body tightened, as did the hand on his shoulder. Her other arm came up and she hugged him, moving close until her body turned and her knees bumped his thighs. He parted his legs so she could slide closer, then accepted the invitation of her open mouth.

It was better—she was better—than he remembered. All hot, welcoming sweetness, with her tongue seeking his. They touched and the fire inside him exploded. He crossed the line, reaching the place where wanting became need and needing didn't begin to describe the pounding hunger rushing through him.

He pulled her closer and it wasn't close enough. They had to become the same person; they had to blend. It wasn't just about their bodies joining; it was more, although he couldn't begin to describe it.

He cupped her face, tilting her head slightly and diving in deeper. He explored her mouth, then retreated to let her do the same to him. Their breathing grew more ragged. He told himself they were getting out of control way too fast, but he couldn't find the strength anywhere. He wanted her and she obviously wanted him.

He pulled back so he could move his mouth to her cheek, then her jaw. She moaned low in her throat. He licked the sweet spot below her ear, the length of her neck, finally leaving a wet trail down to the base of the open vee of her shirt. Her breasts seemed to swell as he approached them. Tight nipples showed through the layers of her clothing. He reached to stroke her. As his forefinger circled the small bud, someone knocked on the door.

Trevor froze. "Talk about lousy timing," he muttered, wondering if he could tell room service they'd changed their mind about eating dinner.

Dana gave a strangled sound that was more groan than laugh. "I guess they got our meals cooked faster than they thought. Just our luck."

He raised his head and looked at her. Her skin was flushed, her eyes wide, her mouth damp and parted. She looked ready to fall into his arms. The passion made her glow. "Dana, I—"

The knocking returned, this time more insistent. "Trevor? Are you in there? Is Dana with you? It's Bill. We need you. There's a medical emergency."

While the passion didn't turn off instantly, it did fade into the background. They pushed off the sofa at the same moment. Trevor headed for the door, while Dana checked to make sure all her clothing was tucked in place.

He pulled open the door. "What's wrong?" he asked.

Bill grabbed his arm. "Thank God. We've been looking all over for you."

"Bill, calm down. Tell me what's going on."

Bill shook his head. "It's Shelly. She's gone into labor."

* * *

Dana followed Trevor down the hall. Her mind raced as she fought to gain control of both her body and her thought processes. The sensual fog was thick, but clearing quickly. She wasn't sure if she was thrilled or crushed by the interruption. Based on the lethargy still tugging at her and the heat radiating from every part of her, she had been ready to make love with Trevor. Talk about a mistake. But knowing he was wrong for her and having the strength to resist him were two very different things.

Let it go, she told herself. Emergency first, personal life second.

They got into the elevator and headed up two floors. Trevor was oddly silent. Dana had been waiting for him to start issuing instructions, but when he continued to say nothing, she turned to Bill.

"Has anyone called for an ambulance?" she asked.

"Yes, but with the storm it's going to take them a while to get here."

She nodded. "All right. After we get to Shelly's room, you find someone in housekeeping. We'll need sheets and towels. Have room service send up some basins along with boiling water. Oh, and contact the front desk. The hotel should have a decent first-aid kit. We'll need that, too."

Bill nodded frantically. "She's going to be all right, isn't she?"

"Sure."

The elevator doors opened and they hurried to Shelly's room. Several people from their seminar stood in the hallway. Bill quickly assigned tasks so that the supplies would be delivered more quickly. Trevor pushed past them and hurried inside. Dana was on his heels.

Shelly lay curled in the center of one of the two double beds. Her long dark hair was tangled, her face pale and sweaty. She clutched her belly.

"They found you," she gasped, her voice laced with pain. "I'm really glad."

Trevor knelt beside her and touched her face, then took her pulse. "Tell us what's happening."

"My water broke a couple of hours ago." Shelly managed a slight smile. "I made a really big mess in the restaurant. The contractions have been coming for a couple of days now. I called my doctor yesterday and he said to go home and stay off my feet."

Trevor checked her eyes, then placed his hand on her stomach. "Why didn't you listen?"

"There was only one day to go. I had a friend who went through this type of thing for nearly a week. I didn't think it was any big deal."

"Guess you were wrong," he said lightly. "How far apart are the contractions now?"

"About two minutes and they really—" She inhaled sharply, then bit down on her knuckles. A moan escaped her.

Dana moved to her side. "Screaming is not such a bad thing, if you feel it will help. I don't think you have the lung power to do any serious damage to the windows."

Shelly nodded, but didn't speak. It was several more seconds until the contraction ended. She gasped, trying to catch her breath.

"Nearly a minute long," Trevor said. "Looks like you're going to have your baby. Give us a second, Shelly. We'll come up with a game plan."

He took Dana's hand and led her to the bathroom. Once there, he closed the door. "I want you to get her out of her clothes. She didn't expect to spend the night, so she doesn't have a nightgown or robe. Cover her with a sheet. Then I'll check to see what's going on. The supplies you asked for should be here shortly and that will help."

Dana stared at him. Something wasn't right. "Trevor, what's going on? You're sweating."

"Tell me about it." His usually smiling mouth was a straight line.

"Is there something wrong? Something with the baby?"

"As far as I can tell, mother and child are both healthy. It's just…" He shook his head. "Do you know how long it's been since I delivered a baby?"

"Oh, is that it? Don't worry. I spent a couple of years as a maternity nurse. If necessary, I'll talk you through it."

His gaze narrowed. "You don't understand. I'm not rusty—I'm terrified. A delivery was the first procedure I ever observed. It was awful. The woman's pain, the blood, which I wasn't used to yet. I'd been up studying all night, I hadn't had anything to eat for about a day and, well, I passed out. Ever since then, the thought of someone giving birth makes me nervous."

She bit back her laughter. "You're a surgeon. This is a snap compared with some of the things you do."

"It doesn't feel like a snap."

So now she knew why he'd been so quiet on the way up to Shelly's room. Somehow his confession of inadequacy made her like him more. "If it makes you feel any better, I don't think anyone can tell you're apprehensive."

"That's something." He looked at Dana. "I'll do the best I can, but don't worry about hurting my feelings on this one. If you know what to do and I don't, jump in. The most important thing here is keeping Shelly and her baby healthy until the ambulance arrives."

"You realize they might not get here in time."

Some of the color faded from his face. "That thought has crossed my mind."

He reached for the door handle. She stopped him with a

hand on his arm. "Trevor, you're so good with T.J. Just pretend the baby is your egg and you'll be fine."

He gave her a quick smile. "But with the egg I don't have to worry about the chicken, do I?"

They returned to the bedroom. Bill and his helpers arrived with the supplies, and within a few minutes Shelly was wrapped in a sheet and resting between contractions.

"I can't do this much longer," she murmured. "I'm hot, then cold. My legs hurt—hell, my whole body hurts. Dana, help me."

Dana knelt on the floor and took her hands. "It's all right. You don't have much longer to go now."

She glanced at Trevor, who had rolled up his sleeves and was currently organizing their supplies. He'd already performed a quick exam and his concerned expression warned Dana that the ambulance wouldn't arrive in time.

Another contraction began. "Trevor," Dana called.

Shelly abandoned restraint and yelled out as her stomach jumped visibly with the power of the movement.

He hurried over and offered Shelly a quick smile. "So let me guess. You were trying to avoid having to pay your doctor, right? All this is a carefully constructed plan. You're thinking that because I've been in the seminar for a week, I won't bill you."

Sweat broke out on Shelly's pale face and her expression was grim. "You...caught...me," she gasped. "That was it all along. Plus my husband wasn't really excited about being a coach."

"Now you've got two professionals and no one competing for their time. Pretty clever."

The contraction ended. Shelly sagged back on the bed. "Tell me it's going to be all right," she pleaded. "Is my baby okay?"

Dana saw the faint flicker of concern on Trevor's face,

but she knew Shelly wouldn't pick it up. He patted her hand. "The two of you are doing great. We'll get through this in no time."

He pulled over the low stool someone had brought from housekeeping and settled down. "How strong was the urge to push?"

"It's about killing me."

"I figured. Next time, I want you to go with it. Push hard. Deep breaths and really work it."

Dana stayed with Shelly, offering comfort while monitoring her vital signs. Trevor delivered the baby, giving a few instructions as the head crowned and then appeared. She watched his sure movements. Nothing in his demeanor indicated he was the least bit nervous. No doubt he was too caught up in what was happening to remember the first time he'd watched a delivery.

"Color's good," he said, turning the baby onto its side. "Shoulders are next and—"

A lusty cry filled the room.

Tears filled Shelly's eyes. "Thank God," she said, her voice reverent.

"As I was about to say," Trevor said. "Healthy lungs. Okay, one more little push. There, that's it. Shoulders are coming out now. Easy. What do you know? Shelly, you've got a son."

He leaned forward and placed the squirming, screaming newborn on his mother's belly. Shelly's tears flowed faster and Dana found she had to wipe her own cheeks dry.

She looked at Trevor. "You did it."

His hand found hers and he squeezed. "We did. Thanks."

He glanced back at the baby, then rested his free hand against the infant's cheek. Dana felt something flicker to life inside her. It wasn't just participating in an event as miraculous as a birth. It was more than that—something about sharing the moment with Trevor. No matter what, they would always have this in their past.

Her heart seemed to shift just a little and she knew what she'd just experienced was a whole lot more dangerous than simply wanting him.

Chapter Nine

Dana waited while Trevor unlocked his door, then she followed him inside the room. Their wineglasses were still on the coffee table, as was the ice bucket, although most of the ice had melted.

A large cart stood just to the left of the door. She wrinkled her nose. "I have a bad feeling that everything is going to be cold...or warm, depending on what you ordered."

"Nothing complicated," Trevor said as he raised silver covers and studied the contents of the plates. "Salad, steak, potatoes. It doesn't look very appetizing now."

She crossed to the sofa and pulled out the wine bottle. "That's okay with me. I'm way too excited to be hungry." After emptying both their glasses, she poured them each cold wine, then handed him his. "I can't believe how smoothly that went. You were great."

"Thanks." His smile was rueful. "You were a big help.

I know I wouldn't have fallen apart, but it was a lot easier with you there.'' He squinted at the window. Outside it was dark, but the rain had let up. ''I wonder if they're at the hospital yet.'' The ambulance had left a half hour ago.

She glanced at the clock. It was already after ten. Funny, she wasn't the least bit tired. It was adrenaline, she told herself. The situation had been unexpected and she hadn't had time to do more than react. Now she was sailing on those chemicals flowing through her body. In a little while she would crash and get tired and maybe a little shaky.

Trevor took the bottle from her and set it down. He raised his glass to her. ''Here's to Shelly and her new son.''

''To them both. They have an exciting start to a wonderful relationship.'' She touched her glass to his, then took a sip. The wine was cool and crisp. ''How are you feeling?''

''Relieved,'' he said. ''You?''

''A little wired. It takes me a while to wind down from things like that.'' She shrugged. ''It's been a while since I was directly involved in patient care. At times I miss it. Now that I know everything is fine, I can say it was fun.''

He raised his eyebrows. ''That's not the word I would choose.''

She placed her free hand on his chest. ''Come on, Trevor. It wasn't so bad. Admit it. You got a real kick out of helping her.''

''I'm willing to admit that the thought of assisting in another birth isn't going to make me break out in a cold sweat, but I refuse to believe it was fun. Give me surgery any day.''

She laughed. He joined in, then suddenly they weren't laughing anymore. When he took the wineglass from her hand and set it on the table next to his, she thought about protesting. She was enjoying her drink. Then he cupped her face in his hands and she couldn't think about anything except the fact that he was going to kiss her and she was going to let him.

His mouth was sure and firm as it caressed hers. Sweet kisses, sensual, demanding, arousing. Her entire body absorbed the sensation of being so close to him. She inhaled his scent, reveled in his heat, his masculinity. She leaned into him, pressing her breasts against his chest. Her arms wrapped around his neck and she felt the short hairs tickling the back of her hands.

He didn't have to urge her to open for him. She parted her lips to admit him, then met him with a warm brush of her tongue against his. He responded in kind and they began an ancient ritual of pleasuring each other.

The kiss went on forever. He rubbed his palms against her back before sliding them lower to her rear. When he cupped her there, she arched against him, wanting to be closer, nearer, a part of him. She moved her belly against him, feeling the strength of his desire. A shiver ran through her, starting low in her stomach and moving up her chest. He wanted her. There was physical proof. This wasn't a dream or a moment of boredom. He *wanted* her.

"Dana," he murmured as he broke the kiss long enough to suck on her earlobe. Tiny lightning bolts jolted through her. She felt her breasts swell.

"Trevor, I…" Words failed her as he claimed her mouth again. He explored all of her, tasting and touching. She followed him back and did the same, reveling in the contrast of his smooth teeth, the soft skin on the inside of his lower lip, the sharp rush of his breath when she lightly nipped him there.

He moved his hands back up her spine, then brought them around to her rib cage. She moved away enough to allow him to slip higher until he cradled her breasts in the palms of his hands. He took their slight weight, rubbing them gently, moving in tiny circles, his fingers inching closer and closer to her nipples until they at last touched the taut peaks.

She swallowed a moan of pure pleasure. He tweaked the tips between thumbs and forefingers, teasing until they nearly vibrated. Each flick of his touch sent a ribbon of fire down her belly to the place between her thighs. Already she felt the heat and dampness as she readied for him. The combination of sensations was so intense she thought she might faint.

Just as passion overwhelmed her last chance at rational thought, he pulled away. Not so he could touch her somewhere else, but so he could look at her.

He tucked her hair behind her ears, then stroked her cheek. Desire tightened the muscles in his face, making him even more beautiful.

She wanted him. She'd wanted him from the moment he arrived in town. In that respect, she was no different from the rest of her nursing staff. Perhaps some of her passion came from the past, from what she remembered about the last time they'd been together. He'd been her first and he'd made the experience wonderful. Whatever had happened later, she'd clung to that fact. With Trevor, lovemaking had felt right. Not too awkward, not too strange, but perfect.

No doubt she was making a huge mistake that she would regret for a long time. But no way could she walk away from him. She had to know if it was how she remembered. Her body was on fire and he was the only one with the ability to control the flames.

His mouth twisted slightly. Panic flared in her belly. What was wrong? Why had he stopped? "Having second thoughts?" she asked, pleased that her voice sounded so normal. He wouldn't be able to guess that she was suddenly terrified he didn't want her.

"Hardly. Just wondering."

"About what?" When he didn't answer, the panic grew. Great. She'd just made a complete fool out of herself. What had she been thinking?

She took a step back. "Okay, no problem. I understand you don't want to...well, you know."

"Dana, don't." He grabbed her arm and held her in place. "It's not what you think. I do want you." Need darkened his eyes. If that hadn't been enough to convince her, he took her hand and pressed it against his arousal.

He jumped when she rubbed her palm against him. "Enough," he said with a faint gasp. "You can't touch me like that. I'm afraid I'll embarrass myself."

Fine. He was aroused and he wanted her, but still, something was wrong. She could feel it. "Trevor, I'm confused. What's going on?"

He led her to the bed and sat down, then pulled her next to him. He pressed her onto the mattress and settled beside her, supporting his head on his hand.

"I want you," he said, resting one hand on her stomach. His smile turned wry. "More than you know. Worse, more than is safe. I need to be careful so I don't, um, finish too early." When she frowned, he added, "It's been a long time."

According to Angie it hadn't been long at all. She didn't like that thought, so she pushed it away. Obviously this was a mistake, she told herself. "How long?" she asked.

"I haven't made love since I left my wife. That would make it nearly two years."

His words hung in the silence. Dana stared at him, searching his face for a hint that he was lying. "Two years?" she asked, her voice incredulous.

He winced. "Unfortunately, yes."

"But I thought—"

He cut her off with a kiss. "You thought wrong. I don't know what they've been saying and I don't want to know. The truth is, I haven't been with anyone in a long time."

She believed him. Her heart surged and she knew she was in even more trouble than before. But she wasn't going to think about that now. There were more urgent matters.

She wrapped her arms around him and pulled him close. "Then we have some catching up to do."

His slow, sexy grin made her insides melt.

"I'm glad you feel that way." He brushed his mouth against hers. "I have good news and bad news. The good news is I have protection. Not that I was hoping we'd do anything and brought condoms, but I do have the ones Shelly had delivered."

Dana giggled. "Good, because I'm not prepared to deal with birth control. It's been a while for me, too."

"Thank you," he murmured, and kissed her.

Her mouth parted and he entered her. She got lost in the passion for a while before remembering he'd wanted to tell her something else. "What's the bad news?"

Trevor cleared his throat. More nerves, she thought in surprise.

"Despite what everyone says," he told her, "there haven't been a lot of women in my life. So don't expect Don Juan. I want to make you happy, Dana, but I need your cooperation. I want you to tell me if I'm doing something you like or don't like. All right?"

He looked so damn sweet at that moment. Obviously nervous about the confession and her reaction, but determined to be honest. How was she supposed to resist him?

"So far you're doing great," she said.

"You, too."

He dropped his mouth to hers and at the same time reached for the top button on her blouse. She couldn't decide what to concentrate on...the feel of his lips moving against her, the sweeping strokes of his tongue or the way his knuckles gently bumped against her breasts. Every part of her was throbbing with desire. She wanted to touch him, to be touched by him, to be under him, with him inside her, claiming her. She wanted this to never, ever stop.

When he reached the last button, he pulled her shirt free of the waistband of her jeans and pushed it open. Still kissing her, he moved his right hand behind her back and reached for her bra. She felt his fingers fumble with the hook. The elastic stretched as he wrestled with the small fasteners. She was torn between letting him try to get it open and offering to help.

He drew back. "Just so you know I wasn't lying about being out of practice."

There was something almost vulnerable in his eyes. Something that drew her in as no practiced, smooth move would have done. Without thinking, she unzipped her jeans, then took his hand and placed it on her belly. She urged him to move deeper, then gasped as his fingers touched her curls and her damp center.

"Just so *you* know I really want you."

His gaze locked with hers. Something powerful and electric crackled between them. "You have no idea what you're doing to me, Dana," he said, his voice thick with passion.

He rolled onto his back, drawing her up on top of him. From that position it was easy for him to undo the hooks. Together they pulled off her shirt and bra. He put his hands on her waist and urged her to slide along him until her breasts were directly over his mouth.

She was about to protest the awkward position, when his mouth closed over her already taut nipple. Liquid heat raced through her as her whole body focused on the single point of perfect pleasure. She braced herself with her hands, pushing against the mattress so that she could stay there for always. She wanted him to keep touching her like that, his tongue circling the sensitive peaks, his lips drawing her in and sucking. When he switched to her other breast, she had to bite back a cry of pure enjoyment. She moved her hands so she could stroke his head, all the while murmuring his name.

He shifted, rolling them onto their sides. Once there, he traced a line from her forehead, down her nose, ending at her mouth. Then he outlined her lips with the tip of his finger. The tender gesture nearly brought tears to her eyes.

"You're doing everything perfectly," she told him.

"Yeah?" His smile was boyish, half proud, half embarrassed. "Good. I want to."

This was a side of Trevor she didn't know. The physically perfect, always together man was gone and in his place was someone...normal. She could resist the paragon, but not the possibility of a real, nearly everyday kind of man.

She kissed him. First on the lips, then on his cheek and his nose. Stubble darkened his face and rasped against her tongue. She liked the taste of him. And his scent and everything else about him.

When he tugged at her jeans and panties, she raised her hips to help him. They still lay on their sides, with one of her legs bent and up against his hip. He completed a lazy pattern, tracing a circle from her shoulder, along her side to her hips, then crossing down her thigh, gently rubbing against that secret place between her legs, moving up her belly to her breasts, ending back at her shoulder.

They stared into each other's eyes while he did this. She tried not to notice the journey was taking longer and longer as he spent more time exploring her feminine place. Finally, he slowly inserted one finger inside her. She felt herself convulse around him. They both sucked in their breath.

"You're a little overdressed," she told him as she tugged on the collar of his shirt. While she was naked, he was completely clothed.

"I know, but it's better this way. I'm afraid if you even look at me, I'll explode."

She touched the tip of his nose. "I *am* looking at you."

"I'm not worried about you staring at my face."

"Why not? It's a very nice face."

"I'm glad you think so."

"I do. Very much."

His fingers slipped down her thigh, and once again it became difficult for her to talk. He found the core of her and circled that place. Her body rocked with the rhythm he created; her breathing increased; her eyes closed. Every part of her focused on that one sweet spot.

He moved slowly, carefully, occasionally dipping inside her. She found herself tensing, wanting to rush the process. She forced herself to hold back, to let him set the pace.

Trevor couldn't believe what was happening—that Dana was in his bed, letting him make love with her. She was more beautiful than he remembered. Time had rounded her curves and added spice to her personality. Before, in high school, she'd showed promise. Now she was all that promise fulfilled and more. So much more.

Her body trembled against his. He moved slowly, wanting her to enjoy the journey as much as he. She was obviously ready for whatever they would do. He continued to circle around that tiny spot of pleasure, occasionally brushing over it, then moving lower and torturing himself by entering the place that would soon provide his own release. Assuming he didn't lose it completely.

He grinned, knowing it was embarrassing as hell for a man his age to be worried about reacting like a seventeen-year-old. Her breath caught and he returned his attention to her. A flush started on her chest and moved up to her face. Her fingers clutched at the bedspread under them, her hips thrust forward and back in a rhythm as old as biology.

He wanted her to find her release. He wanted to be the one to provide it. As he started to move faster, her body strained toward his. She opened her eyes, but her gaze was unfocused. Her mouth parted. He leaned forward to kiss her. She drew him in, sucking hard on his tongue. At the same time, he brushed over that aroused spot.

She cried out and shuddered. Keeping his thumb circling around her, he dipped a finger inside and felt the rapid contractions signaling her release. He stroked her there, too, moving in and out in counterpoint.

The release went on for several seconds. Finally, when she relaxed, he lightened his touch, then drew his hand away. She broke the kiss and stared at him.

"Wow," she murmured. "I mean…wow."

Pride filled him. "I'm glad you liked it."

"'Like' doesn't exactly describe the experience."

"Good."

"No, it was better than good," she teased.

He grinned. "Okay, how about extraordinary?"

"Hmm, closer. I'm not sure I can put it into words." She pressed her face into his chest. "Hold me, Trevor."

He wrapped his arms around her and drew her close. This was right, he told himself. Having Dana next to him, her body still warm and trembling from their lovemaking. He could do this for a long time and not grow tired of being with her.

After a few minutes she reached for the buttons on his

shirt. "I assume it's okay for me to look at you now," she said.

His arousal flexed painfully. "I wouldn't complain."

"Good."

"Oh, I think it's going to be better than good."

She chuckled. "How about extraordinary?"

"Undoubtedly."

With his help, she removed his clothes. While she pulled back the bedspread and climbed between the sheets, he found a condom in the nightstand and slipped it on. Then he knelt between her thighs and looked at her.

Contentment added to her beauty. Blue eyes gazed at him; a smile tugged at her lips. Her short hair was tousled and unbelievably sexy. He could feel the pressure building.

"I'm afraid this isn't going to take very long," he told her.

"I left my stopwatch at home, so you're safe."

She placed her hand on the back of his neck and drew him down. With her lips nearly pressed against his she said, "I suspect this isn't going to be your only performance of the night."

He slid into her welcoming warmth and groaned in contentment. Nothing had ever felt so good...or so right.

"Want to bet on that?" he asked as he withdrew, only to thrust in again.

"Sure. Name your wager. I know I'm going to win."

The pressure increased as he pulled out and slipped in again. "I believe this is what Shelly would call a win-win situation."

Dana cupped his cheeks and smiled. "Just do it, Trevor. You can dazzle me with style later."

"If you insist."

"I do."

As he buried himself in her, he reminded himself it was

terribly rude to ignore a lady's direct request. And then he couldn't think of anything except how much he wanted her and needed her. And then he couldn't think at all.

Dana opened her eyes to find sunlight streaming in through the window. She rolled over and realized she didn't know where she was.

Something about the hotel room was familiar. She blinked and then it all came back. The rainstorm, Shelly giving birth, the celebration afterward, the lovemaking.

She sat upright and glanced around frantically. Lovemaking? She and Trevor had... "What was I thinking?" she muttered, then knew the answer to that question. She hadn't been thinking at all. That was the point. And now she would pay the price.

She knew better. Trevor wasn't the kind of man to be interested in anything but a short-term affair. He didn't believe in happily ever after. Even if he did, even if a miracle occurred and he thought he wanted her, she couldn't get involved with him. It wasn't just because he was the object of desire for every woman on the planet. He was also a doctor and she knew better than to get serious about someone like that.

But telling herself all the logical reasons it would never work didn't stop her from wanting the dream to be true. If only— How many times had she whispered that in her life? If only her mother had found someone. If only they hadn't been so poor. If only Trevor hadn't talked about their night together. If only it could have been different...then and now.

Sound intruded and she cocked her head, trying to figure out what it was and where it was coming from. The shower. He must be in the shower, which meant if she worked quickly, she might have time to escape.

Dana climbed out of bed and searched for her clothes, which were scattered on the floor. Despite her need to leave his room before he realized she was awake, she had to stop and smile. Last night had been amazing. As she bent to pick up her bra she remembered how he'd fumbled with the hook and eye closure at the back. Images filled her mind of all the times they'd made love.

He'd told her he hadn't been with anyone since he and his wife had split up. At first she hadn't been sure she could believe him, but as the night wore on, she knew he'd told the truth. He'd been so tender and sensitive to her needs, but also very *eager* to be with her. And he'd certainly had the recovery time of a man who hadn't—

She broke off the thought when she realized she was blushing. But it was impossible not to remember how he'd reached for her in the night, how he'd drawn her close, touching and stroking her until she was ready, until her body had welcomed him as he'd entered her and made her climax again and again.

The sound of water stopped suddenly. Dana sprang into action, first collecting her clothes, then starting to pull them on. But she was still minus her shirt when Trevor stepped out of the bathroom.

They'd been intimate many times the previous night, and for most of them the lights had been on. So she should be familiar with his body. Or at least immune. But the sight of him, naked except for the white towel wrapped around his waist, made her knees go weak. Broad shoulders; the pattern of hair on his chest; long, powerful arms and legs; tanned skin. How was she supposed to resist this?

"You're awake," he said as he walked toward her. "Gee, and I was hoping to climb in bed and cuddle some more."

He pulled her close and hugged her. She told herself to

resist, that this was all a mistake, but he was too tempting. He smelled of soap and himself. She could no more turn away than she could stop breathing. But she had to be strong. If she didn't, she was going to get her heart broken again. This time there was a lot more on the line and she would find it harder to recover.

With that in mind, she stepped back. A lock of damp hair fell across his forehead. Dana had to physically turn her back on him to keep from smoothing it in place. This was going to be more difficult than she'd first thought.

She pulled on her shirt and fastened the buttons. Only when she was completely covered did she turn around to face him.

"Neither of us was thinking last night," she said. "I understand that and I want you to know it won't be a problem." She tried to smile and had a feeling she failed pretty miserably. "What I'm trying to say is that *I* won't be a problem. I know it didn't mean anything, so don't worry that I'll get all weird and emotional on you."

Trevor stared at her. She tried reading his expression, but his face was an impassive mask. He didn't bother reaching for clothes or sitting down. His only physical act was to cross his arms over his chest.

"Go on," he told her.

"Yes, well, like I said, it's not a problem. I'm willing to admit the sex was terrific, so I won't be able to pretend it never happened, but I don't feel the need to talk about it. We can go back to the hospital and just be co-workers again. I think that's probably for the best." She reached for her shoes, then straightened. "Oh, I would prefer that you not discuss this with anyone. I don't want to be the object of hospital gossip and I don't imagine you want that, either."

Dana finished her speech. She was pretty pleased with

how it came out, especially considering she hadn't had time to practice. As she waited for his response, she was less than pleased to realize a part of her hoped he would protest. That instead of calmly agreeing her plan was sensible, he would sweep her into his arms and tell her he cared about her, maybe even loved her.

You're a fool, she told herself silently. When are you going to get over him?

She didn't have an answer for that. The trick with Trevor was never to be in a position where getting over him was necessary. Unfortunately, she might be too late for that.

He stared at her for a long time. She still couldn't read his expression. Something flashed across his face. Something that, if he'd been another kind of man, she might have labeled as hurt. But this was Trevor MacAllister and she knew better. She doubted he'd ever been in love even once in his life.

Chapter Ten

He was a doctor and he knew intellectually that words didn't physically wound. Yet he felt as though she'd ripped open his chest and left him to bleed to death.

Trevor stood in the center of his hotel room and listened to Dana as she went on about how she appreciated his understanding in this matter and how important it was for them to maintain a professional relationship.

"I know your career is important to you," he heard himself say, as if from a distance. "You've worked hard to be where you are."

She flashed him a grateful smile. "Thanks for understanding."

"Of course I understand. It's not that difficult. You busted your butt in college, you work long hours, you're very successful. Why wouldn't I get it?"

Her blue eyes widened. "Trevor, what's wrong? Are you angry? I would have thought you'd be pleased with what I was telling you. I know you don't want me making things difficult.''

She had no clue what he wanted, but that was reasonable. He wasn't so sure what he wanted, either. The one thing he knew was that he didn't want to be having this conversation.

He walked to the edge of the bed and sat down. Her expression was wary, as if she wasn't sure what he was going to do or say next. He glanced at his chest, but there was no open wound, no blood, no physical evidence that she was ripping out his heart.

''About last night,'' he began, then had to stop to clear his throat. He was setting himself up to be slammed down, but he couldn't stop the words. ''Do you regret it?''

She smiled. ''No. Of course not. How could I? The sex was amazing.''

She continued to talk, but he didn't hear the rest of it. He supposed that in time he would be pleased she'd enjoyed his technique, such as it was. He didn't fool himself. He hadn't been with dozens of women and he wasn't perfect in bed. Everything he'd done last night had been in an effort to please the woman he cared about. Not because of ego, but because of heart.

He shivered, then realized the temperature of the room was fine. His chill came from the inside. At least he hadn't told her the truth. That was something. He could go back to the hospital, the rumors would continue and no one would know that he'd wanted more than a night of great sex.

It was the same as it had been all those years ago. In high school he'd loved Dana, but it hadn't mattered. Once again, she'd captured his interest and his affections, and it still didn't matter. As a young man, he'd adored her. As a grown man, he'd wanted to love her. She, however, wasn't interested in that. At least not from him.

"Trevor," she said, breaking into his thoughts. "You won't say anything, will you?"

She looked so damned pretty standing there. All worried and earnest. It just didn't occur to her that this was more than a one-night stand. She couldn't comprehend that he had depth and feelings, that something might matter to him. She was still reacting to what had happened all those years ago.

The irony was, while he'd been in the shower he'd fantasized about telling her how he felt about her. Worse, he'd toyed with the idea of proposing. Thank God he'd come to his senses in time.

"No, I won't say a word," he told her. "About anything."

The drive back to Honeygrove was awkward. Not only because he couldn't think of anything to say to her, but because of the contrast to the ride down to the seminar. He kept thinking about how much they'd talked and laughed. If he'd known becoming lovers would have changed everything, he would have tried harder to resist.

For once, even a sunny day and the open road weren't enough to make him feel better. All he wanted was to get them back to the town-house complex so they could say goodbye and be done with it. Flashes of their week together kept drifting through his mind. He had too many memories of Dana. Her laughing in the different classes. Her look of horror the first time she'd dropped her egg. The way she'd been so calm and competent while helping Shelly deliver her baby. The fire in her eyes while they'd made love.

And now he was supposed to return to his regular life, as if none of this had ever happened. No problem, he told himself. He'd buried himself in work before; he could do it again. It was probably for the best. After all, Dana still wasn't willing to give him the benefit of the doubt.

He wrestled with that, wondering if he was judging her too harshly. She'd been fine at the seminar, but then they'd been away from the hospital gossip and everything that went with it. Maybe if they had a chance to spend time together away from everyone else, it could work. He knew he was interested, but was she? Could he risk asking? Could he risk passing up this opportunity, knowing he might not have another chance with her?

He pulled into the town-house complex and stopped in front of her place. As she climbed out of the passenger seat, he leaned over, opened the glove compartment and popped the trunk. They met behind the car. He handed her the suitcase she'd brought.

"Thanks for driving me home," she said. Her gaze was direct, but he read the questions in her eyes. She wasn't sure what was going on. Great, that made two of them.

"No problem." He wondered what else to say. Thanking her for a good time wasn't right. He didn't dare admit his feelings, because it was unlikely she would believe him. "Dana, I—"

He what?

She looked at him. "Yes, Trevor?"

"I'd like to see you again. Not at the hospital," he added hastily. "I'm talking about us going out."

She stared at him as if he'd started speaking a foreign language. "Why?"

So much for sweeping her off her feet. He didn't doubt that she'd enjoyed their time together, especially last night, but it had obviously meant more to him than to her.

"Right," he said. "Why? Good question, and I don't

have an answer with me now. Never mind. Sorry to bother you." He turned away.

She grabbed his arm. "Trevor, wait. I'm serious. Why do you want to see me? You're already dating Angie and Sally, and those are only the two I know about." She gave him a smile. "It's not that I don't like you—I do. I think you're a terrific surgeon and, despite everything, a lot of fun. But the last thing you need is another woman in your life. And I don't like to get involved with someone unless it'll be exclusive."

So now he knew the rumors. He had an idea about who Sally and Angie were, but he wasn't interested in dating either of them. "I told you I haven't been out with anyone since I've moved here." He shrugged. "I guess my word doesn't matter."

"I don't understand. They've both talked about going out with you. They mention days, times, places. Are you telling me they're lying?"

"I'm telling you I haven't been on a date in months. How often am I supposed to be seeing them?"

She drew her eyebrows together. "Almost every night, it seems."

"I'm pretty rested for a guy with that kind of social life. You live next door, Dana. You hear my television. You know when my car pulls out of the garage. Last night I didn't make love like a guy who's been getting it on a regular basis. Don't look so confused. This isn't hard to figure out. You tell *me* what's going on."

With that he returned to his car and started the engine. After hitting the remote control to open his garage door, he drove inside and parked. As much as he wanted Dana to come running after him and tell him that she'd been wrong about everything, he knew it wasn't going to happen. After all, she had no reason to believe him and every reason to think he was lying.

But that truth didn't stop him from wanting it to be different, from wanting *her* to trust him. He wanted her to see beyond what the world saw, to understand that the man inside had little to do with the world's view of Trevor MacAllister.

He wanted too much. Where Dana was concerned, he always had.

Dana was the first to arrive at Granetti's. It was barely four in the afternoon, so the after-work crowd hadn't started to fill the place. She snagged a corner booth and sat facing the door so she could see when Katie and Lee walked in. She'd been back from the seminar nearly a week and she desperately needed to talk to her friends. Between the rush of attempting to get caught up from all the work she'd missed and coordinating their busy schedules, this was the first available moment the three of them could squeeze in.

Dana refused the waiter's offer for a drink, preferring to wait until her friends showed up. She stared off into the distance, trying to figure out what was wrong with her. It wasn't just too much work to do. She was always rushed, so that wasn't news. It was the lingering aftereffect of everything that had happened, she decided. Dealing with the reality that she and Trevor had made love.

She shuddered at the thought. Not out of horror, but out of longing and the forbidden memory of how wonderful everything had been between them. Despite being thirty and not even close to being a virgin, she hadn't had lots of men in her life. She was selective. Sometimes, according to her mother, too picky. Which made her decision to sleep with Trevor even more out of character. But that wasn't what was bothering her. It wasn't what they'd done; it was how he was acting now.

She sucked in a deep breath and told herself she'd gotten exactly what she'd asked for. He was polite, friendly and completely professional. Not by a smile or a wink did he hint that they'd ever been more than colleagues. If she hadn't actually been naked with him that night, she would swear nothing had ever happened and nothing would. But she *had* been there. She remembered, perhaps in too much detail, all they'd done. She also remembered his request to continue seeing her.

What she wanted to know was why.

"Obviously it's a pressing problem," a voice said.

Dana glanced up and saw her two friends standing by the table. She jumped. "I didn't see you come in."

"We could tell." Katie slid into the booth. "I thought your voice sounded funny when you called. What's wrong?"

Lee settled next to Katie and motioned for the waiter. "Don't bother denying it, Dana. I heard it, too. You know you're going to end up spilling your guts, so just give in with grace and dignity."

Despite her confusion and the tension filling her body, Dana had to laugh. These two had been her friends since grade school. She trusted them implicitly; they were the family she'd always wanted. She'd asked to meet with them because she valued and needed their counsel.

While they gave their drink orders and decided they would wait a bit to have their early dinner, Dana tried to think of a delicate way to bring them up to date with what had been happening.

The waiter returned with three diet sodas and a basket of garlic bread. Katie took a piece and said, "Don't bother with the idle chitchat. Just cut to the juicy part."

Her eyes were bright with laughter and Dana knew she was teasing. Still, it was good advice.

"I spent the night with Trevor at the seminar."

Their reaction was better than she'd hoped. Lee had been taking a drink of her soda and she nearly spit a mouthful across the table. Katie about choked on her bite of garlic bread. They looked at each other and then at her.

Lee cleared her throat. "Never mind what Katie said. Feel free to start with the idle chitchat. How was the weather? Did you have a nice room?"

Katie dismissed her with a wave of her hand. "Ignore her. Tell us everything. Are you okay—emotionally, I mean? Was it wonderful? Horrible? How do you feel?"

Dana covered her face with her hands. "I'm so confused."

"Maybe Lee's right," Katie said, concern in her voice. "Why don't you start at the beginning."

Dana nodded and tried to get control. After a couple of deep breaths she felt better, so she told them about the week she and Trevor had spent at the seminar.

"He was different," she said. "No, that's not true. He was the same as he always is around me. Friendly, fun. I guess the difference was I didn't have to listen to Angie and Sally talking about their dates with him."

"Were there other women at the seminar?" Lee asked. "Single women?"

"Sure. A few were obviously interested in Trevor, but he didn't encourage them. I never had the impression he was on the prowl, if that's what you're asking."

Lee and Katie exchanged a look. "What has you confused?" Lee asked. "The fact that you two spent the night together?"

"It's not that exactly," Dana said. "Okay, I guess some of it is that I sort of like him." She held up her hand to keep them from saying anything. "Not in a romantic way, but as a friend. When we're together, he's someone I can respect and I enjoy being with. I guess the problem is reconciling that man with Dr. Love who dates anything in a skirt."

"Why is being friends a problem?" Katie asked. "You two work together now, right? You're neighbors. I'm with Lee. I don't understand the problem." She nibbled on her garlic bread. "Unless you want it to be something else and are afraid he doesn't share your feelings."

"I don't want it to be anything else," Dana snapped, then shook her head. "Sorry. I know you're trying to be understanding and supportive. If I look at this logically, it's not that big a deal. Trevor and I attended this seminar together. We got along great and spent many hours in each other's company. No problem. So one night things got out of hand and we ended up in bed. The big question is what happens now."

"What do you want?" Katie asked.

"What does Trevor want?" Lee leaned forward. "That's it, isn't it, Dana? You're not sure of your feelings because of something Trevor said."

She felt herself blushing. "This would be the downside of being so close to you two for all these years. You can read my mind." She sighed. "Yes, that's part of the problem. Although a lot of it has been the fact that I feel so awkward around him at the hospital. We've been painfully polite, and I hate it. I want things to be the way they were before."

"So what did he say he wanted?" Katie asked.

Dana swallowed, half-afraid her friends would laugh at her. Even though she'd been there that night he'd made love to her over and over again, and heard his words the next morning, a part of her had trouble believing that Trevor MacAllister was actually interested in her.

"He said he would like to see me again. You know, like dating."

Katie and Lee exchanged a look.

"What?" Dana asked. "What are you both thinking?"

"Nothing," Lee said. "What did you tell him?"

"I said I wasn't interested."

"Are you crazy?" Katie asked. "Jeez, Dana, he's good-looking, he's successful, you've said he's fun to be around and you like him. Why on earth wouldn't you want to date him?"

"Do I have to remind you what happened the last time Trevor and I were involved?"

Katie shook her head. "No. I remember. But it was a long time ago and people change. I'm sure he has grown up. He would have to have with his demanding career. Besides, I always thought there was something odd about that situation. I don't think we had the whole story."

Dana remembered what Trevor had told her, about Joel being the one to spread the rumors. She knew Katie was right in her suspicions, but this wasn't the time to go into that.

"He's a doctor," Lee said, as if that explained everything.

Katie rolled her eyes. "Doctor, schmoctor, do we really care that much about what men do for a living?"

"Yes," Dana and Lee said together, then laughed.

"You two are taking our little pledge way too seriously."

"That couldn't be because you've already broken it, could it?" Lee asked, then raised her hands in surrender. "Let's not get into that right now. Dana has a more pressing problem." She leaned forward and rested her hands on the table. "It seems to me that the real issue isn't Trevor—it's you. If you were completely uninterested in him—"

"She wouldn't have slept with him," Katie said, interrupting.

"I was getting to that," Lee said. "You wouldn't have spent the night with him and you wouldn't have worried about dealing with him afterward, except where it involved work. So some part of you isn't willing to let this go."

"You're in love with him," Katie said flatly.

Lee groaned. "Katie, don't go there."

"I'm not in love with him," Dana said. Even as she said the words, though, she probed her heart. Nothing about the organ seemed tender or out of the ordinary. "I'm really not," she repeated with conviction. "It's just…" Her voice trailed off. "I don't know what it's just."

"There's potential," Lee said. "That's what has you worried. You're not sure he's what you want, but if there's a chance, you don't want to risk walking away."

"Maybe." Dana wasn't sure. Trevor? Could she ever really trust him?

"Oh, just go for it," Katie advised. "Date him, see what the relationship feels like. If it doesn't work, at least you'll have him out of your system."

"She does have a point," Lee said.

Date Trevor? Dana wasn't sure. The idea had merit, she supposed. It wasn't as if he were a toad or someone she despised. But there could be complications. "What about hospital gossip?"

"You're both grown-ups," Lee said. "You can be discreet. No one has to know."

"You have to try," Katie said. "What if he's the one? Wouldn't you hate yourself knowing that you'd lost your chance at something wonderful?"

"I don't know about wonderful," Dana muttered. "I don't think it'll amount to anything at all."

"Then all that's happened is you've spent a few evenings with a nice man. There are worse fates."

Lee took a piece of garlic bread. "This is where I become the voice of reason and point out that the man *is* a doctor, so tread carefully."

"Ignore her," Katie murmured.

"Ignore me at your peril," Lee said. "We signed our agreement for a reason. I'm willing to admit Katie got lucky, but what's the chance of that happening with all three of us?"

"Slim," Dana admitted.

She was still confused, but slightly less so. If nothing else, dating Trevor *would* get him out of her system, which would be a good thing. She could think of their time together as practice for dating someone else, someone she could really get involved with. After all, she couldn't focus on her career forever. Trevor was a lot of fun and she already knew they were great in bed together. She wouldn't mind a repeat of that night.

"All right," she said slowly. "I'll do it. I'll tell Trevor that I would like us to date, and then we'll see what happens."

"Wonderful." Katie squeezed her arm. "This is going to be great."

Lee grinned. "What I wouldn't give to be a fly on the wall during that conversation."

"What conversation?" Dana asked.

"Oh, just the one where you tell him you're interested in going out with him."

Dana's mouth opened, but she couldn't speak. They would have to have that conversation. Oh, dear Lord, what on earth was she going to say?

Chapter Eleven

Dana stood outside Trevor's front door and fought down the urge to run back to her place. She was actually shaking. Telling herself it was "just nerves" didn't help at all. What had seemed fun and almost easy back at Granetti's was suddenly an incredibly terrifying proposition. What had she been thinking? Was she really going to waltz into Trevor's house and tell him that she was interested in going out with him? Was she insane?

"I can't do this," she murmured. "I just can't. I'll die."

And even if she didn't die, she might feel as though she wanted to, which was about the same thing in her mind.

"Just do it or leave," she said aloud, then wondered what the neighbors would think when they saw her out there talking to herself like a crazy person.

She sucked in a deep breath. She had a lot of flaws, but running away wasn't one of them. After sending up a quick prayer for both courage and the ability to stand whatever humiliation might come her way, she knocked on his door.

It was 7:00 p.m. on a Friday night. She told herself there was a better than even chance that Trevor was preparing to go out on a date. She knew he hadn't left because while she'd heard the rumble of his Cobra when he'd come home, she hadn't heard him pull out of the garage. *Not* that she'd been listening.

So when he opened the door, she braced herself to see him in a suit and tie, his hair still damp from a shower, his face freshly shaved. Instead, Trevor stood before her in obviously old, faded navy sweatpants and an oversized white T-shirt. His feet were bare, his jaw dark with stubble, and the somewhat glazed look in his eyes told her he might have been dozing.

"Dana!" He smiled. "This is a pleasant surprise." He held the door open wide and motioned for her to come in.

"Hi." She stepped into his town house. "I probably should have called first. I hope I'm not interrupting."

He led the way to the living room and gestured for her to take a seat on the sofa. A baseball game played on the television, but the sound was off.

"As you can see, I'm expecting a dinner party of twelve in a little while, but I've got some time before they arrive. What can I get you to drink? Soda? Water? Wine? I have a great sauvignon blanc I've wanted to try, if you're feeling adventurous."

"The wine sounds great," she told him, thinking that the liquor might help her relax. While she'd expected to feel a little nervous, she hadn't thought she would be hyperventilating at the thought of what she wanted to talk about.

He got the wine out of the refrigerator, opened it and poured them each a glass. When she took it, she was embarrassed to realize her hands were still shaking. So much for at least pretending to be calm and in control.

She perched on a cushion on the left side of the sofa. He settled halfway between the middle and the right side. Close enough that she could almost feel his heat...almost, but not quite.

Despite her nerves, her body was thrilled to be back in his presence. Erotic dreams had haunted her since their night together nearly a week before. Images came to her during the day. It wasn't the lack of warning that broke her concentration as much as the intensity. She would be working on a schedule or talking to a supplier, when all of a sudden she was back in bed with Trevor, his hands stroking her, his arousal filling her and taking her—

"Dana?"

"Huh?" She stared blankly at him. "Did you say something?"

"Several somethings, but you weren't paying attention. Is everything all right?"

That question was better than his asking what she was thinking, she told herself. She looked at him, at his handsome face and the smile hovering at the corners of his mouth. "I'm fine, but you look tired."

"I am," he admitted. "Long week with too many surgeries."

"I noticed how many," she said. "You took a couple of emergencies."

"I did what I could. There was that three-car pileup and I was already at the hospital. It wasn't a problem."

"Maybe not," she told him, "but not every surgeon would have agreed so readily."

"Call me 'Saint Trevor,'" he said lightly.

She took a sip of the wine. It was delicious. "I like this," she said, raising her glass.

"It's from a winery in Southern California in the Santa Ynez Valley. Not very well-known, but I enjoy their wines. I visited them a couple of times when I was in L.A. I guess now I'll have to have the wines shipped to me. The place is more than a weekend from here."

A few minutes of silence followed. Dana glanced around the room, trying to think of something to say. Her stomach had settled down some, but that was counteracted by the heat in her blood and her hormones screaming for her to attack Trevor. She decided it would be better to resist. At least until she found out how he would react to what she had to say.

"Dana, tell me what's wrong," he said.

She set the wine on the coffee table and smiled brightly. "Wrong? Nothing's wrong."

"You're fidgeting, and rubbing your hands together. Either something is bothering you or you've got some kind of skin condition. If it's the latter, you should be seeing a dermatologist instead of a surgeon."

"No, I don't have a skin condition. It's just..."

How on earth was she supposed to bring this up without sounding like a complete idiot? She knew that most of her discomfort came from the fact that she was about to put herself on the line. After all, there was a chance Trevor hadn't meant what he'd said "that morning." It could have simply been postsex chitchat. Maybe he hadn't been interested in her all.

But he *had* been interested, she reminded herself. She'd felt the physical proof over and over again. In fact, thinking about it was enough to—

Quit stalling! The voice inside her head was so loud she was afraid Trevor could hear her. But he didn't say anything. Instead, he waited politely for her to tell him why she was visiting him on a Friday night.

"It's about the other morning," she said at last. "You know, after."

After she'd had the most incredible experience of her life.

He nodded. "What about the other morning?"

Foolishly, she'd hoped he would guess without her prompting him. Fear swelled inside her but she ignored it. After all, it wasn't as if she actually cared about Trevor. If she was risking romantic involvement, then she would have a right to be terrified. But only her pride was at stake.

"I wasn't very gracious," she admitted. "I'm sorry about that."

"I understand," he told her, his eyes unreadable. "It was an unexpected thing for both of us."

"Um, yes, that, too. It's just...I wasn't sure what you meant when you talked about, well, seeing me."

He sipped his wine. "What didn't you understand?"

She sucked in a breath. So he wasn't going to make this easy. "Why you said it. Why you mentioned wanting to see me again. The thing is..." She exhaled and tried another deep breath. It didn't work at keeping her calm. So she decided to just go for speed. If she blurted it all out quickly, maybe it wouldn't be so embarrassing.

"I didn't mean to brush you off like that," she started, her words running together. "It's not that I'm not interested in dating you—it's just there's so much to deal with. We have our past relationship, although I've decided I don't think you were the one to spread the rumors. And then there's the hospital. There's so much gossip and I wouldn't want anyone to know and—" She had to stop for air.

"That is a lot," he said.

She'd hoped for more of a reaction. She still couldn't tell what he was thinking. "That's about everything," she said. "I, um, thought that if, um, you were still interested in seeing me, you know, on a personal basis, that, well, I'd like it, too.''

Her voice had dropped with each word, so that by the end of her short speech she was barely whispering.

Trevor didn't answer right away. Her tension increased, as did her dawning realization that she'd just made a huge mistake. He hadn't meant what he'd said that morning. He was just being polite at the time. There wasn't any attraction between them. She was a fool.

She was about to rise to her feet and bolt for the door, when he put his glass on the coffee table and leaned toward her.

"Dating?" he asked.

It wasn't the word itself; it was the way he said it. Caressing the syllables, surrounding it with meaning, making her skin tingle and her thighs go up in flames.

She could feel the heat on her cheeks, but she nodded. "Yes. Dating."

He smiled. It was the extraspecial one designed to reduce unsuspecting women to puddles, and she was no exception. The flames in her thighs spread to the rest of her body.

"Sounds like fun," he said.

The relief was tangible. She sagged back against the cushions. "Oh, good."

"When would you like to start?" he asked.

"Whenever it's convenient for you, but there have to be a couple of ground rules."

His smile faded. "Why do I know I'm not going to like them?"

If telling him she was interested in dating him had been hard, then the rest of what she had to say was impossible. She forced herself to do it anyway. "First, I don't want anyone at the hospital to know. We're both in high-profile jobs and the rumors could make our work difficult."

"I agree," he said. "I won't be telling anyone, except possibly my father, and I'm sure he can be discreet."

Walter was going to know? She didn't want to think about that.

"What's the second rule?" he asked.

"I don't date with a crowd," she said. "I would need this to be exclusive. You have to promise not to see anyone else. This is a deal breaker for me, Trevor. If you can't give up the other women, then I won't go out with you."

He stared at her for a long time. "If you think I'm the kind of man who would date more than one woman at a time, why are you willing to trust my word?"

It was a fair question. "I'm not sure, but I am. I suppose it's because you don't lie."

He was silent for a while. Finally he nodded. "All right, Dana, I'll give you exclusive. Despite what you think about me, I've never dated more than one woman at a time in my life. I am, by nature, monogamous, so faithful is easy for me. Any other ground rules?"

Don't break my heart. But she didn't say that one aloud. She couldn't. After all, her heart wasn't engaged, nor was it going to be. She was in this for the fun and nothing else. At least that was the plan. She ignored the voice in the back of her head that whispered something else might be going on. Something she wasn't willing to recognize yet.

"No, that's it for me." She cleared her throat. "That's really all I had to say."

"Great." He rose to his feet, forcing her to do the same. "Tell you what. Let's get started tomorrow. I'll pick you up at seven. Dress casual."

Then, before she knew what was happening, he'd ushered her to his front door and shown her out. She wasn't sure what it meant or what would happen now. Yet a part of her was sure she'd just done something that would change her life forever.

Trevor stared at the closed door and wondered where he'd gotten the courage to calmly discuss dating with Dana, then show her out. He knew it was the right thing to do. She had some strong opinions about the two of them and he was beginning to see that the only way to get through to her was to keep her off balance. But given the choice, he would rather have pulled her into his arms, kissed her until they were both weak with longing, then taken her upstairs to his bedroom and made love with her.

An intriguing idea, but not practical. Not for right now.

He returned to the living room and tried to watch the baseball game. He barely recognized either team, let alone found the score interesting. His mind raced. He was torn. On the one hand, he was thrilled that Dana wanted to start a relationship with him. For a while he'd been afraid that their night together hadn't meant anything to her. Now he knew that she'd been affected, too. Although not in the same way. After all, he'd realized that he loved her. She'd realized that dating him wouldn't be too horrible.

But while he was pleased to be in a position where he would be able to see her, he was also furious. He was still fighting his reputation and her assumptions. Until she believed in him, until she took the time and trouble to see him for the man he was, they would never have a chance at making anything work.

For now, though, he would concentrate on the opportunity to be with her. He had several ideas about how to make the most of their time together. Dana might not have fallen in love with him, but she'd been just as surprised and pleasured by their lovemaking. He didn't doubt the memories were haunting her, as well. He would use that to his advantage, he decided. Not by seducing her, but by playing hard to get.

Trevor wore jeans, a long-sleeved shirt rolled up to the elbows and cowboy boots. After their week at the seminar, Dana told herself she should be used to seeing him in casual clothing. And she was. What she wasn't used to and what she might never grow totally comfortable with was how gorgeous he was.

He'd showered and shaved, so the fantasy of the previous night—damp hair, freshly shaved jaw—was now a reality. She felt her heart flutter as an assortment of other organs and body parts also took notice of him. She couldn't help thinking how much she wanted him and how wonderful it had been to be with him.

"Hi," she said, and held open the door. "You're right on time."

"It's one of my best qualities," he said as he stepped inside, leaned close and kissed her cheek.

Dana had been hoping for a more *vigorous* greeting. In fact, if he'd taken her in his arms and really kissed her, she'd been willing to start the date with dessert. Not that she would ever have admitted that to him or any other living soul.

"You look pretty," he said.

As he'd requested, she'd dressed casually in tailored cotton pants and peach T-shirt. "Thanks. How was your day?"

"Not bad. I had to check on a couple of patients at the hospital. Otherwise, it was quiet."

She'd figured as much. She'd spent her Saturday getting caught up around the house. While she hadn't actually been listening for sounds from his place, she'd heard enough to tell her that he had indeed stayed in for much of the day. Alone.

"Good."

He smiled. "Are you ready?"

"Sure. Let me grab my purse."

She locked the door behind them and told herself the tightening sensation in her stomach did *not* come from nerves, even though she knew it did. One would assume that after spending the night with him, a mere date would be simple. But she found herself trying to think of something clever to say so that he would like her.

"Where are we going?" she asked.

"Not far." He led the way back to his town house.

Dana followed uncertainly. "Did you forget something?"

"No." He ushered her inside. "I know you have this strange idea that I'm out at a different party every night, but that's not true. I thought it would be easier to convince you of the fact if we went on what I consider a very nice, very typical date."

As she stood in the center of his living room, she wasn't sure what to think. The dining-room table had been set for two. There were even fresh flowers for a centerpiece.

"I'm cooking," he said. "Nothing fancy. Steaks, a salad and baked potatoes."

"Sounds delicious."

"Wait until you see what we're having for dessert."

Her thighs trembled. She didn't want to wait.

"I have a couple of videos for you to choose from." He pointed at two small plastic cases resting on the kitchen counter. "I hope at least one of them will appeal to you. But before dinner and our movie, I'd like you to look over my house plans with me. Some of the rooms aren't exactly what I want, but I can't figure out what's not working. I thought you might be able to help me.''

It was not the date she'd imagined, but as he described the evening, she couldn't think of anything she would rather do more. Far better to be here with Trevor where they could enjoy each other's company, than to spend the night in a loud restaurant or club, where they couldn't really talk.

''Sounds like fun,'' she told him.

''Are you sure? We can go out if you'd prefer.''

His hazel green eyes darkened slightly, as if he weren't completely sure of her reply. She knew he would do whatever she requested. There was something charming about his uncertainty. Trevor might be a skilled surgeon who radiated confidence the way the sun radiated light, but sometimes, with her, he was just a guy trying to do the right thing. The flashes of vulnerability left her weak with wanting. How was she supposed to resist him?

''I love what you've planned for the evening and I can't wait to have you cook for me.''

''You're going to love it,'' he promised.

And she knew that he was right.

He pushed the video into the VCR and returned to the sofa. Dana had discarded her shoes earlier and sat on the couch with her feet curled under her. They each had a glass of red wine, the last from the bottle they'd shared at dinner.

Trevor took his time about setting the controls because he wasn't all that anxious to return to her side. Not that he wasn't having a good time; he was. But Dana was making it damn hard to stick to his promise that nothing would happen between them tonight. He was determined to make her want him, but more than that, he wanted her to realize who he was. She had to get past the facade and the rumors. Making love would only complicate the situation.

Still, it was one thing to think rationally while alone and quite another to act that way when faced with a beautiful woman who was obviously expecting more.

Dana hadn't said anything, but he'd read her body language. She'd stood close while he was cooking the steaks, had touched him when they'd looked over the plans for the house. Even now, she sat in the center of the sofa, giving him nowhere to escape when he sat down. She was going to be right there, all soft and sweet smelling, tempting him to the point where he didn't know how he was supposed to resist her.

He sat next to her, and decided that not being intimate didn't mean they had to act like strangers. He put his arm around her and she snuggled up.

"This is nice," she told him.

"I agree." He pushed the Play button on the VCR and the tape started. "I'm glad you picked this movie. I saw it when it was first in the theaters, but I haven't had a chance to rent it since."

Dana glanced at him. He felt her sharp gaze, but didn't dare return it. He wasn't sure what she would read in his face. Her remark about things being nice hadn't been about the movie at all, but it was safer to comment on that than to agree she felt entirely right in his arms.

Her head rested on his shoulder; her right breast nestled against his chest. Their thighs brushed and he knew it wouldn't take much to convince her to let him make love to her right there on the couch.

"I wouldn't have minded the other movie," he said as several previews played. He'd chosen a recently released romantic comedy along with a film about the ill-fated Apollo mission to the moon. She'd picked out the latter.

"I like this one. I saw it in the theater, too, so it's been a while for me."

The movie began and Dana relaxed against him. He felt her breath against his neck and the warmth of her body. He'd been aroused for hours and he had to shift somewhat to ease some of the pressure. Yeah, not making love with her had been a great theory, but in reality it was frustrating as hell.

He told himself it was for a good cause, that they would both be better off in the long run. After all, he wanted more from Dana than just a few weeks of play. Sound advice that made him groan silently every time she snuggled closer.

Despite the distraction, he managed to get through the movie, even losing himself in the story a few times. They fit well together, he thought. His wanting had subsided to a manageable ache. Still, when the credits started and Dana turned to him, her eyes wide with expectation, he wasn't sure he would have the power to resist.

"That was great," he said, freeing his arm and getting to his feet. "Did you like it as much the second time?"

"Yes." She rose quickly.

He stretched. "It's been a long week. All those surgeries. You must have been playing catch-up, too."

"I was, but I'm not that tired."

The overhead light illuminated her short blond hair. He found himself wanting to bury his hands in the silky strands as he pulled her close for his kiss. He wanted her; he needed her. And he would do the right thing and let her go…at least for tonight.

He glanced at his watch. It was just after midnight. "I don't want to tire you out on our first date. If I do, you won't want to see me again."

"I'm really fine," she said, sounding confused, but collecting her shoes and slipping them on.

He ushered her out of his place and walked her back to her town house. They stood in front of the door. He could see the questions in Dana's eyes. In a way, he understood. She didn't know what was going on, and if he explained it, he would lose his advantage.

How could he tell her that she mattered to him and therefore he wanted to go slowly? That this wasn't just about sex, at least it wasn't for him. He wanted a chance to make her care about him. He was willing to put off pleasure in the hope of getting a more long-term gain.

Still, when she looked up at him, he couldn't resist taking her in his arms. He held her gently, enjoying the feel of her pressed against him. He tried to keep her from pressing too close so she wouldn't be able to tell he was aroused, but it was no use. Dana wrapped her arms around his back and leaned in so they touched from shoulders to thighs. No way could she miss his excitement.

"I had a great time," he murmured into her ear, then touched his lips to the tempting spot just below her lobe.

"Me, too." Her voice caught. "Dinner was terrific."

"I've been on my own long enough that I've learned how to be domestic." He smoothed her hair off her face and brushed her lips with his. "Thanks for going over the house plans with me. You made some great suggestions."

"My pleasure. The place will be beautiful."

Her mouth parted. It was an invitation...one he didn't dare accept. He kissed her cheek, stepped back and said, "Good night, Dana. I'll call you tomorrow."

He started down the narrow path that would lead him to his place. When he reached the turn, he couldn't help looking back. Dana stared after him, her fingers resting against her mouth, her eyes wide with confusion. Apparently she'd been expecting a lot more and was stunned he hadn't delivered. Good, he thought with satisfaction that wasn't quite enough to distract him from his own aching desire. Now she would have something to think about.

Chapter Twelve

"You're deep in thought about something. Should I come back later?"

Dana glanced up and saw Katie standing in the doorway to her office. "No, please. I could really use an interruption. What are you doing up here?"

Katie plopped down in the seat in front of Dana's desk and tucked her light-brown hair behind her ears. "I've been playing hooky for a couple of hours. Wedding plans." She smiled sheepishly. "There's a lot more to do than I thought. My mom is helping, but it seems one detail after the other keeps cropping up."

"You don't have to sound apologetic," Dana told her. "I still think it's great."

"Even though Mike's a doctor?"

"Katie, look at yourself. You're so happy you glow. Why would anyone want to discourage you from being with the man who makes you feel that way? You two are perfect together. Quit looking for trouble and enjoy this time.''

"You're right. I guess I'm a little nervous. I mean, getting married is a big step.'' She laughed. "It's not that I'm afraid of spending the rest of my life with Mike. I know we'll be happy. It's really about the wedding. I guess I've been reading too many of those bridal magazines. I'm starting to dream about china patterns.''

"I've seen the one you picked out. It's beautiful.''

"I refuse to talk about place settings, silverware or stemware.'' Katie dismissed the subjects with a wave of her hand. "Okay, so now you know what's bothering me. Tell me what's going on with you? Any more dates?''

"Yeah, Trevor and I have been seeing each other pretty regularly.''

Katie shifted in her seat, as if getting comfortable so she could settle in. "Tell me everything.''

Dana didn't know whether to laugh or scream. "Nothing's changed.''

Katie stared at her blankly. "What do you mean, nothing's changed? It's been three weeks. Last I heard, you were seeing him nearly every night. He cooks. You cook. You go for walks, watch videos, that kind of stuff. You can't mean to tell me you guys haven't...'' Her voice trailed off. "You know.''

"Believe me, I know.'' She heard the edge in her voice and knew it came from frustration. "I'm serious, Katie. The man is driving me crazy. He's sweet, he's attentive, we have a great time together, but—'' She shook her head.

"Nothing?''

"Nada. He gives me these short little kisses good-night.'' She leaned back in her chair and rubbed her temples. "I swear, I could be a nun for all he notices me. Oh, there's plenty of hand-holding and hugs. He's not completely inattentive.''

"I don't think many nuns hold hands," Katie teased.

"Oh, thank you very much. That makes me feel better.''

"Dana, come on. You've got to lighten up. The fact that Trevor is choosing to act like a gentleman is a good thing.''

"How do you figure?''

"It means he cares.''

Dana looked at her. "Oh, really. So men only sleep with women they don't care about?''

"No. I didn't mean it that way. But I was talking about this with Mike.''

Dana groaned. How humiliating. "Tell me you're kidding.''

"I'm not. Anyway, I told him you'd been seeing Trevor for a while now and he, you know, wasn't getting physical.''

Dana's cheeks flamed. She had to swallow before she could speak. "Tell me you didn't really confess all to him.''

"Of course I did. Mike wasn't shocked.''

"Maybe not, but I am.'' She knew her friend was only trying to help, but still, this was going too far.

"Do you want to hear what he had to say or not? I thought it was very interesting.''

Dana consoled herself with the thought that it couldn't get worse. "Go ahead. Enlighten me.''

"You're not taking this seriously, but you're my friend and I care about you, so I'm going to tell you anyway.'' She glanced at the door as if to make sure they were alone. "Mike said that guys act differently when they really care about a woman. They don't want to mess things up, so they'll take it more slowly. You know, act like a gentleman, make her feel special, that sort of thing.''

"Uh-huh. So far you're not making me feel a whole lot better. After all, Trevor and I already did the wild thing."

Katie raised her eyebrows. "The wild thing? I'll have to remember to use that on Mike tonight. Anyway, he thinks that's what's going on with Trevor. That he really cares about you, so he's giving the relationship time to develop."

"That or he just doesn't want me."

"Oh, please. If he didn't want you, he wouldn't have made love with you."

"Maybe he decided he didn't want me after we'd done it and he knew what he was getting."

Katie glared at her. "I should slap you. Dana, you're a wonderful woman. Of course he wants you. If he didn't, why would he bother dating you?" She raised her hand. "Don't even consider answering that one. You know I'm right."

Dana mulled over how she'd begun to doubt herself. She and Trevor had been seeing each other regularly and he hadn't tried anything. At first it hadn't been a problem for her, but now she was starting to wonder. Was something wrong with her? With the relationship? Had she offended him by insisting on exclusivity and he was punishing her?

She dismissed the last thought. Trevor had his flaws, but he was a decent guy and she admired him. No way would he play that kind of game.

"I'd like to think you're right," she said. "I guess I do feel he likes me or he wouldn't spend so much time with me. I am, to quote Lee, just wallowing in my sock drawer of self-doubt."

"Better than hanging out in the trash can of regret."

"Huh?"

Katie giggled. "Never mind. The point is, you should be happy that he's going to all this trouble."

"What I should be and what I am are two different

things.'' She sighed. ''I appreciate your advice and Mike's. It's just hard. And confusing. Sometimes I feel...'' She wasn't sure what she felt.

''Oh, I've been doing what you suggested,'' Katie said. ''I've been asking about Trevor and so far no one has said a word about the two of you dating.''

''Thanks. I figured no one knew because my staff hasn't even hinted that they were aware and they're not people who keep things to themselves.'' Ironically, while she appreciated Trevor's respecting her wishes that they keep their personal lives private, a part of her wanted everyone to know they were going out. Mostly because she was tired of avoiding Angie and Sally. It's not that she thought Trevor was still seeing them, but she didn't want to listen to them go on about him. Their speculations made her uncomfortable.

Katie rested her chin on her hand. ''I'm beginning to think there's a lot less to Trevor's reputation than we realized.''

''What do you mean?''

''While I was asking around about him, one of your nurses 'confessed' to a hot date with him. But it was the same night you two had been out. I wonder if the talk is more wishful thinking than reality.''

Dana nodded slowly. ''I've thought the same thing myself. Short of confronting Angie and Sally, there's no way to be sure. So for the moment, I'm avoiding them.''

Katie's mouth twisted with concern. ''Are you happy, Dana? Is he good to you?''

At last an easy question. ''He's wonderful,'' she said simply. ''Dating him makes me feel good. We don't go out a lot, but I enjoy spending the time at home. When he's had a long day of surgery and I've been caught up in my work, it's nice to unwind together. But it's more than that.

When we talk about work, he really listens to my day and respects my opinion. Later, if something comes up I can tell by what he says that he was actually paying attention. We laugh at the same jokes. He always helps with the cooking and the cleanup afterward. He even lets me drive his car.''

"That is serious.'' Katie smiled. "So the only area that isn't working is sex.''

"I'm sure it would work fine if we'd just do it.''

"Maybe it's not a bad idea that you don't.''

"Why?''

Katie stared at her. "Promise you won't get mad.''

"So I'm not going to like this, right?'' Dana took a deep breath and made an x over her heart. "I promise.''

"Sounds to me like you're falling for him.''

Dana shook her head. "No, I'm not. I refuse to. Trevor is a fun playmate, but he's not the kind of man I'd get serious about. Really. There isn't a problem. I consider this practice, nothing more. He's helping me get back into the whole dating process, and when this is over I'll be ready to get serious about someone suitable.''

"Who are you trying to convince?'' Katie asked softly. "Sounds to me the person you're selling this to is yourself.''

Dana pressed her lips together. Katie was a good friend and simply calling things as she saw them. However, that didn't necessarily make her right. "I know you're trying to help.''

"Oh, a polite way of telling me you think I'm wrong. That's fine. When you figure out the truth, I'll get to say 'I told you so.'''

"If you're right about this, I promise you can say it as many times as you would like.''

"Good. I can't wait." Katie chuckled. "So what's the plan for tonight?"

"Dinner with his folks."

"Oh, really?"

"Don't say it like that," Dana told her. "It's not what you think. He's hardly taking me over to meet Mom and Dad. It's just one of those dinner parties Walter and Maggie are always having."

"Sure."

"What else would it be?" Dana asked.

"Something more personal. A chance for the family to spend some quality time with Trevor's new girlfriend."

"I'm not Trevor's girlfriend."

Katie grinned. "If you say so."

"I'll have to call my insurance agent and add you as a driver," Trevor teased. "You drive my car as much as I do."

Dana downshifted as she approached the stop sign. Once she'd halted, she looked at him. "I can't help that I adore driving your car." She squeezed the leather-wrapped steering wheel. "Mine is a mode of transportation. Yours is a carnival ride."

With that, she shifted into first, pressed on the gas, released the clutch and took off. By the end of the block, she was already cruising at five miles above the speed limit. She glanced at the speedometer and sighed. "This car is a problem for me. It's too easy to go fast. So I guess I'm going to have to be careful if I don't want to get a ticket."

He touched her cheek. "If it makes you happy, I don't mind if you drive my car all the time."

"Really? Great. I'll start planning a cross-country trip."

As she smiled at him, Dana felt something strange in the pit of her stomach. It wasn't just desire, although she was wrestling with plenty of that. It was something else…a warm glow that had nothing to do with wanting Trevor in her bed. She liked how he joked with her and teased her. They laughed a lot together, and she'd forgotten how fun that could be. She liked that he didn't mind cooking dinner, that he really seemed to care about how her day went and rarely got angry about anything. She enjoyed his conversation, his intelligence.

Not that she was falling for him, she reminded herself. That would be foolish. Trevor wasn't the kind of man it was safe to care about. Fortunately for her, she had her emotions firmly under control.

She made a right turn, then eased into his parents' driveway. As she slowed the car, she noticed there weren't any unfamiliar vehicles parked nearby.

"Are we early?" she asked, then glanced at the clock on the dashboard. Trevor had said they were to arrive at seven and it was just a couple of minutes to the hour.

"No. Why?"

"I don't see anyone else here yet."

"Who were you expecting?"

She raised the hand brake and gave him the keys. "Walter and Maggie usually invite a couple of dozen people to their parties."

"This isn't a party. We're having dinner with my folks. Just the four of us. I thought I'd mentioned that."

She thought about what he'd said to her. Would she like to go to his parents' house for dinner? At the time she'd just assumed it was another party. She hadn't realized it was going to be this intimate.

Thinking of Katie's teasing about Trevor taking her to meet Mom and Dad, Dana grimaced. It served her right for assuming.

"Is this a problem?" Trevor asked. "We can cancel."

"No. Of course not. I really like your parents." It was enough of the truth that Trevor climbed out of the car and escorted her to the front door without asking more questions. She really *did* like Walter and Maggie. It's just that she wasn't expecting to have to make conversation with them for the entire night. Plus, what would they think about Trevor's bringing her home like this?

"What did you tell them about us?" she asked.

He knocked on the door. "That we were dating. I figured my promise not to mention anything to people at the hospital didn't extend to my immediate family."

"Of course not," she murmured, wishing he had kept their private life to himself. What would Walter think about her dating his son? Would they resent her? Would they assume there was more of a relationship than there was?

Maggie flung open the door. "I knew it was you, Trevor. Why on earth are you knocking? This is your home."

"I know, Mom, but I was trying to be polite. You know, show off for my girlfriend."

Maggie laughed and pulled Trevor close for a hug. He kissed her cheek. Then the older woman squeezed Dana's arm and invited them both in.

Dana could barely acknowledge the greeting. Her brain focused on one word. *Girlfriend.* Had Trevor really said that? Did he really think that about her? She knew they were dating, but that implied a certain… She sucked in a breath. Okay, she wasn't sure what it implied, but it was way more than she was ready to admit to.

They moved into the study, where Walter greeted them. Drinks were poured and they settled down on the old comfy leather sofas.

Dana had always liked this room, with its oversized fireplace and bookcase-lined walls. She enjoyed the fact that the latest mysteries and romances shared shelf space with medical journals and books. The furniture wasn't new, but it was comfortable and well used. A lot of happiness lived in this room.

"Your father tells me you've been working hard this week," Maggie said. She sat close to her husband, her body angled toward him, her free hand resting on his leg.

"No more than usual."

"You took an emergency case Tuesday and again yesterday," Walter said.

Trevor shifted. "They weren't that big a deal."

"Sure they were," Dana said. "You already had a full schedule and—" She stopped and looked at him. "Why are you smiling at me like that?"

"Be careful, Dana. People might start to think you like me."

She knew he was teasing, but she couldn't help the flush that heated her cheeks. "Trevor!"

He hugged her close. "Don't worry. Your secret is safe with me."

She glanced at his parents and saw they were smiling indulgently at them. Dana wasn't sure if she should pull away from Trevor or just endure the embrace. Only it wasn't tough to be in his arms. Given the choice, she would like him to touch her more.

Conversation turned from the hospital to what was going on with one of Maggie's charities. She did a lot of fundraising for different local organizations. As she talked, Dana watched her, noticing her quick smile and the way she punctuated her comments with hand movements. Walter and Trevor both paid close attention to her conversation and Dana could see the affection radiating from them.

Maggie MacAllister couldn't have been more different from Dana's mother. For one thing, Maggie had started her own business before she met and married Walter, and in a time when women generally chose more traditional roles. She hadn't bothered waiting for someone to come rescue her; she'd made her own way. Dana admired her and wanted to be like her. However, when Walter had proposed, Maggie had made the decision to give all her time to her family.

Dana reminded herself that thirty-plus years ago, women hadn't had as many options. Still, she suspected Maggie would make the same decision today, while she, Dana, would want to find a way to combine family and work. Her career was too important to her to give it up.

Like Maggie she didn't need rescuing, but she did want something in her life. Something more than she had now. As she studied the older couple sitting across from her, she realized what she wanted was a love strong enough to last for years. Walter and Maggie had to have been through some tough times. Every marriage required a fair degree of work and had ups and downs. Still, despite everything, their love was a powerful force.

She felt an odd restlessness building inside her. She tried to tell herself it was because Trevor hadn't made love with her and she wanted him to. But she suspected it was more than just that. She needed...what? A relationship? A commitment? Maybe just someone she could love and trust who would love and trust back.

Was she making a mistake, wasting her time with Trevor? He wasn't the one for her—he couldn't be. His lifestyle was so different from hers.

Dana looked at Trevor's parents. They were good people with strong values. They had raised their son to respect those values. Was she selling him short by assuming he didn't believe in the same things? What about all he'd told her about his ex-wife. She was the one who'd been unfaithful, not he. Walter wasn't a bad man and he wouldn't let his son be one, either. Maybe she'd been wrong about Trevor from the beginning. After all, she now believed that he hadn't spread the story about her in high school. Maybe the rumors at the hospital were just that…rumors. But how could she be sure?

After dinner Dana helped Maggie clean up. "I do this just often enough to keep Walter guessing," the older woman said as she loaded the dishwasher. "Sometimes I even do laundry."

"Whatever does he think?"

Maggie laughed. "He thinks I'm amazing. And after thirty-five years I like knowing that."

Thirty-five years. Dana wondered what it would be like to be with someone that long. "You obviously love each other very much."

"We do, but don't think it's been easy. We've worked at this marriage." She brushed her dark hair off her face. "There were times when I thought about leaving him—or killing him." She smiled. "I'm sure he thought about strangling me in my sleep, too. But we got through it. Mostly, I think, because we were committed to each other. He makes me happy. Unfortunately, not enough of my married friends can say that about their spouses. But Walter is absolutely the one person I want to spend my days with. I think about him and I still smile. It's lovely."

"I envy you that."

Maggie winked. "I suspect you have a little happiness of your own to be pleased about. I've seen the way you look at Trevor."

Dana didn't know what to say. She wasn't sure how she was looking at Trevor, but she knew she didn't love him, nor was she planning to.

"He's a lot of fun," she agreed, wondering how she was going to get out of the situation. She didn't want to have to say anything that wasn't true, but she didn't want to hurt the older woman's feelings, either.

Maggie leaned against the counter. "Yes, he is. But don't let that charming exterior fool you. He's been hurt in the past."

"Trevor told me about his ex-wife."

Maggie's expression hardened. "That one. It was so awful. Walter and I disliked her from the start. But what were we supposed to do? We didn't want to say anything—after all, the worst thing would have been to force him to choose. Of course, being young and thinking he was in love, he would have sided with her. Then we could have lost him forever, or at least seriously damaged the relationship." She sighed. "Children are a great joy, but they're also a challenge. That was one of our challenging moments."

Dana told herself it was none of her business, but she couldn't help being curious. "Why didn't you like her?"

"We were sure that Vanessa didn't really love Trevor. She seemed much more interested in marrying someone attractive. A good catch. She wanted to be part of a 'beautiful couple,' but she wasn't interested in commitment. She was horrified when she found out Trevor was actually interested in his work, and that he didn't want to play all the time."

"It must have been hard for you to watch him involved with someone who didn't really care about him."

Maggie nodded. "I can't remember anything more difficult. The worst part was, we were right. Walter and I so wanted to be wrong about her. But that's behind him." She smiled. "We're very happy that you and Trevor are going out."

Dana swallowed. "Uh—"

Maggie held up a hand to stop her. "Don't worry. I swear I won't be an interfering mother. You don't have to worry about that. I just wanted you to know that Walter thinks the world of you, as do I. We're both so thrilled that Trevor has found someone who believes in him.'' She paused expectantly.

"He's very sweet," Dana managed, not sure what else the other woman wanted. "He even lets me drive his car."

"Oh, really? That's impressive." Maggie laughed. "That boy and his car. I guess they don't outgrow the need for toys, do they?" She folded her arms over her chest. "I probably shouldn't tell you this, but Trevor hasn't seen anyone since he and Vanessa divorced. For a while he was so hurt he could barely work. I don't think it was that his heart was broken as much as he felt betrayed. He'd really believed in her and trusted her, and she let him down."

Dana was uncomfortable with the conversation, but she didn't know how to stop it. Worse, she was starting to feel sympathetic toward Trevor. "I know that was really hard for him."

Maggie nodded. "It's so strange how women always assume the worst about him. I don't know why that is. We're just so pleased that you've taken the time to see the man inside. I promise you, he's worth loving, Dana. I know I sound like a proud mother, but I'm telling you the truth, woman to woman. You can't do better than Trevor."

Dana was still thinking about her words when they pulled up in front of her town house. If Maggie was trying to do a sales job, she'd gotten the customer very interested.

Trevor left the motor running as he came around and opened her door. "I had a great time tonight."

"Me, too." Dana glanced back at the car and figured that, once again, he was not coming inside. What was going on? Why didn't he want to make love with her? She bit back a groan of frustration. Damn the man anyway.

He stopped in front of her door, gave her the smile that

always left her weak in the knees, then kissed her cheek. She was still fuming when he disappeared into his garage. A thousand thoughts circled in her head. She was confused about her feelings for Trevor, she felt as if she'd just lied to his mother and, worst of all, her entire body was on fire and no one was around to put out the flames.

Chapter Thirteen

Trevor stepped out of the shower and stared at himself in the mirror. He needed a shave and there were dark circles under his eyes, the result of too many restless nights. Nights he'd spent lying awake, wishing he were with Dana instead of in his bed alone.

After wrapping the towel around his waist, he reached for his electric razor, then stopped. He couldn't keep doing this, he thought. Night after night of seeing Dana, playing the gentleman suitor, spending time with her, being close but not touching her. He was tired of waiting for her to come around, of waiting for her to want *him*. They were either in a relationship or they weren't, and he knew the answer to that question. He might not like it, but he couldn't avoid the truth forever. There was no point. Just as there was no point in them dating.

He put the shaver down, then walked into his bedroom and dressed quickly. He didn't bother with shoes and barely ran a comb through his wet hair. On his way out the door, he stopped long enough to pick up his keys, then went across the walkway to her front door and pounded.

He'd heard Dana pull up just as he'd stepped into the shower, so she hadn't been home long enough to change. She'd stepped out of her shoes and now stood in her foyer in her stocking feet.

"Trevor?" She glanced at her watch. "I wasn't expecting you for another hour. Is there a problem?"

She was so damned beautiful, he thought grimly as he walked into her town house and stalked into the living room. How was he supposed to say goodbye? What choice did he have? They couldn't keep on this way forever. It would kill him.

He turned to glare at her. "I can't do this."

"Go out tonight?" Her expression softened. "I know you had a grueling day today. We can stay in or just reschedule. Either is fine with me."

She looked so damned earnest, he thought. Staring at him as if his every word mattered. This would have been a whole lot easier if she'd been surly or at least mildly unattractive. But no, she had to go and be all sweet and understanding. Worse, despite the fact that she'd had a long day, too, she looked adorable, with her hair mussed and most of the makeup long since faded from her face.

She moved toward him and placed her hand on his upper arm. "You don't have to be entertaining all the time," she told him. "I like the evenings when we stay in and relax. You're very easy to just spend time with. Does that sound like fun, or would you rather be alone?"

He felt himself weakening because he liked what she said. She made him want to believe that she cared about him...the man he was, not the reputation. But he couldn't change his mind. Too much was on the line. Besides, it was impossible. He couldn't stand being this close to her, smelling the scent of her, wanting her. The situation was driving him crazy.

"I can't," he said forcefully as he took a step away from her. "This isn't going to work."

"What isn't? Trevor, what's happened? I can tell something is wrong. This isn't about work or being tired, is it?"

He looked at her. Lord help him, why did he have to fall for her? Life could have been a whole lot easier if he'd just been able to forget all about her.

He took a step toward her and grabbed her upper arms. "It's been over a month," he said. "We've seen each other more nights than not and we've reached the limit of my ability to act like a gentleman."

Her mouth parted in surprise and it was all he could do not to kiss her right then. Not the casual kisses he'd played with in the past few weeks, but a real kiss, the kind that engaged the heart as well as the body.

"I thought I could make you..." He released her and turned away. What was the point. "I have to go," he said, and started for the door.

A hand on his back stopped him. "You thought you could make me want you?" she asked.

While he hadn't been responsible for what had happened in high school, perhaps she thought he deserved punishment and this was her revenge. Fine. Let her have it. "Yes. That's what I thought."

"Oh, Trevor. I have a bad feeling we've been working at cross-purposes here."

She moved in front of him. The expression on her face wasn't triumph or even pleasure at his discomfort. Instead, she gazed at him, as if making sure what he said was true. Whatever she saw when she looked at him must have confirmed her suspicions, because she nodded, then raised up on tiptoe.

"I've always thought the whole idea of a man acting like a gentleman in matters such as these was highly over-rated," she said, then pressed her mouth to his.

At first he was too stunned to react. Her lips moved against his, touching, discovering. Her hands clutched at his shoulders, pulling him closer.

"This would be so much better if you would cooperate," she murmured.

Then he got it. The message that she wanted him—wanted him with the same fire and intensity that he wanted her—came through. Desire and need, ignored and sup-pressed for weeks, flared to life. He wrapped his arms around her and hauled her hard against him. He angled his head, opened his mouth and invaded her.

She met him, welcomed him, circled around him, stroked him, explored him. Her fingers cupped the back of his neck, as if she were concerned about keeping him in place. Had he been able to talk, he would have reassured her that he wasn't going anywhere. At least not without her. The only place he wanted to be was in her arms.

He pulled back enough to trail kisses along her jaw and down her throat. Her head rolled back and she groaned her pleasure.

"Yes, Trevor," she whispered. "I want you, too. If you only knew how much."

The words eased the pain inside. He hadn't been wrong to trust her. Perhaps she didn't care as much as he did, but she was interested in a relationship, interested in him. That was enough...for now.

He returned to her mouth and devoured her. Moving his hands up and down her spine, he rediscovered shapes and heat and curves. When she tugged on the front of his

T-shirt, he went with her, allowing her to lead them to her bedroom.

They tried not to break the kiss, which meant they stumbled slightly on the half flight of stairs leading to the second level. Her bedroom, like his, was in the back of the town house. He had a brief impression of a floral print comforter covering a queen-sized bed, light wood furniture and open drapes. She cupped his face.

"Don't move," she told him, then stepped to the window and pulled the cord, drawing the thick fabric shut.

The room darkened like twilight falling. He could still see her, but not as distinctly. She crossed to the bed and pulled back the covers, then returned to his side. But instead of stepping into his embrace, she twisted her hands together in front of her and wouldn't meet his gaze.

"This is a silly thing to mention," she said. "But I am a nurse and it's really important. However, I don't want you to get the wrong idea about me. It's been a long time since I, well..." She shrugged. "You know."

He didn't know. If they weren't standing in her bedroom and her breathing wasn't still unsteady, he might be concerned. As it was, he cupped her cheek. "What are you talking about?"

"Protection." She said the word, then sort of hunched forward as if expecting an attack.

Protection? He swore silently. "I didn't bring any." Going to his place to get his recently purchased condoms might break the mood, but he cared about Dana too much not to respect her body that way.

"I figured as much, what with you wanting to end it and all."

He swept his thumb across her lower lip. "I was a little premature with that idea."

"I'm glad you think so." She smiled, but still couldn't

meet his gaze. "Um, the point is, I have some." She pointed at the nightstand. "It's a new box," she continued in a rush. "I was sort of hoping we would do this and I didn't want to get caught without them, but I don't want you thinking that I—"

He swooped down and covered her mouth with his, cutting off the rest of what she had to say. He'd gotten the point and the details didn't matter. It was enough that she'd wanted him and had planned for them to be lovers. Contentment filled him. Contentment and desire.

As she kissed him back, she tugged on the hem of his T-shirt, pulling it up, then running her fingers from his stomach to his chest. Every muscle rippled, first in anticipation, then in delight. When her fingertips grazed his nipples, he thought he might explode right there. She moved her hands around and repeated the caresses on his back, then slipped lower and cupped his rear. Responding to the silent invitation, he pressed against her, rubbing his hardness against her belly. Her breath caught in her throat and she laughed.

"Do that again," she whispered.

Her words were as exciting as the feel of her body. He repeated the action, rotating his hips, cupping her behind and pulling her up so that he could excite her, as well. Her thighs parted slightly. She brought her hands up to his shoulders and clung to him.

"Trevor."

She said his name as though it were an incantation and he the source of the magic. But this wasn't about him; they created the fire and need together.

"I want you," he told her, then licked her ear.

"Yes. I want you, too." She shuddered. "Trevor, please."

She didn't define her plea, but he knew what she wanted,

because he wanted it, too. That he never stop. That they spend the rest of eternity in each other's arms. That the desire never end.

He reached for the zipper at the back of her dress and pulled it down. She shrugged and the navy fabric pooled at her feet. He quickly tugged off his T-shirt, shoes, socks and sweats while she stepped out of her panty hose. Then he took her hand and led her to the bed.

He touched her face, stroking her cheeks and outlining her mouth with his fingers. Her eyes were huge and dark, the pupils so dilated he could barely see the blue irises. She rubbed her hands against his chest. His hardness tightened with every touch. Pressure built inside, but he was in no hurry. For some reason, he felt as if they had eternity.

He drew her onto the bed and stretched out next to her. This time, when he reached behind her and unfastened her bra, the tiny hooks released easily. He chuckled. "I'm getting better."

"Have you been practicing?"

"Only in my mind."

She sighed. "Good answer."

He drew away the bra and gazed at her breasts. They were perfectly shaped, with peach-colored nipples that puckered into tight buds. He cupped her throat, then drew his hand down the center of her chest. He stopped at her belly.

"Do you remember when we did this all those years ago?" he asked.

She looked at him and smiled. "Of course. I think I remember every detail of that night. You made my first time wonderful."

"Ditto."

She sat up and stared at him. Her breasts bounced with

the action and he had trouble keeping his attention on her face.

"What did you say?" she asked.

"You made my first time pretty wonderful, too."

She shook her head. "Are you telling me you were a virgin that night?"

"Yes. Why is that so hard to believe?"

"I don't know." She braced herself on her arm and angled toward him. "I guess there are a lot of reasons."

He rolled onto his back. "Don't tell me it's because of what everyone said about me. Go ahead and think that if you must, but I don't want to hear about it."

"That's some of it," she admitted. "Trevor, you were the most popular guy in high school. You had a million girlfriends."

"No. I had two. Including you," he added, before she could ask.

"But I thought you were going out all the time."

"You thought wrong."

He said the words lightly, but Dana sensed the truth in what he told her. She was having trouble concentrating on the conversation while trying to remember all that she could about their first time.

"A lot of girls in high school claimed to have slept with you," she reminded him. "I can think of five or six right off."

"Cheap talk. I'll admit to having a lot of female friends, but that's not the same thing. We talked, we hung out, but there wasn't anything physical between us. With my first girlfriend, we did a lot of petting, but never went all the way."

She remembered so much about that night. How she'd been excited and scared at the same time. Things had gone fast between them, but she'd been as responsible, if not more responsible, for that. She'd been so desperate to show him she loved him. As if becoming lovers would somehow prove their feelings. Now, with the hindsight of an adult, she knew that making love with him hadn't proved anything. But that wasn't something she would have understood then.

His hand rested next to her. Close to her thigh, but not touching. Not moving, not doing much of anything but taunting her. Her whole body was one giant flame, waiting for him to send her into oblivion. But first there was one other question.

"This is none of my business," she began.

"But you're going to ask me anyway."

She nodded. "How many, Trevor? How many women have you made love with?"

"Less than fifty," he said, his voice teasing. "Enough conversation, Dana. I want to make love with you."

That phrase distracted her. She sank onto the mattress and opened her arms to him. He gathered her close and kissed her. One of his hands buried itself in her hair; the other found and stroked her breasts. With each touch, the tension increased until she felt as if she would simply be reduced to ashes from the heat.

She was liquid desire. There was nothing she would have refused him. When he tugged at her panties, she helped him pull them off. When he knelt between her legs, she opened to accommodate him. When he gently parted the folds of her feminine place so he could give her the most intimate kiss of all, she yielded to the madness and allowed him to pleasure her.

She drew her knees back and tried not to moan too loudly. But it was difficult. He licked all of her, then found the tiny point of pleasure and loved it until she was shaking. He circled her, surrounded her, brushed against her; then, when she was so close to her release that it wasn't even necessary to breathe, he gently inserted a finger inside her.

The combination of sensations flung her into a release so incredibly complete she had no control at all. She was vaguely aware of crying out something, perhaps his name, perhaps just a few unintelligible sounds. She raised her hips and begged him to never stop. He stayed with her, touching her lighter and lighter, drawing every last ounce of pleasure from her.

When breath returned to her body, she found herself in his embrace. Perspiration coated her body and shudders continued to ripple through her muscles. She was both incredibly content and embarrassed.

"It's never been like that for me," she said by way of an explanation, and turned her face into his chest.

"I'm glad. I want this to be as incredible for you as it is for me. I enjoy making love with you. I want to bring you indescribable pleasure."

She giggled softly. "I've long suspected you're an overachiever, but in this case, I'm not going to complain."

She raised her head and looked at him. He was so stunningly handsome, yet at that moment, she didn't care about his looks. He was special to her. It wasn't love and never would be. They were in a relationship destined for failure. But right now she wasn't going to think about that. She was simply going to enjoy the man and how he made her feel.

He brushed the hair off her face and smiled. As he shifted, something grazed against her thigh. His arousal. She touched him there, feeling the length of him beneath his briefs. A shudder rippled through him as he surged toward her. She pressed her mouth to his chest and tasted him. The crinkly hair tickled her nose.

"I want you inside me," she murmured against his skin.

"Yes," he growled.

While he peeled off his briefs, she opened the nightstand drawer and removed the unopened box of condoms. She felt herself flushing. "I didn't know what kind to buy."

He glanced at the box. "Right now I don't care, as long as they work."

When he was naked, she helped him put on the protection, then settled onto her back. He entered her slowly, reverently, as if this time were precious to him. She was glad this mattered to both of them.

He moved in and out of her. Something quickened inside her and she tensed for the inevitable release. As she drew back her knees, he stared down at her.

"Four," he said.

She didn't understand at first. Then she got it. He was answering her earlier question. How many lovers?

"Four including you," he added.

She was stunned. Questions filled her mind. About the stories she'd heard and what people said. About the fact that she'd been his first and in all the years they'd been apart there had been only three other women. Then he moved faster and nothing mattered but how he made her feel.

She pushed down, driving herself into the tingling he created. She felt her body begin to tense. She hadn't expected to experience a release again, but she couldn't help herself. As he stiffened and called out her name, her body began to convulse around him, pulsing rhythmically as the climax filled her.

She couldn't catch her breath, couldn't do anything but absorb the sensations. Then she glanced at him. Trevor opened his eyes. He was still caught up in the passion, and as their gazes locked she felt a connection she'd never experienced before.

* * *

"You don't have to make breakfast," Trevor insisted.

Dana stood up and crossed to the closet. "You've got to be starving," she told him. "I know I am. We never had dinner last night." She pulled on her robe and smiled at him. "I want to do this, Trevor. Consider it my morning-after thank-you."

"If you insist." He stretched and the sheet slid down his thighs, exposing the most interesting parts of his body.

Dana paused in the doorway and looked at him. Morning light illuminated the room and him. She could see the perfect shape of his chest, the hard muscles of his flat belly and arms. She supposed they should both be exhausted after all the lovemaking the previous night, but she felt revitalized and alive. And it was all because of Trevor. He had been so incredible. Loving and giving, making love with her over and over.

"You can go back to sleep if you'd like," she said.

"No, I'm getting up. Do you mind if I take a shower?"

"Please." She motioned to the bathroom. "There are fresh towels in the cupboard in the hall."

She walked to the kitchen and opened the refrigerator. As she collected eggs, vegetables and cheese for omelettes, she thought about the previous night. Something had her worried. Probably because their evening had been about more than just great sex. The physical she could handle fine. It was the emotional that had her concerned. For reasons she didn't understand, she was feeling close to Trevor. She'd enjoyed being with him, not just touching him, but laughing with him and talking about different things. They'd lain awake for hours discussing their goals for the future. She'd been surprised by how many things they had in common.

She supposed what made her nervous was that she really cared about Trevor. He'd become a good friend and someone she enjoyed having in her life. She was also starting to sense the potential for something more on her part, and that terrified her. She couldn't risk their getting close because she wasn't about to put her heart on the line. Intellectually, she understood that if she really wanted to achieve her goal of a husband and children, she would have to risk trusting a man. But the concept frightened her. She'd watched her mother for too many years to be comfortable with letting someone have that kind of power over her. She didn't want to be dependent. She wanted to make it on her own.

Of course she'd already done that. She'd set career goals and achieved them. She tried telling herself that getting married didn't necessarily mean handing over the power to her life. With the right partner, she could still retain her identity. At least, that was the theory. When she thought about Katie and Mike, she believed it was possible, at least for them. But what about for her?

Maybe...with someone she could trust. Someone not so dynamic. Trevor would be too risky. She was afraid of him because she knew she could love him too much. Far easier to keep things as they were, using him for practice, then finding someone suitable later.

She diced vegetables, then grated cheese. After getting out the omelette pan, she reached for the carton of eggs.

"What are you doing?" Trevor asked, horrified.

She looked up. He stood in the doorway to the kitchen, hair still damp from his shower, a towel wrapped around his waist. Her body responded to his perfection with the same muscle-twitching, bone-melting, everything-quivering dance it always did in his presence.

"Making breakfast," she said. "Omelettes."

He crossed to her side and snatched the carton from her.

"Eggs? You want to cook eggs? What will the children think?"

It took her a second to get the joke. "You can't mean T.J."

"Who else? I'm shocked, Dana. I thought you were more sensitive than this."

She opened her mouth, but didn't know what to say to him.

He set the carton on the counter and wrapped his arms around her. "Bagels," he said. "I'll take you out for bagels or pancakes or waffles. Anything but eggs."

"But I—"

His mouth settled on hers and she decided she didn't want to talk all that much. The heat flared.

"What about breakfast?" she asked when she caught her breath.

"Later," he murmured, leading her back to the bedroom and stretching out beside her. "Much later."

Chapter Fourteen

Dana sipped her morning coffee and didn't care that it had that burned tinge the hospital cafeteria seemed to pride itself on. She didn't care about the rain, the six calls she had to return before noon, the run in her panty hose or the three surgeries that would require rescheduling and completely mess up two days' worth of work.

She felt like Snow White from the Disney movie. Everything was lovely as she went about her days. She would swear that she heard singing and that little forest creatures greeted her at every turn.

Dana laughed. Okay, the little forest creatures were a bit of a stretch, but she was one happy lady. Her weekend had been perfect. Except for going home to get a couple of changes of clothing and some more condoms, Trevor hadn't left her place until Monday, when they'd both had to be at the hospital. They'd made love, laughed, ordered in food, cooked, made love again...and again, talked about their pasts, their futures, their hopes. Oh, and they'd made love some more.

She leaned back in her chair and sighed in contentment. It was Wednesday and she was still glowing. Perhaps it was because they'd spent the past two nights together, too. Monday at his place and Tuesday at hers. It was very convenient for both of them. If either forgot something, it wasn't far to go pick it up.

Dana stared at the paperwork on her desk, but didn't really see it. She couldn't remember being happier with anyone before, ever. It wasn't just the sex, although that was quite amazing. There was more. Something about being with Trevor that made her feel good about herself. It was as if, with him, she felt complete.

"I'm not getting serious, though," she reminded herself aloud. "This is dating fun. A temporary, albeit lovely, situation. Nothing more."

She would be a fool to expect more. After all, she was talking about Trevor MacAllister here, not some regular guy.

Angie strolled into her office and sat in the chair opposite hers. "'Morning, boss. You're looking really happy about something."

Dana smiled. "I'm having a good hair day. What's going on?"

"You'd asked me if I could trade shifts and it's not a problem. I'm happy to do it."

"Thanks." Dana made a note on her schedule. "I know you hate working in the late afternoon, but I need someone with your experience for the OR."

Angie shrugged. "I'll be forced to sleep in, so that works for me. After all, I've been having some very late nights."

A knot formed in Dana's stomach and she would have sworn the temperature in the room dropped about thirty degrees. Did Angie mean what Dana thought she meant? She couldn't be talking about Trevor. Dana knew exactly what he'd been doing every night since Friday. They'd been together...sleeping in the same bed.

She swallowed hard. Except for Monday night, when they'd agreed that they actually had to spend some time sleeping, so she'd gone home about ten-thirty.

"Wild social life?" she asked, working hard to make her voice sound normal. She wasn't completely successful, but she didn't think Angie would notice the difference.

"Hmm, you bet." The pretty young nurse leaned back in her chair and closed her eyes. "I can't believe how wonderful Trevor is. And not just in bed. While he's a real—" She stopped and shrugged. "Sorry. I'm sure you don't want details."

"That statement couldn't be more true."

"But it's not just that," she continued. "He's also funny and sweet and wonderful to be with. The only fly in the ointment is Sally. I hate that he's seeing her, too."

Dana couldn't believe it. No way was Trevor seeing all three of them. He just plain didn't have time. Besides, she knew in her heart he wouldn't do that to her. Would he?

While part of her wanted to believe in him, another part wondered how well she really knew him. Was she expecting too much? Did she have the right to assume their relationship meant as much to him as to her?

There was one way to find out. She sucked in a breath and clenched her hands into fists. "When did you see him?"

"Saturday and last night. He saw Sally on Friday, but I don't think he's seen her since. So that means I'm winning, right?"

If she hadn't been sitting, she would have collapsed with relief. Since Friday, the only night she and Trevor hadn't spent together was Monday, although they'd shared the evening. So he couldn't have seen Angie or Sally.

She opened her mouth to ask the young woman why she was lying, then pressed her lips together. She didn't want to get into this right now. Asking Angie that question was the same as announcing her relationship with Trevor to the entire hospital, and she wasn't ready to do that. She didn't want to deal with the rumors and speculation. To be completely honest with herself, she didn't want everyone to know they were dating because she didn't want any pity when they broke up. Even if she were the one to end the relationship, everyone would assume it was the other way around. She'd already had enough humiliation where he was concerned.

Angie looked at her and raised her eyebrows. "You're not answering. Don't tell me there are things going on with Sally that I don't know about."

"Not that I'm aware of," Dana said. "I can't say if you're winning or not. I suspect you're both in the same boat where Trevor is concerned."

Both lying. But why?

After Angie got her new schedule and left, Dana wrestled with that question. Why would two young attractive women lie about dating someone? Was it the challenge? Did they need people to believe the most eligible doctor in the hospital wanted each of them? If Angie and Sally were both lying, who else had lied? Joel? Girls in high school?

She remembered what Trevor had said about his reputation having little basis in fact. She was starting to believe that was true. He'd claimed to have made love with only four women in his life, including her. She had no reason to doubt that, either. She smiled. Okay, she had a little reason to doubt. He was an extraordinary lover, but some of that was because he took the time to find out what she enjoyed. He was attentive and caring, two qualities tough to resist in bed.

Her phone rang, interrupting her thoughts. She picked it up. "Dana Rowan."

"Nurse? You've gotta help me. I'm running this fever and there are spots all over my body. Is it fatal?"

The voice was familiar, but it took her a couple of seconds to place it. The memories stirred in the back of her mind and then she laughed. "Roger, is that you?"

"Hi, hot stuff. What's going on?"

"I can't believe you called me. It's been forever. What? At least a couple of years."

The man on the phone chuckled. "How many kids did I have the last time we talked?"

Dana thought about the question. Roger was a man she'd dated in college. When the romance hadn't worked out, they'd stayed friends. She'd attended his wedding and had even spent a long weekend with him and his wife a few years back. Their happiness had left her with a combination of pleasure for them and longing for herself. She wanted what they had.

"You had two. Little Emma was about three and R.J. was less than a year."

"Well, Marcie just had another boy and R.J. is nearly two. So it's been way too long. Which is the reason I'm calling. I'm in town on business. I have an unexpected free night tonight and wondered if you'd like to have dinner."

The invitation was tempting. Not only did she always have a good time with Roger, but he was someone she trusted, and a male. Maybe he could give her some advice about Trevor. She could use the opinion of a relatively disinterested third party, not to mention a man's point of view on the situation.

She and Trevor hadn't made any plans for the evening.

She'd assumed they would spend it together, but Trevor would understand.

"I'd love to join you."

"Great. Where?"

She named a local restaurant. "About seven-thirty?"

"Works for me. I'll see you then. Oh, and I can't wait to call Marcie and tell her I'll be seeing a beautiful blonde tonight. Think she'll be jealous?"

Dana laughed. "Not a chance. She knows you adore her so much the rest of the female population barely exists. My bet is she'll tell you to say hi and not give it another moment's thought."

"Yeah, I know." He gave an exaggerated sigh. "I've tried explaining that the male ego likes to know that the woman in a guy's life is at least a little worried about keeping him faithful, but not Marcie. She's got me good and hooked. What can I do?"

"Enjoy," Dana said firmly. "After all, the alternative is to do without her."

"Never. She's my whole life. But we're not going to spend tonight talking about me. Happiness is a thrill for those living it, but it makes boring dinner conversation. Plan to be the entertainment, kid. See you at seven-thirty."

"Bye."

Dana hung up. This was exactly what she needed. A distraction from Trevor and the chance to get some good advice. She glanced at the clock and figured she could still catch him at his office.

After dialing the number, she waited for the receptionist to answer. She gave her name, then prepared herself to explain that this was a personal call. Sometimes getting through to doctors was not simple. But to her surprise, the receptionist immediately asked her to hold on. Less than a minute later, Trevor was on the phone.

"You read my mind," he said. "I was just thinking about you."

A quiver shot through her stomach. The man sure had a way about him. He could disarm her with a phrase.

"What were you thinking?" she asked, her voice low and sultry. "About what we were doing last night?"

"Um, that, too. But don't get me started. I still have a couple of patients to see and I don't think they'd appreciate obvious proof that I'd just talked to a very sexy lady."

"It wouldn't look good, would it?"

"You don't think it looks good?" He sounded hurt.

She laughed. "You know that's not what I meant. It's lovely. More than lovely. It's incredible and perfect and I can't wait until the next time I see it. Better?"

"Definitely better."

"Okay. I always have to watch what I say around you."

"I believe in keeping you on your toes. Otherwise, you intelligent types think you can walk all over a guy."

If only that were true, she thought. Unfortunately for her, in this relationship Trevor had all the power. Still, there was something about him. She sighed. "Yeah, yeah. You're so horribly abused," she teased. "How do you stand it?"

"I figure I'm building character. You don't usually call me at the office. What's up?"

"Nothing important. A friend from college is in town for the night. We're going out for dinner." She paused, not sure what else to say. They had been spending the last few nights together, but she didn't know if she was supposed to check in with him about this kind of stuff. "I, um, thought you might want to know." She tensed, wondering if he was going to laugh at her or tell her it didn't matter.

"Oh."

Dana straightened. He sounded disappointed. "Is that okay?"

"Sure. It's just that my dad called. He and my mom invited us to join them for dinner tonight. They're going to their favorite restaurant on the west side and they thought it would be fun for us to tag along. No problem, though. I'll phone them and explain."

"I'm sorry, Trevor. I'd change my dinner, but we only have tonight. You should go with your folks anyway. You'll have fun."

"I will. Otherwise, I'll just stay home waiting for you. Will you be out late?"

"Not at all." When he traveled, Roger always hurried back to his hotel room so he could have a long chat with Marcie.

"Good. Because I'd still like to see you tonight."

She thought about seeing him. Not just the lovemaking, but being with him, talking and laughing. "I'd like that, too."

"So whoever gets home first will put on something sexy and be waiting for the other."

She laughed. "Now I *am* going to try to get home after you. I want to see you in something sexy."

"I might just surprise you."

She thought about Angie and Sally and the fact that he probably hadn't been dating them at all. "You already do," she told him. "In the most pleasant way possible. See you tonight."

"So Emma looked up at me, smiled and said, 'The water's blue now, Daddy. Just like when Momma cleans.'" Roger shook his head. "I kept telling myself the bright-blue poster paint she'd just poured down the toilet was water soluble, but I still checked with a plumber. That little girl is a constant challenge.''

Dana heard the love in his voice and smiled. "You wouldn't have it any other way."

"You're right." Roger finished his beer and set the glass on the table.

They'd been at the restaurant nearly an hour and had yet to order dinner. There was too much to catch up on.

Roger leaned forward and raised his eyebrows. They were auburn, just a few shades darker than his curly red hair. "All right. You've listened to me tell you about the trials and joys of living with three kids under the age of five. I'm sure my tales of diaper rash and blocked toilets will be the subject of your dinner conversation for the next couple of weeks, but it's time to move on. What's new with Dana Rowan?"

"I already told you about my promotion, right?"

"Yes, and congratulations. You're doing very well."

"Thanks."

Work was the easy part. It was her personal life that was giving her trouble.

"Dana, I recognize that look. Something is bothering you. Tell Uncle Roger. You'll feel better, I promise. If nothing else, I can give you a guy's perspective on the situation."

She looked at his kind face. While he had pleasant features, he wasn't even close to Trevor's incredible physical perfection. In some ways, Dana wouldn't mind if Trevor were a little less handsome. At least then she wouldn't feel as if she had to be in competition all the time.

"I'm seeing this guy," she began, not sure what to tell Roger.

"I figured as much. You pretty much have the rest of your life in order. So is he a good guy or a bad guy?"

"Interesting question." She sipped her wine and thought. "He's good, most of the time."

"And when he isn't?"

"No, it's not that. He's…" How did she explain the phenomenon that was Trevor MacAllister? "He's one of those people who always win. He's good-looking, successful, smart, funny."

"Married?"

"Roger!"

Her friend grinned. "Hey, I know he's not perfect. I was just searching for a flaw."

"He has flaws, just not very many. The problem isn't as much him as everyone else, and maybe me."

"You'll have to explain that one to me."

Before she could, the waiter came over to their table. They ordered. When they were alone, Dana continued. "I knew him back when we were in high school. He was the most popular boy and all the girls wanted to go out with him." She recapped her relationship with Trevor, then and now. She explained about the nurses who claimed to be dating him and her recent realization that they were lying about some or maybe all of the time they'd spent with him.

"I just don't understand," she said. "Exaggerating is one thing, but flat-out lying? It doesn't make sense. Why bother? Didn't they know they would get caught?"

"Maybe they have their own reputation to think about," Roger said. He shrugged out of his sport coat and hung it over the back of the chair. "These are young, attractive women. He's a successful, single doctor. I would guess they're interested, not only in him, but also in being perceived as desirable. If the hottest thing to hit town in twenty years is taking them out, or so everyone thinks, then they can ride his coattails. Women are just as concerned about status and perceptions as men."

"Agreed." What he said made sense...sort of. "I'm starting to get the impression this has happened to Trevor all his life. Everywhere he goes people—women, really—assume the worst about him."

"Based on how you described the guy, I should hate him without even meeting him," Roger said. "But if this is the price he pays for being so high up on the food chain, count me out. It's not worth it." He shrugged. "Of course, no one is offering me his position, and no one is going to let him walk away from his."

"You mean he's trapped?"

"Sure." Roger leaned toward her. "Let me fill you in on a little secret about men. There's a lot of talk that guys aren't interested in love and commitment. That we all want to score with a different woman every night. That's just not true. Sure, at times every man looks at an attractive woman and thinks, 'Yeah, I'd like to bag her.' But it's just a passing thought. Cheap talk and wayward hormones. Nothing else. The truth is, we want to be married. We like knowing that someone in the world loves us and cares about us. Someone who will be there when we get home. We like the familiarity, the routine. We really love our wives and our families."

"I know you're like that," she said. "I've seen those qualities in other men, too. But Trevor—"

"Sounds to me like Trevor hasn't had a chance to experience that yet. Has anyone bothered to look past the reputation to the man underneath?"

"He was married before."

"Obviously it didn't work out, and I'm willing to bet he wasn't the reason."

She remembered what Trevor had said about Vanessa's cheating on him. "No, his wife was the problem."

Brown eyes softened with concern. "You're going to

have to think about this, Dana, because the man is important to you. I've known you a long time and I've watched you grow up. You're a wonderful woman and you deserve an equally wonderful man in your life. Trevor sounds decent. You might have to give him a chance.''

''I'm dating him.'' Well, they were doing more than dating, but she wasn't about to discuss that with Roger.

''You're going through the motions, but it seems to me that you're holding something back. Be careful when you do that. If you don't give it all, you'll risk losing him. Don't let it take losing him for you to figure out what you've got.''

The waiter brought their salads. Dana waited until he was gone. ''I'm not sure what I have.''

''Does it matter? You're already in love with him.''

She'd speared a piece of lettuce and was in the process of bringing the fork to her mouth. She froze, then carefully lowered the utensil to the plate. She felt hot and cold at the same time. Love? Never! Their relationship was about having fun and friends having sex. Nothing more.

''I am *not* in love with him.'' The idea was insane. Love Trevor? She'd learned her lesson already. Besides, loving anyone would be too risky. She didn't want to be that vulnerable ever.

''He's a doctor,'' she continued. ''I refuse to be involved with a doctor. I know what that's like. They're never around. They care about everyone but their family. It's insane and impossible.''

Roger chewed, then swallowed. ''Maybe, but it's also too late. Face it, Dana. You're gone on the guy.''

''No, I'm not. He would never be interested in someone like me. Not in the long term.''

''Why?''

"Because..." Her mind went blank. "Well, just because. Besides, I'd be crazy to trust him."

"Seems to me you'd be crazy to let him go."

"Trevor wants someone glamorous."

Roger shook his head. "Trevor wants someone who will love him for himself. Take away the good looks and you'll find a guy just like everyone else on the inside. He wants what we all want. Loving acceptance and a place to feel safe. You can do that, Dana. I suspect you already do. Why won't you admit you're crazy about him?"

Because if he betrays me again, he'll destroy me. But she didn't say that aloud. Roger might guess the truth, but she refused to confirm it by broadcasting all her faults to the world.

"It's not that I don't like him. It's just—"

The hairs on the back of her neck rose. Dana stiffened, then raised her gaze. Their table was in the back of the main dining room. Secluded, but with a clear view of the entrance. Standing by the front door were Maggie, Walter and a very angry Trevor. His gaze locked with hers. His expression was hard, his eyes dark with betrayal. Dana felt the blood drain from her face.

"What's wrong?" Roger asked. "You look as if—" He turned around and saw the trio by the door, then returned his attention to her. "Tell me you told him what you were doing tonight."

"I said I was having dinner with a friend."

He swore. "But you didn't happen to mention that friend was male, right? Don't answer that." He glanced at Trevor again.

As Dana watched, the three of them spoke quietly to the hostess, then left the restaurant. Dana realized she was shaking. She put down her fork and tried to draw in a steadying breath.

"The good news is, the man has it bad for you. The bad news is, he thinks you just cheated on him. That isn't why his first marriage broke up, is it?"

Dana stared at him in horror, then nodded.

"So this is a major button for him."

Her stomach knotted, but for once not from tension. What had she done? "I—I don't know what to do."

Roger stood, walked around the table and pulled her to her feet. "You're going to go to his place and wait for him. When he gets there, you're going to tell him that it's not what he thinks." Roger pressed one of his business cards into her hand. "If he doesn't believe you, he can call me. Hell, he can call my wife. Unlike some people, I was bright enough to tell her who I was having dinner with."

"I didn't keep it a secret on purpose," she protested. "I just didn't think to tell him."

"If you want to keep him, you're going to have to start thinking. Tell him the truth. Tell him that you're scared, but you really care about him and you want another chance. Tell him this matters. He looked hurt, so expect him to lash out. But he obviously cares about you. That will help."

Dana nodded. Her eyes burned and she knew she was close to tears. "I'll try," she said.

She knew Roger only wanted to make her feel better so she attempted a smile. She had a feeling it didn't come out very happy. Her mouth felt numb, as did her body. She couldn't stop shaking. She had the most horrible feeling she'd just destroyed something very wonderful, losing her chance before she'd even been sure she wanted one.

Chapter Fifteen

Trevor sat in his garage for a long time before turning off the convertible's engine and climbing out of the car. Maybe coming home had been a mistake. Maybe he should have gone with his parents to another restaurant. Perhaps company would have distracted him from what he'd seen—Dana having dinner with another man. And not just dinner. He'd noticed her long before she'd glanced up and seen him watching. He'd observed the heads bent close together, the intensity that radiated from both people.

The pain in his gut increased. He tried to erase the image, but it had burned itself into his brain. In some ways it was the horror of the past repeating itself. Once again he'd allowed himself to believe in a woman and she'd betrayed him.

Trevor pulled open the door and stepped into the town house. It wasn't that big a deal, he told himself. He and

Dana weren't married; they were dating. Did he have any right to complain?

"Damn straight," he growled, and made a fist. But before he could pound his hand into the wall, he reminded himself he had two surgeries scheduled for the next day. He couldn't risk injuring himself for the sake of his pride.

Without physical release, the anger and frustration bubbled inside him. He paced the length of the living room, turned and repeated the pattern.

He cared about her. That's what got to him, eating him from the inside out. He'd thought she was different. He'd thought *she* cared. In his heart he'd wanted their relationship to have meaning for her, too. He'd wanted her to see that he was all she needed in a man. He'd wanted...

"All of it," he muttered. "Marriage. Commitment. Family. Forever."

He'd been a fool. Dana was just like the rest of them. He'd made a mistake in thinking he could love her and have that love returned.

He sank onto the sofa and concentrated on ignoring the pain. This wasn't as bad as finding Vanessa, he told himself. After all, she'd been his wife and her betrayal had been more—

More what? Personal? Direct? More meaningful? Did a betrayal have meaning? He shook his head to try to clear it. In the end, it didn't matter a damn. He'd trusted Dana and she'd let him down. End of story.

He rose to his feet. Maybe a drink would help him forget. He wouldn't get drunk—he couldn't work with a hangover, either, but maybe something to take the edge off. He didn't dare go for a drive. Not until he was under control.

He crossed to the wet bar. A soft knock on the door halted him in midstride.

He knew. As surely as he believed the sun would rise in

the morning, he knew who was out there on his porch. He told himself not to bother answering. She had nothing to say that he wanted to hear. Yet even as he repeated the instruction to pretend he wasn't home, he moved toward the door and flung it open.

She stood illuminated by porch light. Her eyes were wide, her face pale. Even her light makeup couldn't hide the ashen undertones of her skin. Her mouth trembled and she twisted her purse strap in her hands.

The obvious signs of nervousness should have made him feel better. But they were too little, too late. He stared at her, not inviting her in, not speaking. Just staring. Wondering what combination of facial features had first drawn him to her. What words had she uttered? How had she smiled to allow him to believe again, to hope that this time there was a chance?

"I can explain," she said, her gaze steady. "It's not what you think."

He stepped back from the door, neither inviting her in nor telling her to leave. She entered on her own, then crossed the foyer and followed him into the living room.

He chose not to sit down. Instead he leaned against the wet bar and glared at her. She continued to look back at him, her chin high as if with pride, but her faint trembling giving away her apprehension.

"I told you I was having dinner with a friend from college," she said. "That's true. Roger and I knew each other back then."

"You conveniently left out the fact that you were having dinner with a man, and an ex-boyfriend." He added the last, firing blindly, wondering if it was true. When she flinched and blushed, he knew it was. The pain in his gut intensified anew.

"Trevor, please. I'll admit I didn't say Roger was a man,

but only because I didn't think of it. He's just a friend. If I was sneaking around, would we have gone somewhere public?''

"Certainly. You didn't expect me to be there." He turned away, not wanting her to read his agony. "Dammit, Dana, I was out with my parents. How do you think this made them feel? What are they supposed to think?" He held up his hand. "Stupid question. I take it back. They're supposed to think the truth. That you don't give a damn about me or what's going on here.''

She sank onto the sofa and bowed her head. "That's not true. I do care. I don't know why I didn't tell you about Roger, but I swear it was just an accident. I'm not interested in him. There's nothing going on. He's happily married to a terrific woman. They've got three kids and are madly in love.'' She opened her purse and pulled out a business card. "He said to call him if you didn't believe me. He'll tell you. You can even call his wife. He doesn't have anything to hide and I haven't done anything wrong. I'll admit to poor judgment, but not to anything premeditated.''

"So if you didn't plan to make a fool of me everything is fine?'' His voice vibrated with fury.

Dana flinched. "Why aren't you listening? Roger is in town on business. He called and asked me to dinner. One of the reasons I went is that he's easy to talk to. I thought he could be a sounding board for me. I happen to have some confusing things going on in my personal life right now. I wanted to get his advice on you, Trevor. You are who we were talking about. I told him how wonderful you are and how I'm not sure..." Her voice trailed off. She sucked in a breath. "How I'm not sure about anything.''

The pain had reached an unbearable pitch. He knew from past experience it would level out there for a few days, then crank down just enough to let him survive. In his head he even knew that in time it would stop hurting altogether. He might never trust again, but the gaping wound would eventually scar over. Yet in his heart he knew he would hurt forever. Because there had been something special about Dana. He'd loved her...he was such a jackass, he probably still did.

She straightened. "Trevor, this is probably not going to make sense to you, but I swear it's the truth. I really like you and I like being with you, but sometimes it's hard for me. You're so successful and so handsome. All these women want you and they say things. I get confused. I thought Roger could help me with that. I wanted to talk about the rumors, about how people made them up. They weren't about you at all."

The click was audible. Trevor wondered why he hadn't heard it before. Everything fell into place. "Exactly," he said.

"What?"

"It wasn't about me. Why didn't I see that before?"

"I—I don't understand."

He folded his arms over his chest. "None of this was ever about me. This so-called relationship was just a reaction to the hype."

"No. That's not what I mean," she told him. "I'm not sure I understand exactly what you're saying, but I think you're telling me I was only interested in what other people thought. That's not completely true. I had trouble because of what the nurses were saying. That they were going out with you and sleeping with you. But I believe you now."

"Gee, thanks. I guess that makes everything better."

His sarcasm made her shudder. "Trevor, don't do this. Don't shut me out."

"What choice do I have? I was taken in by you. I believed you. I believed in us. I thought you wanted what I did. That this mattered.'' He turned toward her. ''I suppose there's a certain justice in all this. I was trying like crazy to prove myself to you, while you were just having fun. You treated me the way you assumed I treated women. For the moment, for the pleasure, with no regard for the future or any feelings on either side. At least there weren't any on your side.''

She sprang to her feet. ''That's not true.''

''Isn't it? Can you look me in the eye and tell me you care?''

She glared at him. ''Yes.''

''How much?''

Her mouth opened, but she didn't speak.

''Love?'' he asked. ''Do you love me? Or is 'like' better? Keeping with words starting with the letter *l* let's just cut to the chase. Lust. That's what this is about. You wanted me in bed—nothing more. Little more. If I'd been the bastard everyone assumes, I would have had this coming. But I'm just a guy, Dana. No better, no worse than anyone else. I didn't deserve this. And you sure as hell didn't deserve me.''

Tears filled her eyes. He braced himself so he wouldn't react. She reached out a hand to him. They were half a room apart, so he didn't have to worry about her actually touching him. He could stay strong as long as she didn't get too close.

''It wasn't ever like that,'' she whispered. ''I do like you.''

''I don't believe you.''

''How can you not? It's true.''

''Gee, Dana, you're telling the truth and someone is doubting your word. Now you know what that feels like. Not much fun, is it?'' He walked to the front door and put his hand on the knob. ''I'll give you that you might have had some feelings for me, but I'm willing to bet you never once thought about letting yourself fall in love with me. If anything, you saw that as something to be avoided.''

Her mouth parted. The guilt made her turn away. Even though he'd known the truth, he was still disappointed to read it on her face. He'd hoped for more.

''I'm sorry,'' she whispered. Tears spilled over her lower lids. ''I'm so sorry.''

''That's not good enough. I'd wanted more than this from you. From both of us. I thought—'' He opened the door. ''I won't bother boring you with what I'd thought.''

''Trevor, please.''

She crossed to him and placed her hand on his arm. The tears continued to fall. She was beautiful. How was he supposed to resist her?

''Forgive me.''

''I can forgive, but I can't trust you. You still don't see me as a person, and until you do, there's just no point.'' He pulled free of her touch. ''The hell of it is I thought you were the one. Like an idiot, I went ahead and fell in love with you. I'd even planned on asking you to marry me. But you've shown me the error of my ways. This wasn't a give-and-take relationship. You weren't interested in anything but using me up and moving on. All this time, I've been in love alone. I guess I should have seen that. Sorry to make this awkward. Don't worry. I won't bother you again.''

Dana stared at him. His features blurred. She knew it was from the tears, but a part of her believed it was because he was already fading from her life. He'd loved her? He'd wanted to marry her? This couldn't be happening. It wasn't possible. She'd lost him and she hadn't even known she'd had him.

She wanted to beg him to reconsider. To give her another

chance. Yet she'd done nothing to deserve him the first time, so how could she expect him to ever trust her again? She was all he'd said she was.

"I didn't mean..."

Her voice trailed off. There was nothing left to say.

She crossed to her town house and let herself inside. Although the sun had long since set, she didn't bother with the lights. Instead, she walked to the common wall at the back of her living room and placed her hand flat against the cool plaster.

"Oh, T-Trevor," she murmured as a sob caught in her throat.

She'd been such an incredible fool. She'd never bothered to look past her stupid misconceptions and her pride. She'd assumed the worst about him and had acted accordingly. Everything Trevor said was true. She was spiteful and shallow, and she *had* treated him with exactly the same disdain she'd assumed he used in his personal life. How many times had she told herself and her friends that this wasn't serious? That she was just practicing for a "real" relationship? How many times had she deliberately held back her feelings so that she wouldn't get too involved?

She'd never once thought about his feelings or what he might want. She'd blindly gone through the motions, taking instead of giving, assuming the worst instead of allowing him a chance, making him live up to her standards without bothering to inquire about his. She'd promised herself she wouldn't fall in love with him because he wasn't worth the risk. But *she* was the unworthy one. She was the flawed character, while he was the prize.

To her, he'd been little more than a caricature, not a flesh-and-blood man who could feel and be hurt. She'd never thought he could love anyone...not even her.

She sank to the carpet and rested her forehead against

her knees. The shame poured over her, accompanied by regret and a sense of loss. To have come so close to everything she'd ever wanted and to have lost it because she was a thoughtless, self-centered idiot. How could she have acted that way? When had she become so incredibly shallow that she thought she had the right to judge others based on her unfounded assumptions?

There were no answers, no comfort of any kind. Perhaps if she had given her all, it would have been easier to accept her defeat, but she'd never bothered to try. She'd simply taken without thought, had blindly ignored the possibilities and the man. She'd betrayed him in the most soul-destroying way possible. Not by having dinner with Roger, but by taking his affection and his body without giving a moment's thought to the man inside.

He'd loved her and she hadn't bothered to notice. She'd been too sure she was right about everything. She'd never even realized she was falling for him, as well. Roger had been right. She did love Trevor. And now he was gone.

Chapter Sixteen

"**Y**ou look terrible," Lee said bluntly.

Dana had done her best to avoid glancing at herself in the mirror that morning, but she'd seen enough to know Lee was actually being kind. She looked a lot worse than terrible; she looked as if she'd been emotionally beaten up, then left for roadkill. If any of that was true, she had only herself to blame.

"I know." Dana shrugged. "I feel worse than I look, which is kind of scary."

Katie moved close to her in the round booth they had in the back of Granetti's and put her arm around her. "Dana, I knew something was wrong from the sound of your voice when you called. You have to tell us what's going on. We're your friends. We love you and we want to help."

"I know." Dana cleared her throat. It wasn't just that she was fighting tears. Everything hurt. Her entire body felt as if it had been flattened by a steamroller. She couldn't eat, hadn't slept in a couple of days. Basically she was a wreck, and the situation didn't show any signs of getting better. "I figure I can hang on for about three more days, then I'll start making mistakes at work. I just wish there were something I could do."

Katie and Lee exchanged confused glances. Lee leaned forward. "While acting mysterious is, I'm sure, entertaining for you, we can't help if we don't know what's going on. Come on, Dana. Spill it."

"There's nothing you guys can do. I made all the mistakes. I suppose that's what's so incredibly disheartening. I can't blame anyone but myself. I was even proud of my actions. I thought I was so smart. I—" She felt the tears start to form. While she was at the hospital, it was relatively easy to maintain control, but here, among friends, she found herself weakening.

"Trevor and I aren't going out anymore," she said, then wiped her face.

"You broke up?" Katie asked.

"Sort of. I thought..." She covered her face with her hands and tried to get control. After taking a couple of deep breaths, she straightened and looked at her friends. "The truth is, I wasn't thinking." She told them what had happened, starting with her desire to make sure she didn't get too emotionally involved, then ending up with the dinner with Roger and the resulting discussion with Trevor.

"'Discussion' isn't the right word," she admitted when she'd finished. "I don't know what else to call it, though. We didn't fight. He told me what he thought of me, and there was nothing I could say to change his mind. I feel like such a fool. How could I have been so blind? Worse, how could I have acted like that? I never thought of myself as cruel and shallow, but with him, I was both those things."

"Is that really what's bothering you?" Lee asked.

"I don't understand."

Katie glanced at Lee and nodded. "What she's asking is, are you the most concerned about finding out you have some negative qualities? Is that the most upsetting part of this situation?"

Dana realized the point her friends were trying to make. She thought about the past three days, how she hadn't been able to sleep or eat. She felt as if she were living in a void, where time and space had no meaning. She went through the motions of her job, talking to people when necessary, functioning, but not really alive.

"I'm not happy with what I've learned about myself," she said slowly. "Obviously I would like to be a better person. But that's not causing me the real pain. I'm hurting because I lost a chance with a wonderful man. Trevor is all I've ever dreamed about. It never occurred to me he would be interested in me, so I didn't take him seriously."

Dana paused, then winced. "No, wait. I'm done lying to myself, too. I did think it was unlikely Trevor would be interested in me, but that's not the real reason I held back. I was afraid. I didn't want to love him, because he was too close to perfect for me. If I gave with my whole heart and then lost him, I wasn't sure I would survive. I watched my mother all those years. Life passed her by while she waited to be rescued. Several kind, loving decent men wanted to marry her, but she wouldn't have them. She had her ideal and nothing was going to stand in the way of that. Maybe she was right to wait, but I think she took an awful risk. She could have been alone forever. I didn't want that for myself. I wasn't willing to hold out for a fantasy. I wanted someone genuine."

"So when the fantasy came along, you couldn't let yourself trust in him," Lee said.

"I guess." Dana tucked her hair behind her ears. "I can't believe it hurts this much. I had him and I didn't even know. I let him slip between my fingers because of pride. Because I wouldn't believe in him or me."

Katie looked at her. "I keep hearing you say that you lost him and didn't know you had him. I understand that's painful, but I'm not sure that it really matters. You're talking about saving face, Dana, not a broken heart. You haven't said one word about loving him."

Dana knew her friend was right. "I'm afraid," she whispered. "Admitting that will make it worse."

"Admitting that is the only way to get what you want." Lee leaned forward and rested her arms on the table. "Nothing you've described is irreversible. Of course Trevor is angry and hurt, but the bottom line is he wasn't exactly forthcoming with his feelings, either. He never told you he loved you or was thinking about proposing. You were both guilty of hiding what you felt, because you were afraid. Okay, you were wrong in how you acted. You've accepted that and you've learned from your mistake. Next time you won't be so quick to judge him."

"It's not that simple," Dana said, wishing it could be. If only there were a way to convince Trevor of her feelings.

"You're making it more complicated than it needs to be," Lee told her.

"Lee's right," Katie said. "Look at what Trevor objected to. That you held back and never planned on getting serious about him. What if he found out that wasn't true anymore?"

"How?"

"You didn't want anyone to know you two were going out," Lee said. "You were afraid of the gossip and what people would say when it ended, right?"

Dana nodded.

"So, start the rumors that you two are an item. Let them get back to Trevor. Let people know how you feel about him. Be proud of him. Be excited about having him in your life. You've wounded his male pride in a huge way, but I don't think you've changed what is in his heart. If you have, then it's better to know that now, before you get more involved."

"Good point," Katie said. "If this was enough to make him fall out of love with you, then good riddance to him. Otherwise start mending fences. Admit you were horrible to him and tell him why. Tell him you were afraid. He'll understand, Dana. He's a good man. He's worth fighting for."

Their advice washed over her, taking the sting out of the worst of the wounds and giving her hope. Maybe there was still hope. If she could show Trevor that she wasn't afraid to fight for him, that she desperately wanted him, he might be willing to give her a second chance.

"I have to try," she said slowly, still formulating plans in her mind. "If I don't, I'll regret this for the rest of my life. I love him. I won't just let him go."

While talking with her friends didn't take away the gaping hole in her chest, Dana felt more in control when she returned to her office after lunch. She didn't have a plan yet, but she wasn't going to give up without a fight. She was a hundred percent responsible for Trevor's reaction to all that had happened, so it was up to her to fix it. If only she knew exactly how to make him believe in her again.

Before she could outline a few strategies, Sally and Melba walked into her office. The three women discussed a few scheduling issues, then Sally leaned back in her chair and sighed dramatically.

"This has been the best week of my life," she said. "For

the past six days, Trevor and I have been together constantly.''

Dana glanced from one of her nurses to the other. It was now or never. "No, you haven't."

Sally grinned. "I don't mean work. Of course he's been here and at his office. But other than that..." Her voice trailed off and she raised her eyebrows suggestively.

"I'm not talking about work, either. The six previous days include the weekend, which Trevor spent with me. And I do mean *with me*. In fact, he was at my place for most of it. We went to a movie, so that got us out of the house, but aside from that, it was just him and me, alone. Three nights ago he was having dinner with his parents." She had to be careful about that one. Three nights ago, her world had come crashing down around her. If she thought about it too much, she might lose control.

"I know the time they met and the name of the restaurant," she continued. "And I know you weren't there."

Sally's mouth hung open. "That's not true," she said. Her face turned bright red. "Of course I was with him."

Melba looked amused. "You know, boss, I've long suspected that Sally and Angie were stretching the truth a bit. Poor Dr. MacAllister couldn't have been doing what they both said and still stayed awake during surgery." She patted Sally's arm. "It's okay. I know why you did it. But come clean. You and the good doctor have never been an item."

Sally straightened in her chair. "Of course we have. It's just—" Her voice broke and she dropped her chin to her chest. "Dammit, Angie was going on and on about how Trevor had asked her out. She was so smug I couldn't stand it. So I sort of made up some details."

Dana had already guessed the truth, but it was nice to

have it confirmed. "If it makes you feel any better, he was never dating Angie, either."

Melba looked at her with interest. "But you have been seeing him, haven't you?"

"Yes."

"Go, girl! Talk about still waters running deep." She leaned forward in her chair. "Tell me. Is he as wonderful as he looks?"

Dana leaned forward, too. The pain in her chest was still there, but it had subsided a little. Trevor was angry and hurt, with good reason. She'd treated him badly. But he loved her and he wasn't the kind of man to give that love lightly. If she could get him to listen, he might be willing to give her a second chance.

"He's better," she said. "He's the most wonderful man in the world. Not perfect, but perfect for me."

"Wow." Melba sank back in her seat. "How long have you been going out with him?"

"A few weeks."

"You've kept it quiet."

"Until we were both sure, we didn't want to be the subject of speculation." She glanced at both women. "You know how people talk."

Melba laughed. "They do go around flapping their lips, even when there's no reason. Are you still keeping it quiet?"

Dana took a deep breath. This was the chance. If she gave permission, word would spread so fast, it would be old news by four. There was risk involved, though. Trevor might not give her that second chance and her humiliation would then be public. However, she'd always been the one insisting on secrecy. He probably thought she was ashamed of him.

"No," she said. "It doesn't have to be kept quiet anymore."

Trevor pulled off his gloves and tossed them into the bin. There was blood on his scrubs, but he didn't have the energy to change right now. The five hours of surgery had been grueling, but that wasn't what had drained his energy. It was Dana. Always Dana.

He'd tried to survive without her for three days and he felt as if he were dying. How would he make it through the rest of his life? He loved her. Knowing that it was probably a mistake, he'd allowed himself to fall for her. He'd fallen hard and fast, and now was faced with the task of reassembling the pieces of his life.

He pushed open the swinging doors and stepped into the corridor. Three nurses stood at one end. They glanced up at him as he approached, then they giggled. He was used to the attention, but this afternoon he had less than his usual patience. He wanted them to leave him alone. Didn't they get it? He wasn't interested in a harem. He wanted one woman by his side for the rest of his life. Unfortunately, she didn't share his feelings or his view of the future.

One of the nurses stepped toward him. He tried to place her and couldn't. Her name tag read Angie.

"Dr. MacAllister, you look tired," the young nurse said. "Did everything go well?"

"The patient is fine. Thank you."

Before he could move on, the woman stepped in front of him. "Dana's my boss. She's really great. You're lucky to have her." She glanced back at her friends, then at him. "We were hoping you'd try out a few more of us before making a decision, but I can't say I'm surprised at your choice. Congratulations."

He stared at her. "What are you talking about?"

She touched her fingers to her mouth. "Oh, I'm sorry. I thought it was okay to mention that you two are dating. Is it still supposed to be a secret?" She chuckled. "Well, you know how hospitals are. It's out now. Have a good evening."

She returned to her friends and the group moved away. Trevor stared after them, not sure he understood what had just happened. People knew he and Dana were dating? But how? He'd never said a word—because she'd asked him to keep quiet. He grimaced, remembering how that had bothered him. He'd been thrilled they were seeing each other, and had wanted everyone to know. He supposed he understood her reluctance, what with their working together. But if he hadn't said anything, how had the rumor started?

His first instinct was to go to Dana and talk to her about the situation. He wanted her to know that he had kept his word. Then he reminded himself it didn't matter. He and Dana weren't an item anymore. Besides, even if he did tell her the truth, she wouldn't believe him.

It wasn't supposed to hurt this much, he thought as he headed for the cafeteria. He'd thought nothing would ever be worse than what Vanessa had put him through, but he'd been wrong. This was worse, because he'd lost the ability to try again. He was done. He'd given Dana everything he had and she hadn't been interested. End of story.

As he entered the cafeteria, someone called his name. He turned and saw Lee, Dana's friend, heading toward him.

"Hi, Trevor," she called. "How's it going?"

"Fine," he lied, figuring she wouldn't be comfortable if he unburdened himself to her. "And you?"

"Not bad." She looked at him and smiled. "Rumors are flying about you and Dana."

"I've heard. I don't understand how they got started. I didn't say anything to anyone."

"I think Dana mentioned it to a couple of her nurses."

He stepped out of line and stared at her. "What? Dana couldn't have done that. She didn't want anyone to know about us."

"I know she thought that at one time, but that was before."

His chest had tightened so much it was tough to breathe. "Before what?"

"Before she realized she was a fool." Lee moved close to him. "I know it makes you uncomfortable, Trevor, but the truth is, you're more fairy-story prince than real-life guy. You can't blame a woman for not being sure it's safe to trust you. Look at all Dana's been through. She grew up poor and neglected. She had her heart broken when she thought the boy she loved had betrayed her. Then that boy, as a grown-up and very attractive man, strolls back into her life. What was she supposed to think?"

"That I meant what I said. That I would never lie to her."

"Convincing the head is one thing—convincing the heart is quite another. She made a mistake. She hasn't said much about your past, but I'm willing to guess you've made a few mistakes of your own—from time to time. You're the only one who knows how far you can bend on this, but I would hate to see two really terrific people lose out on the love of a lifetime just because of a misunderstanding."

He didn't know what to say. He heard the words, but he couldn't absorb them. Not yet.

Lee sighed. "I can't believe this. You're a doctor and I'm encouraging you to get involved with one of my dearest friends in life. Go figure."

With that, she turned and left. Trevor stared after her. Thoughts tumbled through his head. Dana had told people they were dating. But they weren't anymore. Was she trying to get his attention? Did she want him to know that she wasn't ashamed of being with him?

"None of this matters," he muttered as he got back in line, then poured himself a cup of coffee. It was too late for them. Everything was over...wasn't it?

It was close to seven before he was able to go to his locker to change clothes and head home. He was tired to the bone, and confused as hell about Dana. He hadn't been able to stop thinking about her. Lee's words also haunted him. Especially the part about Dana's making a mistake. Lord knows he'd made plenty, starting with Vanessa.

A second chance. Could he risk it? Could he not? If there was even the slightest opportunity, didn't he owe it to both of them to make every effort? After all, he'd never loved anyone the way he loved Dana.

He rested his hand against his locker. Dammit, no. He'd gone as far as he was going with her. She'd had her chance and she'd blown it. He'd seen the worst side of her and he didn't like it.

But if that was the worst she had to offer, wasn't she a prize worth having? He'd seen into the blackness of her soul and knew it wasn't so very bad.

The voice in his head annoyed him. He tried to ignore it. But it persisted in reminding him that when compared with Vanessa, Dana's worst wasn't much at all. A few dark specks rather than a yawning black hole. Dana was many things, but she wasn't deliberately cruel. Considering all she'd been through—all *they'd* been through—was it surprising that she'd had trouble trusting him? He'd wanted her to look past the facade and the rumor, but hadn't he withheld information, thereby making it difficult for her to do that?

"Stop it," he muttered. He didn't want to be reasonable or rational. So what if Dana had told people they were going out? Nothing had changed. She still didn't give a damn about him. He was still just a convenience to her. She still didn't love him. That was the bottom line.

He fumbled with his locker, opened it and reached for his clothes. Then something caught his eye.

Sitting on the shelf was a familiar box. It was just like the one he'd carried T.J. around in during the seminar. He opened it and found a note and an egg. Despite the tightness in his chest and pain, he smiled faintly. Only Dana would know about the significance of the egg. He unfolded the paper and read:

Sometimes it's hard to say egg-sactly what we mean, because we're afraid. Sometimes we find someone egg-straordinary has become a part of our lives, but we can't believe. The lack of faith isn't about that other person, but about a failing within ourselves. Sometimes we want to say we're sorry, but we don't have the right words.

He glanced around, but he was alone in the room. Dana wasn't lurking in the corner, yet he knew she'd been there just a short time ago. He crossed to the phone on the wall and called her office. After a couple of seconds, he was told she'd already left for the day.

Hope flared inside. Hope that he didn't want to think about but that he couldn't ignore. Had she figured it all out? Did this mean she cared? He told himself to just walk away, but he knew that if she came to him and asked him for a second chance, he wouldn't turn her down. He couldn't. Despite everything, he still loved her.

He drove home much faster than usual. When he pulled into his garage, he walked around front instead of entering through the garage. An egg carton sat on the doorstep. He opened it and found the container empty except for a small note: "I'm a broken shell without you."

There was a sound behind him. He turned and saw Dana standing there. She wore jeans and a long-sleeved white shirt. Despite her makeup, she had circles under her eyes and her skin appeared drawn.

"You look like you've been sleeping about as much as me," he said.

"If that means not at all, then you're right." She took a step toward him. "Trevor, I—" She motioned to the note. "What I wrote is funny, but it's also very true. I'm lost without you. I was so busy protecting myself against falling in love with you that I never noticed how much you'd become a part of my life. I miss you. I miss talking to you and hearing your voice. I miss laughing. I miss making love. I miss how you feel when you hold me." She smiled sadly. "I even miss how you smell."

She took another step. "I know I don't have the right to ask for another chance, but I'm asking anyway. You were dead-on about me. I'm embarrassed and ashamed and I have no excuse. I want to tell you I'm a better person than that, but you have no reason to believe me. So instead I'm asking for the time to prove that to you."

She swallowed. He could tell she was nervous. He thought about interrupting her, but figured she needed to have all this said. It would probably be better for both of them if she got it out of her system. And if the truth be told, he didn't mind hearing her confession.

"I was so wrong about you. I see that now," she continued. "I've been a thoughtless fool. I was afraid to believe you could care about me, so I ignored all the signs. Even the ones that said I was falling in love with you."

He'd wanted her to say the words, but he was unprepared for the impact when she did. Even though she continued talking, he dropped the empty egg carton, crossed the three steps between them and hauled her hard against him. His mouth silenced hers.

It was like coming home after being gone a lifetime. She was all that he remembered and more. Her heat enveloped him; her lips parted willingly as she took him in.

"I love you," she murmured against him. "I have for a long time. I love you, Trevor. The man inside as much as the rest of you."

"I love you, too. I don't know that I ever stopped."

Somehow he got the door open and maneuvered them both inside. Then they were in the living room, pulling off clothes, frantically kissing and touching and loving, and then he was inside her...where he belonged.

"I do love you," she said, and caught her breath as her body responded to his. "I want to marry you, if you'll still have me."

"There's no one else I want."

"Did you want a long engagement?" she asked.

"No. I was thinking a couple of days. Why? Did you?"

She shook her head. "Good thing, too. What with this." She motioned to their bodies.

Trevor realized he was making love with her with no barrier between them. Love swelled inside him. He cupped her face. "I want us to have children."

She smiled. "Me, too. You'll be a terrific father."

"You'll be a great mom." He chuckled. "So, if it's a boy, what do you think about calling him 'Eggbert'?"

"Trevor! I don't think so."

Dana wrapped her arms around him and pulled him close. He thought about telling her he was kind of serious about the name thing, but right at that moment, she tilted her hips slightly, drawing him in deeper. Then he couldn't think at all. He could only feel her and their love.

* * *

As they moved together in that age-old rhythm, the miracle occurred. Two did become one, creating a new life. Fortunately for Dana, *and* the baby in question, their child turned out to be a girl.

* * * * *

Well, two down, one to go
But while Katie and Dana have already
broken their vows—
and gotten themselves engaged to doctors—
Lee is going to be different.
She'll never succumb to a doctor's charms.
Or will she?
You can find out in

CHRISTINE RIMMER's

DR. DEVASTATING

the wonderful conclusion to

PRESCRIPTION: MARRIAGE

available from
Silhouette Special Edition
in December.

Meanwhile, turn the page
for a sneak preview....

"Why are we playing this stupid game, Lee?"

"Uh, game?"

"Yes. Game. You looking at me the way you do, and me pretending I don't see. What's the point, when you're attracted to me and—well, I suppose I might as well just say it. I'm attracted to you, too."

"Huh?" Lee almost dropped her water glass. The thing slid through her fingers and clinked on the edge of her plate. Awkwardly, at the last second, she caught it by the rim and somehow managed to ease it to the table without spilling any.

Derek watched her struggle with the glass. And then he nodded, still rueful, a little abashed. "It's true." His expression said it all. He couldn't understand what in the world he saw in her. He considered her totally beneath him, since she was neither gorgeous nor blond. For goodness' sake, her eyes weren't even blue. "I don't know how it happened, but I'm attracted to you."

Amazing, Lee thought. The man really did have an ego every bit as hefty as the two-hundred pound barbell he bench-pressed each time he worked out. But then, he was a doctor, after all. Lee recalled an old joke she'd heard back in nursing school: Imagine an arrogant doctor. But I repeat myself....

Derek went on, a little bewildered, but still utterly sure of himself and his power over disease, injury—and the feminine gender. "I guess what I'm saying is, I think this is something we might as well just go ahead and deal with straight out. I think we can see each other in private and still maintain a viable working relationship. Because I really do believe this is something we're just going to have to get out of our systems."

"Like a viral infection, you mean? Something that has to run its course?"

Lee had meant to inject a note of irony, but Doctor Taylor failed to pick up on it. "Yeah. You could say that. We could agree that whatever happens between us, we won't allow it to affect our work at the clinic."

"Whatever...happens?"

"Yes." He narrowed his eyes at her, in one of those reproving looks he reserved for patients who balked at the course of treatment he'd prescribed. "And what's the problem? Am I not making myself clear?"

"Well, no. I think I'm getting the picture just fine."

"You do?" He looked doubtful.

"Yes. You want us to...date." The word sounded so incongruous to her that she had to choke back a burst of hysterical laughter as soon as she said it.

He blew out a breath and gave her a reproachful frown. "Lee. You're behaving very strangely about this."

Strangely. He thought she was behaving strangely. Well,
ll right. Maybe she was. Derek Taylor was her fantasy.
Ier mind candy. She'd had a very good thing going with
im. A safe, secret, harmless, one-sided, totally mental love
ffair. It had been great.

But he just couldn't leave it that way. Oh, no. He had to
o and make it dangerous. Make it *real*.

And beyond that, there was the little matter of his attitude
bout the whole thing. His arrogance and his ego simply
new no bounds. It was written all over his too-handsome
ace; he thought he was doing her a big favor to give in
nd go out with her.

Well, she didn't need any favors from him.

What she needed was out of here, stat.

"Lee. Say something. Please."

Carefully, she pushed her glass and her plate toward his,
n the center of the table. Easy, she thought. Tread cau-
iously. Remember, you do have to work with the man.

"Lee?"

"I, um…"

"Yeah?"

"Well, Dr. Taylor—"

"Derek."

No. She was not going to call him that. *"Dr. Taylor,"*
he repeated, a real edge in her tone.

They stared at each other. At last, he said too quietly,
'Go on."

She reached for her shoulder bag a few inches away on
he Naugahyde bench of the booth. She pulled it into her
ap, all ready to go. And then, choosing each word with
gonizing care, she told him, "Dr. Taylor, I'm sorry if you
magined I had some…romantic interest in you. But I
romise you, I never intended for you to think I wanted
nything more than a strictly professional relationship with

you. I love my work. And going out with you is way too
likely to cause problems—for me, for you, and most im
portantly, for the work we do.''

His fabulous face had taken on a totally blank, disbe
lieving expression. She thought of how a Ken doll migh
look if Barbie went and told him she was leaving him fo
GI Joe. "You're telling me you won't go out with me.'
Clearly, getting turned down was a new experience for him

"Yes. I think it's for the best. I think that we—''

"Just a minute." The words were pure ice. She did he
best not to flinch at the sound of them. And the blank look
was gone, too. Suddenly, he bore no resemblance to a Ke
doll at all.

"Yes?"

"Are you saying you're not attracted to me in the least"
That I *imagined* those looks you're always giving me?''

Lee knew what she should answer: That's exactly wha
I'm saying. But she just didn't have it in herself to tell a
lie that big. So she hedged, "Whether I'm attracted to yo
or not isn't the issue here.''

"I think it is."

"Well, I'm sorry, but I can't agree with you.''

"You *are* attracted to me. Admit it. I just want the damr
truth, that's all!''

Take 2 bestselling love stories FREE

Plus get a FREE surprise gift!

Special Limited-Time Offer

Mail to Silhouette Reader Service™

P.O. Box 609
Fort Erie, Ontario
L2A 5X3

YES! Please send me 2 free Silhouette Special Edition® novels and my free surprise gift. Then send me 6 brand-new novels every month, which I will receive months before they appear in bookstores. Bill me at the low price of $3.96 each plus 25¢ delivery and GST*. That's the complete price, and a saving of over 10% off the cover prices—quite a bargain! I understand that accepting the books and gift places me under no obligation ever to buy any books. I can always return a shipment and cancel at any time. Even if I never buy another book from Silhouette, the 2 free books and the surprise gift are mine to keep forever.

335 SEN CH7X

Name	(PLEASE PRINT)	
Address	Apt. No.	
City	Province	Postal Code

This offer is limited to one order per household and not valid to present Silhouette Special Edition® subscribers. *Terms and prices are subject to change without notice.
Canadian residents will be charged applicable provincial taxes and GST.

CSPED-98

©1990 Harlequin Enterprises Limited

FOLLOW THAT BABY...

the fabulous cross-line series featuring the infamously wealthy Wentworth family...continues with:

THE SHERIFF AND THE IMPOSTOR BRIDE
by Elizabeth Bevarly
(Desire, 12/98)

When a Native American sheriff spies the runaway beauty in his small town, he soon realizes that his enchanting discovery is actually Sabrina Jensen's headstrong *identical* twin sister....

Available at your favorite retail outlet, only from

Silhouette ®

Look us up on-line at: http://www.romance.net

SSEFTB3

Bestselling author

LINDSAY McKENNA

continues the drama and adventure of her
popular series with an all-new, longer-length
single-title romance:

MORGAN'S MERCENARIES

HEART OF THE JAGUAR

Major Mike Houston and Dr. Ann Parsons were in the heat
of the jungle, deep in enemy territory. She knew Mike's
warrior blood kept him from the life—and the love—he
silently craved. And now she had so much more at stake.
For the beautiful doctor carried a child. His child...

Available in January 1999, at your favorite retail outlet!

Look for more MORGAN'S MERCENARIES in 1999,
as the excitement continues in the Special Edition line!

Silhouette®

PSMORGMERC

For a limited time, Harlequin and Silhouette have an offer you just can't refuse.

In November and December 1998:

BUY **ANY** TWO HARLEQUIN
OR SILHOUETTE BOOKS and
SAVE $10.00
off future purchases

OR BUY ANY THREE HARLEQUIN OR SILHOUETTE BOOKS
AND **SAVE $20.00** OFF FUTURE PURCHASES!

(each coupon is good for $1.00 off the purchase of two
Harlequin or Silhouette books)

....

JUST BUY 2 HARLEQUIN OR SILHOUETTE BOOKS, SEND US YOUR
NAME, ADDRESS AND 2 PROOFS OF PURCHASE (CASH REGISTER
RECEIPTS) AND HARLEQUIN WILL SEND YOU A COUPON BOOKLET
WORTH $10.00 OFF FUTURE PURCHASES OF HARLEQUIN OR
SILHOUETTE BOOKS IN 1999. SEND US 3 PROOFS OF PURCHASE AND
WE WILL SEND YOU 2 COUPON BOOKLETS WITH A TOTAL SAVING OF
$20.00. (ALLOW 4-6 WEEKS DELIVERY) OFFER EXPIRES
DECEMBER 31, 1998.

....

I accept your offer! Please send me a coupon booklet(s), to:

NAME: _____

ADDRESS: _____

CITY: _____ STATE/PROV.: _____ POSTAL/ZIP CODE: _____

**Send your name and address, along with your cash register
receipts for proofs of purchase, to:**

In the U.S.	In Canada
Harlequin Books	Harlequin Books
P.O. Box 9057	P.O. Box 622
Buffalo, NY	Fort Erie, Ontario
14269	L2A 5X3

PHQ4982

The BENNING Legacy

**An absorbing new cross-line miniseries in
Silhouette Special Edition and Silhouette Desire from**
Jackie Merritt

**Three sisters find that true love uncovers the secrets of
the past...and forges bright new tomorrows!**

Starting June 1998 in Silhouette Special Edition:

FOR THE LOVE OF SAM—June 1998 (Special Edition)
Spunky younger sister Tamara Benning had a sneaking
suspicion that there were long-buried Benning family
secrets. But she had a budding secret of her own....

A MONTANA MAN—August 1998 (Desire)
Tamara's older sister Sierra's adventure begins with the
Man of the Month

And coming this December in Special Edition,
the conclusion...the Benning family secrets
are finally unraveled in **THE SECRET DAUGHTER.**

Available at your favorite retail outlet.

Silhouette ®
™

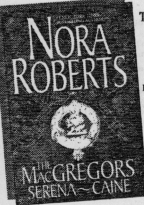
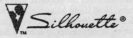

Silhouette®

COMING NEXT MONTH

#1213 THEIR CHILD—Penny Richards
That's My Baby!
Horse breeder Drew McShane had selflessly married pregnant ranching heiress
Kim Campion to give her baby a name. As their darling daughter illuminated
their lives, Drew began to realize how much he truly adored Hannah's mommy.
Could he convince his wary wife they were destined for love?

#1214 HEART OF THE HUNTER—Lindsay McKenna
Morgan's Mercenaries: The Hunters
He never let anything—or anyone—get to him. But when Captain Reid Hunter's
latest mission meant guarding Dr. Casey Morrow, it irked him that the feisty
beauty fought him every step of the way. Now her achingly tender kisses might
turn this world-weary cynic into a true believer in love!

#1215 DR. DEVASTATING—Christine Rimmer
Prescription: Marriage
Devastatingly handsome Dr. Derek Taylor had inspired many of nurse
Lee Murphy's fantasies. Suddenly all her secret yearnings sprang to life when
the dashing doc began paying an awful lot of attention to little old mousy her!
Could it be that sometimes dreams *do* come true?

#1216 NATURAL BORN LAWMAN—Sherryl Woods
And Baby Makes Three: The Next Generation
Justin Adams was a by-the-book lawman—no exceptions. Until the day he
caught a desperate Patsy Longhorn swiping a bottle of baby medicine for her
feverish tyke. After taking the penniless mother and son under his protective
wing, the softhearted sheriff vowed to safeguard their future—with him!

#1217 WIFE IN THE MAIL—Marie Ferrarella
Shayne Kerrigan was in quite a quandary! His irresponsible brother had run
off—and the lonely widower had to break the news to his sibling's jilted mail-
order bride. All too soon, Shayne and his children were under sweet Sydney's
spell. Could Shayne convince her to become *his* Christmas bride?

#1218 THE SECRET DAUGHTER—Jackie Merritt
The Benning Legacy
A lifetime ago Blythe Benning had bid goodbye to her college love—as
well as their beloved baby. Now Brent Morrison was back, eager to rekindle
their passion—and to locate the daughter he'd never met. But when their
quest unearthed a shattering family secret, it seemed their lives might never
be the same....